Native New Yorker **Laurie Gwen Shapiro** is the author of two previous novels, *The Matzo Ball Heiress* and *The Unexpected Salami*, an ALA notable book. She codirected the film *Keep the River on Your Right: A Modern Cannibal Tale*, which received an Independent Spirit Award. She is at work on both a new novel and documentary. Visit her Web site at www.lauriegwenshapiro.com.

THE ANGLOPHILE

LAURIE
GWEN
SHAPIRO

RED
DRESS
INK
™

THE ANGLOPHILE

A Red Dress Ink novel

ISBN 0-373-89529-1

© 2005 by Laurie Gwen Shapiro.

www.RedDressInk.com

Printed in U.S.A.

For the Englishmen in my life, past and present.

Acknowledgments

Thanks to: My husband, Paul O'Leary, Mark Newgarden, Megan Cash, Pete Bonastia, David Lawson, Nick Wheeler, and my brother, David Shapiro—travel companions on various stateside and British adventures.

Also: my smart friends,
Corey S. Powell and Joanna Dalin; Farrin Jacobs;
Richard Porter, the Beatle Brain of Britain;
Hartsdale Pet Cemetery; Uncle Sam Morrison;
Marla Egbert Nitke; Nancy Yost and Michael Cendejas;
and Jeanette and Julius Shapiro for their
incredible emotional support.

He was a veray parfit gentil knight.
        —Geoffrey Chaucer, *The Canterbury Tales*

Looking through the bent-backed tulips
To see how the other half live
Looking through a glass onion
        —John Lennon, "Glass Onion"

If you are real, sit down on that big footstool and talk,
I want to hear about you.
        —Frances Hodgson Burnett, *The Secret Garden*

PART 1

America the Beautiful

PREFACE

An Englishman in the Loop

There's a certain type of Englishman who has a way of standing out in an American crowd, even though he would be appalled to know it. Case in point: the soft-spoken one on my two o'clock Chicago skyscraper tour writing notes about the celebrated Rookery Building in an innocuous spiral memo book. One clue to his breeding is the screamingly expensive silver pen. But it's his looks that plain give him away. With his broad shoulders, thin glasses, wispy strawberry blond hair, exposed pasty-white neck and stretched Anglo-Saxon nostrils, he is my quintessential type: Christopher Robin, all grown up into a strapping gent. Back in the graduate studies offices of New York University, I'm the renowned sucker for the *Brideshead Revisited* extras. So now, while he's busy writing, it's a safe opportunity for me to ogle that brown leather trench coat with the argyle scarf loose around the collar.

Gary Marino, an old friend from my freshman dormitory floor at SUNY/Binghamton, is my sole contact in the city until tomorrow's linguistics conference kicks in. He has his own eye candy on this tour, a blond woman who, if his tastes hold true to seventeen years ago, is *his* quintessential type.

A woman on the tour raises an arm. "Just a few more minutes to defrost?" she tunefully drawls to our volunteer docent from the Chicago Architectural Foundation. "It's so toasty warm in here."

My linguist's ear pins this middle-aged unrooted accent on a Southern childhood and a Los Angeles career.

"Brilliant idea," the Brit seconds, a quiet statement followed by like-minded pleas from the rest of my fellow chilled excursionists.

Our guide, a likeable man whose chiseled face is spoiled by a wiggly pink growth on his chin, checks with the guard assigned to the magnificent skylit lobby remodeled at the turn of the century by Frank Lloyd Wright.

"Yes, we can linger," he reports back to us in his pleasingly thick voice. "Those in need can even pee into a historical toilet."

"I have to piss like a racehorse," Gary says to me at the start of the sanctioned break.

"Thanks for sharing."

When Gary grins, he time-travels before my eyes to our freshman year.

"I'm dying for chocolate. See you after your piss."

As I head for the newsstand I notice the Englishman look up and briefly follow me with his eyes. Did he catch me giving him an admiring gaze? Is he wondering whether Gary is my boyfriend, or am I just spinning tales to entertain myself?

I look back and he doesn't turn away. Instead he smiles at me from across the lobby. When Gary returns I can barely focus on his rant about his transplanted Easterner specialty pickup: the Midwestern woman who suddenly realizes that there might be more out there beyond the wheat. Gary rolls his eyes when he's figured out my distraction. "You couldn't possibly be interested in the *brilliant* guy from England."

I've gobbled up my York Peppermint Pattie. "Noticing him, that's all."

CHAPTER 1

The Anglophile

I distinctly remember kissing the cover of *Oliver Twist* when I finished reading it during one of my school recesses. Although the little protagonist was hip-deep in a welter of stink and his only meal came from a cauldron of gruel as he dreamed of jacket potatoes or a parade of lusty puddings, I often thought that if Oliver Twist was an English boy, even a dirty one, he must still be pretty darn cute.

It was a big read for a nine-year-old, I don't think I got half the words. But my teacher brought it in for me one day from her personal collection. She told me it was about the British kids I was always asking about. If she thought I could read it, I was determined to try. Only one other time did she bring a book specifically for a kid in the class, a book about the Civil War she handed to the one rich kid, Owen Zuckerman, from Jamaica Estates, one of the few truly fancy neighborhoods of my borough. No one felt left out as far as I know, as Owen and I were the class bookworms.

During recess, two of my classmates, Paul Schwartz with his flat face and pinprick eyes and his best buddy Cameron Hernandez, often pretended to be boxers. Paul feinted with his left hand, and Cameron parried with his right. The girls clustered on the far side of the yard played all the jump rope and chanting games that were popular in our neighborhood. The clique of pretty black girls was always in the right corner with their double Dutch game, two ropes rotating inward with inconceivable speed, and the pretty white girls busied themselves in the left corner with quick-action hand games like Miss Mary Mack—in my lofty opinion only a slightly more sophisticated take on patty-cake. I had a friend in each chanting-girl camp and despite some of the other girls' audible moans, Janie and Heidi each asked repeatedly if I was sad and wanted to join in. But I excused myself and finished all of Lewis Carroll on a tree stump inside the schoolyard. In light dappled by the iron bars protecting us from that noisy Long Island Expressway, I ignored the car horns and the racing motorcycles and the showdowns of "Listen, fuck you, mister, *YOUUU* GET OUTTA THE CAR."

I was an even bigger reader at home. Before Dad got back from his electrician's day, I sat happily on the living room couch reading while my two noisy brothers wandered our hallway with metal salad bowls on their heads and two cans of condensed milk for their field phones—this military march always occurred after the

Channel Eleven afternoon rerun of *Hogan's Heroes.* Here were two Colonel Klinks with a pecking order: Colonel Gene and Major Alan, who only pretended to be macho so he didn't get the shit beaten out of him by his big brother. Now and then, my brothers acknowledged my presence on the couch by gunning me down.

When Dad started getting ill Mom insisted my wild brothers play in the somewhat ramshackle kitchen, the farthest room from the master bedroom, now the Diamond sick bay. A white sheet stained beyond help with grape Hi-C made a nice picnic tent on the cracked-tile kitchen floor.

One afternoon during this uneasy stretch of time I served Gene and Alan my version of cream tea under the tent. They were quite appreciative as they were exhausted from hours of bravely softening the D-Day beach so that the other marines could land. Instead of scones served with full cream and strawberry preserves, I substituted reconstituted orange juice and a Mallomar cookie for the men at war. When they'd refueled they raced back out to the hallway with the popgun, a late fifties Davy Crockett hand-me-down rifle from an older cousin, already in college, a gun that was repaired near its butt with string held down by superglue. My brothers never minded that they had a preloved weapon. They lived for its bang that scared the hell out of our elderly neighbor, Mrs. Weiss.

Alone again under my tent, I replaced Christopher Robin as the God Figure ruling over the Hundred Acre Woods. I didn't need my brothers for company. The very hungry hedgehogs, blackbirds and field mice gathered around me as I fed Pooh Bear lime Jell-O.

"Dad will get better," I promised him. I knew his animal friends were listening as I kissed him on his patchy forehead. "No more crying! We need a setting too for Owl, and Rabbit and Rabbit's friend Small, if we can talk that beetle out of the Heffalump trap, we'll be all here, because I've given up on Eeyore."

"Mom, she's talking weird again!" Alan screeched down the hall. "She's frightening me."

"Idiot!" I was humiliated at being listened to on the sly. How dare he after I'd served him high tea!

"Freak!"

I threatened to tell Mom that he was stashing her *Redbook*s, and that wherever there was a woman in the ad, he'd draw pubic hair all over her crotch.

When Alan started bawling I had to admit I was never going to turn him in.

I'm a year younger than him, but most people who meet our clan today assume he has to be the baby of the family. Even back then, I never let Alan boss me. He was a crybaby. I only feared Gene's occasional smack when I smart-mouthed Mom.

Mom rushed in the kitchen, her face covered in white wrinkle cream. "Quiet, all of you. Dad is resting."

After stupid Alan was out of sight, I'd shifted imaginary texts, and invited sickly Colin from Frances Hodgson Burnett's *The Secret Garden* into my picnic tent. I was sure that like his cousin Mary Lennax, I could convince him to smile.

The Secret Garden was hands down my favorite book

back then. It was damn sexy—*The Thorn Birds* for the under-twelve set. There was unrequited lust going on there amidst the daffodils and bluebells, even if the young protagonists were cousins. The nine-year-old me wanted to be Mary, holding Colin's hand. I didn't know the term "sexual undercurrent" yet, but I sure sensed it.

I wanted my own family to possess whatnots and spend crowns and pence, or climb creaky staircases and stroll around regatta meets with straw-brimmed hats. I wanted a safe English haven outside my doorstep—a bright green meadow or better yet a tucked-away garden with zinnia creeping up trellises. To see colorful flowers planted at every corner, a table set with dainty teacups, silverware and sugarcubes, wouldn't that be heaven? A sanctuary you could well imagine housed happy elves and fairies with magical faces staring up at little innocents, or talking caterpillar friends with sticky wings because they had just crawled out of a chrysalid.

But I was a lower middle-class Jewish American living in a charmless Queens apartment with a storage closet filled with Bar Mitzvah and wedding souvenir yarmulkes embroidered with names of cousins and children of my parents' friends.

My living room showcased a tacky painting of a rabbi doing a squat dance—the official Guinness Most Prolific Painter, Morris Katz, banged it out on canvas. According to my mother who had won the painting as a door prize in the Elechester Apartments' community room weekly bingo game, it was painted in less than three minutes with Katz's trademark toilet paper methodology.

★ ★ ★

My father died when I was nine and three quarters.

With three kids it was all Donna Diamond could do to get through daily bills. We were already in trouble because Dad had been ill for over a year, and hadn't worked much when he was sick.

The day of my dad's funeral, Alan searched his bureau drawers for appropriate pants to wear. Although he was only eleven, he didn't bother my mother, a spiritual wreck scouring the listings pages for a better job than her secretarial spot at the Book of the Month Club. Gene was the one who begged her to stop her weepy job search. "But we need food on the table," I heard her say. "Tomorrow," my brother replied. "Tomorrow, you'll look." Alan anxiously asked Gene—now a de facto father figure at the age of twelve—if he should go wearing the holey slacks, or the one with the reek. The pants smelled moldy because when Dad's checks stopped coming, Mom still insisted on using our faulty washing machine instead of the communal ones in our apartment building's laundry room. It was her machine, and ownership gave her pride.

When he was well, Nate Diamond was a character in our neighborhood, notably funny for a man who had a way with lightbulbs and cabling. I absolutely adored him. He never skimped on kisses for his wife or kids, even for his two war-obsessed little men. We didn't have elaborate toys like the ones kids in Forest Hills paraded on Austin Street, but Dad always brought us something fun from the dollar-store on Kissena Boulevard, like Silly Putty or Mad Lib pads. He told us fabulous tales about his great-uncle Mickey Diamond who took a running jump west in 1929 to escape the Depression, and who then married and begot the long line of fabulous Diamond cowboys of Lubbock, Texas. Alan in particular would beg Dad for more tales of the family cowboys lassoing their matched Jewish bulls, Moishe and Schlomo.

Before his death Dad joked with my painfully shy mom that his gravestone better not read, Here Lies Silly Daddy. That's apparently what I called him as a toddler when he tickled me until I called out "rhinoceros," our family's version of crying "uncle." In almost every photo in our house that had Silly Daddy in it, he was laughing his head off, his round brown eyes closed in delight. He needn't have worried about what would be destiny's decree: after he finally passed on a golden afternoon, Mom wrote down what she wanted my aunt Dot, her sister-in-law, to order: Nate Diamond, 1935–1979, *Devoted Father, Devoted Husband, Loving Brother. Forever Missed.* Without asking my mother Dot added the symbol for the Ten Commandments and the two Lions of Judah on either side. But when my mother saw them at the unveiling, she nodded her approval. Yes, my father wasn't religious, but his mother was, and she knew what Dot knew, that Dad would want to respect his immigrant momma who preceded her son in death by a mere five years.

Donna Diamond was (and still is) withdrawn and thin. Back in the postfuneral days, she was forever unpeeling the shiny silver wrappers of Wrigley's spearmint gum so she could pop another stick to clean her cigarette breath. Mom's smoking got worse after Dad's fall to lung cancer. She once stopped for a year, but picked it up again when she became convinced that she would never remarry. Dad knew he would die and wanted her to be happy when he was gone. But there were few takers for a middle-aged mother of three with big debt hanging over her.

I never talked about our situation with my friends. Even my closest pals were never invited back home. Who would want to admit that we were too broke for a new toaster and had to remove burned bread with tongs, or that Mom spent an hour a day clipping coupons, or that our food was stored in cloudy orange Tupperware containers that she scooped up at a rummage sale for a quarter each?

Luckily when it was time for college I won that undergraduate scholarship to Binghamton, including housing. My mother wanted me to go to New York University who had offered me a partial scholarship, tuition only.

"It's the same cost as Binghamton if you live here, and take the F Train into the City."

"I'll visit all the time. I'll take the bus home. It's not expensive from Binghamton."

Mom squeezed a bony fist by her thigh. "I want my little girl here."

I went to Binghamton anyway, after Gene talked to her. I could hear Mom sobbing in the kitchen as she admitted to him that she wasn't giving me room to grow. Gene knew I needed to get away back then. My guilt was swallowing me up. I even secretly applied to the English program at Yale. For the pricey Ivy League application fee, I used my Hanukkah money from Mom's much-older half brother. My uncle Sam, a World War II veteran, had half-decent money from his partnership in a Bronx catering hall, but I didn't tell Sam, or my mother, or even Gene that I got in. I knew that with the paltry scholarship Yale offered I'd kill Mom with humiliation when she was forced to say that it was impossible.

We could never afford that junior year abroad in London, so dating New Yorkers and New Jerseyans of Anglo-Saxon heritage was the closest I got to my beloved Brits back in college.

Besides, it didn't cost anything to travel to England with a library book.

CHAPTER 2

London Calling

Gary whispers in an awful imitation of a British butler voice: "Lord Faggot of Faggot Manor—"

"He's not gay." I hush him quickly with an angry look.

I can't get over how Gary really hasn't changed since college, save a few physical details: his once-skinny physique has widened out by quite a few inches, and two gray hairs peek out of his left sideburn. But his mild bigotry and harmless puffery is cozily familiar, as is the royal-blue turtleneck he's wearing. He used to order the exact same item in threes from the L.L. Bean catalogue—a half-successful effort to prove to the frat brothers that he wasn't a Bensonhurst cliché of gold chains and scenic disco shirts.

"I'll stop."

"Good, homophobe. Plus, I don't even need the Englishman. I'll have you know I'm seeing someone really nice now."

Gary's smile is speculative. "What's his name? Wait, let me guess—uh, Chris?"

That's a standard joke amongst my college friends—I hold the unofficial Guinness record for *Jewess Who Has Gone Out with the Most Christophers in All Its Variants.* There were two serious boyfriends, Chris and Kris; and four short-haul runs, Christopher, Chris, Christian and the Christopher who preferred to be called by his initials, CK.

"Kevin."

"Kevin what?"

"Who are you, the president of my aunt's synagogue?"

"That the aunt with the skunk?"

"Hey! When did you meet her?"

"At graduation. C'mon, Kevin who? Fess up."

I hate him right now. "Kevin Bernstein."

He smirks. "You're dating a Jew? *Auntie Dot* will be pleased."

"Jesus. You really remember her from that long ago?"

"Her name was *Dot.* She had a pet *skunk,* and she had those eyebrows—" Gary snorts, because my aunt's over-plucked eyebrows are always redrawn in with dark brown liner at right angles. How do you tell your elders that there should never be sharp turns in makeup application? (My mother, forever Dot's submissive sister-in-law, says, succinctly, "You don't.")

"You know what she said to me?"

I cringe. "Do I want to hear this?"

"'Gary, *you* talk to her, hon. I want my niece to respect her heritage. Doesn't your mother want you to date Catholic? Tell Shari that Christ is in Christopher.

He's not our guy. She won't listen to her old aunt, so maybe she'll listen to her friends.'"

His raspy impersonation of two-pack-a-day Dot is so spot-on that it makes me a little sick. I'm mad all over again at Dot so inappropriately riled up at my graduation ceremony—my roommate, not normally the fink, had spilled the beans about my many Christian Chrisses. Not so privately, Dot took it upon herself to chew me out, invoking her status as activities chairwoman of her Catskills synagogue—a reinforcement of her cultural commitment that made her as proud as her ownership of three successive de-stunked skunks with their "spray" capabilities removed at four weeks. (She's also treasurer of a nationwide skunk-enthusiast group.)

Our guide loudly claps his hands by the front door. "Folks, who's ready to brace the cold again? If we walk faster, it won't hurt so much." He is commendably chipper as the frigid early afternoon wind bullwhips our faces. This man has years of knowledge still to impart as the windowed tips of Chicago's revered skyscrapers glisten pink in the bright cold sky. We've already heard why in 1871 architects hovered like vultures over Mrs. O'Leary's burnt city, the exact location of the St. Valentine's Day Massacre, and the date Enrico Fermi launched the nuclear age.

As we exit the office lobby I tug at a stubborn forty-year-old zipper on my *zingy turquoise wool Very Twiggy* coat I bought last month on eBay from CarnabyJane, a seller in Sussex. Costly for a vintage buy, especially with the overseas postage, but I splurged to cheer myself up about the lack of progress on my dissertation.

"Still buying dead women's clothes?" Gary teases after the zipper finally zips. He looks downward and shakes his head in further disdain. "I didn't even see the boots. How are those fuckers still around?"

"I just resoled them for the sixth time."

Gary is appalled. "Give them a retirement party. Do you want me to take you to Neiman Marcus later? The girls in my office buy their boots there...."

If Dot could hear this conversation, she'd nod vigorously. On my first Thanksgiving break from Binghamton, when she saw me in my favorite thrift store dress in the worst condition, a yellow mini with a cigarette hole, she rapped her stick of celery on one of my mother's many chipped plates, and decreed, "You can't go back to college looking like a ragpicker. The time has come for some adult clothes." She demanded a shopping trip to Macy's. "You need nice sweaters, and slacks—we'll make it a day." She did buy me a good black cardigan and new faded black Levi's that came in awfully handy. But mostly I wore my prized juicy-colored slightly tatty Mod dresses with tights all through a chilly, snowy Binghamton winter, warming my ankles and feet with my proudest thrift score, a pair of deep purple go-go boots.

The brutal wind continues to batter as the tour race-walks the three blocks to the next Windy City architectural jewel. Face red raw, Gary complains that cold days in his current hometown are even worse than the ones in Binghamton, and ten times worse than New York City's doozies. So his big plan is to bring a corn-fed gal back East next year, when he's done ten years in Chicago. "I'm cold and I'm thirty-five, old as the hills. Cold and old. Time for a wife."

I snort. "Have someone in mind then?"

"Not the one I'm dating. Hailey's too bitter."

Bitter in Gary Marino's universe means sarcastic, which is okay for girls you hang out with in the dorm floor lounge when you watch *Letterman,* but it's not okay for girls you actually date for a long run. Although Gary is a funny guy, sarcasm is not his forte—even though he's an account executive for a major ad agency. Gary's humor would fit right into the Delta House living room, but a lot of the time I find his manner a pleasant shift away from the sardonic take on life so prevalent in my Ph.D. set. Hell, I'm bitter, too, a "second-rate existential-ist," as one short-haul Christopher so meanly put it just before he gave me the heave-ho.

Opposite a public Calder sculpture, our guide breez-ily informs us that the name Chicago is derived from the Algonquian word for the onion grass that grew around Lake Michigan. His words are freezing midair. With my sleeves pulled down over my hands, only my fingertips have warmed; I feel like a chicken in a par-tially defrosted state.

I steal another peek at the Englishman. Despite my growing lust for the man on the tour, I want out. I should have listened to Gary and gone with him to the neighborhood bar he frequents in Lincoln Square, the one with the crackling fireplace, but I idiotically pushed him on his first poorly pitched suggestion: "Well, there's a weekly architecture tour for people into Chicago's culture shit."

"I like your coat. Very stylish," the Brit says from somewhere right behind me. I lost track of where he was during my wandering thoughts, and I turn around with a start.

"Didn't mean to scare you."

"It's okay, and thank you."

"It looks vintage, is it?"

"Yes."

"Quite a lovely blue. Like a robin's egg."

"It's British," I spurt out.

"Oh? Did you buy it in England?"

"No, on eBay. From a woman in Sussex. Or was it Essex?"

"Maybe Middlesex," he offers.

"So much sex in England."

He looks at me curiously, perhaps to sort out if my weak pun was an accidental come-on or I was deliberately the siren.

"That's quite an old joke, you know," he says evenly. I'm not sure what to say next.

Gary taps me. "Whaddaya think—time to say sayonara to the skyscrapers?"

I reluctantly nod to Gary, and give this sexy stranger a parting grin. I'm a taken woman anyhow. My English friend gives his own careful parting smile that acknowledges my obvious interest as reciprocated. Another lifetime, I promise myself.

Gary is so very Gary as he informs our guide about our defection: "Hey listen bro, the two of us are freezing our effing butts off. My pal and I need something hot to drink."

"I see," the tour leader harrumphs. "Just twenty more minutes and then I let you loose. You can't suffer for a little history?"

I could easily be guilted into staying, especially with my flirtation still on the tour, but I can tell by my old floormate's face that he's truly had enough. So I add, just to soften the crass defection, "You were fantastic. I learned so much, thank you." I mean what I say. If only I had as much passion for my work as this man does for his.

After a cautious sideways step in my direction, the Brit quietly asks, "Where're you headed?"

The guide frowns at him.

"Dunkin' Donuts," I whisper.

"Right. It'll be warm there, I suppose?"

"We're banking on that."

The guide's mood has taken a downturn as he starts the trivia again. "Oak Park is worth a ride, even in this weather. There are nine, count them, nine Frank Lloyd Wright-designed houses in this residential neighborhood—"

Gary silently counts out three fingers and the two of us tiptoe out of sight as quickly as possible when the guide isn't looking.

"Poor guy was disgraced," I say, but only after we're safely inside Dunkin' Donuts, waiting in line behind other Arctic refugees.

"Why, because a couple of people left his tour slightly early on a cold day?"

"You could see he took pride in his expertise."

"Yeah, but I bet half of the others wanted out, too. So what did the lord say to you?"

Before I can answer him, I hear "Mind if I join you two?" in that devastating English accent.

I'm all smile, a Jane Austen coquette. "Sure, go right ahead."

A pretty young blond woman (the one Gary was ogling on the tour) has followed suit as well. Except for her iced-pink lipstick, everything about her clothing is winter-white, a supposedly edge-of-fashion color-co-ordinated concept that has few takers back in deter-minedly black-clad Manhattan.

Gary's mood instantly jazzes up. "Hi," he says with an open grin.

"I'm f-f-f-frozen," she says and then smiles with teeth whiter than her pants.

"We were thinking of some hot chocolate."

"Cocoa," says the Brit. "Good idea. Yanks say London is cold, but Chicago is positively freezing."

"Are you also from out of town?" Gary says to the woman. In my Masters of English Literature mind I have dubbed her *The Woman in White,* but Gary would never in a billion years get that Wilkie Collins reference, so why even share? When I tried to explain the pilgrim-age that inspired Chaucer's *Canterbury Tales* the day he made me toast pizza in his dorm room, he pretended I was holding up a chunk of kryptonite and collapsed theatrically.

"No, I live here. I swore to myself I would finally take the tour."

That's all the information he needs. Gary leaves my

side to chat her up. They're flirting in one line while I'm chatting with my Brit in the alternative one closer to the door.

There are three hungry and cold customers still ahead of the Brit and me.

I rub my cheeks to warm them up and ask, "Are you visiting America?"

"I'm here from London for the week—work-related."

"The receptionist in my hotel said she's never seen the mercury drop so low in March. Even in a city used to wind, it's caught everyone off guard."

"Oh, I see. It is dreadful, isn't it?"

"Yes," I say. Silence. I think for a few long seconds: should I probe further? The always-cautious English make me wary of talking too much. Being a world-class chatterbox—my everyday manner—is something that fellow New Yorkers think nothing of. I'm a linguist who feels self-conscious in the face of a perfect little Brit accent. My profession helps keep my outer-borough nasal twang in check. But there are telltale words and phrases that sell me and every other striving native Noo Yawker right down the river: *a dozen aiggs, dine-o-saw, a glass of waw-da* and *Harry Pott-a.*

These mile-a-minute thoughts are once again punctured by that highborn BBC voice: "I hate to break this news, but I do believe your lad is ditching you." A few feet ahead, Gary is nodding earnestly and ordering for the blonde.

"Who, Gary? He's an old buddy. He's definitely not my *lad.*"

"Then he won't mind if I pay for your cocoa." I study

him for a moment. He's got a good poker face but he's flirting—his eyes are his tell.

"No, he wouldn't," I say coyly.

"It's warm in here, just as you foretold."

"Yes it is. Are you defrosted yet?"

"Almost, except for my eyeballs."

The word eyeballs is always funny and my laugh is appreciative.

The Brit beams and says, "Where are you visiting from?"

"New York City." Well, that's what he asked. Why rush to tell the man matching my fetish to a T about my boyfriend back in Manhattan? I'm just flirting, too. "Gary and I have been great pals since college. One weekend he kidnapped me—well, he very *convincingly* convinced me to drive all the way from upstate New York to Indiana just to see a college basketball game. We bonded during the road trip."

"Did you go to Cornell then?"

"No, SUNY Binghamton. You've probably never heard of it," I say, a bit deflated. Yeesh. Will my lowly state-school past thin this privileged man's enthrallment?

"You're right, but let me try another one. Was that basketball game at Notre Dame?" he asks with a small but just as wolfish smile. This chap is definitely interested.

"Yes, as a matter of fact. You played basketball in England?"

"Me? Oh heavens no. I rowed."

"What British rower follows American basketball?"

"This one."

"Name four players!"

"Not the university ones, I'm afraid. But the NBA, sure, I could do it."

"Go ahead then."

"Shaq, of course. Kobe Bryant, he's a natural—shame about the legal problems. Jason Kidd, and Jefferson and Martin, they're also Nets. There's Reggie Miller in the Indiana Pacers, he's brilliant, and there's that forty-year-old bloke, Karl Malone—"

"Okay!" I stop him with my upturned palm as I chuckle. "I believe you. That's amazing. I can't think of one athlete from your neck of the woods except—who's that soccer guy, you know, *Bend It Like Beckham*—"

"Beckham," he says with a wink.

I'm officially in love.

"We had an uncle doing a stint in Boston who sent my brother and me an overseas subscription to *Sports Illustrated.* That got us hooked. I worshipped Wilt while Nigel was the Dr. J expert."

Nigel, I echo in my brain. I have never met even one American named Nigel. I have a brief vision of Nigel and his so-far nameless brother reading *Sports Illustrated* taking turns tending a raging peat, stoking it with an antique poker topped with a family crest.

I guess I was smirking again because he says, "Humorous stuff, is it?"

"No, uh, I was just thinking that you'd love what Gary does for a living. He's an executive on the Bulls account, and has season passes."

"Really?"

"Really."

"You're making me bloody jealous here. I tried to get tickets to tonight's game, but my concierge told me even nosebleed is like asking him for front row seats to Oprah."

"I'm going tonight."

"*Really!* Brilliant!"

"The girl Gary was supposed to go with came down with chicken pox from her cat—sounds weird, I know—and when I called him to tell him I was in town—"

Gary slides into the conversation as soon as he hears his name, a bag of donuts and cocoa in his hand: "I told her it was her lucky day."

I playfully poke Gary. "I'm not so sure about her story."

"Why?" asks Gary.

"Who ever heard of cat pox?"

Gary shrugs. "I've never heard of it either. But it's exactly what she said to me."

I turn back to my Brit, who is still looking amused: "I told him my work here kicks off tomorrow, so yes, I'd love to go to the game."

"So you like Notre Dame basketball?" the Brit asks.

Gary is floored. "You follow ND in England?"

"Well, I've heard of it of course—"

"My dad went to ND. *Fucking* loved it."

Now I remember the whole issue with Gary's father's "enchanted" college years, one of the big topics of conversation during our epic road trip. Gary's rejection from the school still was a sore spot for him. How could it have happened? He was a legacy applicant with a ninety-one percent high school average. Either of those qualifications alone should have gotten him in. Gary had been wait-listed to no avail. His theory was that he was rejected because he was coming out of a public school and he asked for financial aid. Gary's father wasn't big money like so many other legacy applicants; his Dad had attended ND in the sixties on scholarship. Yet Gary still refused to say a bad word about the school.

Gary's family was richer than mine, but that's not saying much. In his mind he was poor.

To keep alert on the eighteen-hour drive from Binghamton to Notre Dame, Gary needed someone like me along, a chronic talker. I calmed down about being abducted once we left the New York State border, and dutifully kept the conversation going through Ohio Amish territory, Cincinnati and Gary, Indiana, Michael Jackson's hometown. Gary stopped the car there for a corny photo op, which was of course Gary standing in front of a big green Welcome to Gary sign banked up with snow. Back in the car I sang, "Gary, Indiana, Gary, Indiana, Gary Indiana, let me say it once again!" A private joke with myself: "Gary, Indiana" was the song that most annoyed my oldest brother, Gene. Our mother listened to the original Broadway cast soundtrack album of *The Music Man* at least twice a week, humming along as she painstakingly ran over our old living room rug with a carpet sweeper. The music wormed its way into Gene's brain. I'm not sure how I escaped its insidious power.

The Brit speaks again: "So there's a story going around that you abducted this young lady for one of their basketball games."

Gary snorts, and then a distant memory washes over

his face. "I forgot all about that road trip! I friggin' kidnapped you!"

"There was nine inches of snow in Indiana! You were insane to make me go!"

Gary can't talk for laughter. Finally: "Man! What a trip that was. Remember how we spun out fifteen miles before getting to the stadium?"

"Remember it? Gary—we almost *died*."

Gary's laughter subsides after a glance toward the stool behind the window where his little lady friend is perched. "Shit, listen guys, I have to get back to that chick. Digging me, big time. I just wanted to refund your cocoa, Miss S. When you're in Chi-town you don't pay."

"Too late, my new friend has already offered to pay."

Gary barely contains himself, but keeps his commentary to a knowing smile. The Brit is expressionless again, but I suspect we're his entertainment for the day.

"I'll be over by the window, but first I have to take another horse piss. Give me a minute to finish the job, and then come over and join us."

"He's a bit off-color, but he's a wonderful pal," I say when Gary's out of earshot again. "We lived a few doors down from each other in my college back east—"

"Ah, ah, ah. Never apologize for school chums. My mate Reece was almost sent down fresher year for streaking. Cost his father plenty quid to keep him there. Took the committee a week to take a decision on that. His old man had to cough up an endowment to keep him through to tripos. But he was a good bloke all the same."

He chuckles out loud, and I laugh too even though I haven't the faintest clue who or what tripos is. There's one more rollicking memory of his school days: "Bloody Andy served everybody drinks with fish ice at our last reunion."

"Fish ice? Is that another British expression?"

A laugh. "No, just the ice that fish gets shipped in. Salmon fish ice it was. Nasty stuff."

I bet Gary would enjoy hearing about these fellow pranksters, but he has returned from the bathroom and right now he's having a fine time ogling the contours of the blonde's blinding white sweater.

"So, you're from New York City," he says.

"Yes, I'm living there again. Gary's also a New Yorker, by the way, from Bensonhurst—that's a part of Brooklyn. You can ask him about Knicks games. That's his secondary team."

"I'm going to New York after Chicago; never been." My unprotected heart jumps at the news. *Boyfriend, boyfriend,* I tell myself as he continues, "Had to add a few days on, of course. How can you come to America and not see New York?"

"You'll love it. And trust me, Downtown needs your pounds to rebuild." I'm blushing a bit as I sneak another face-saving look toward the front of the line. What is taking so long? We're ordering donuts here, not steaks. How many boxes of donut holes has that man ahead of us ordered?

"Maybe you could show me around?"

This time I look him straight in the eyes. "Of course I will." Did I just say that? It sounds like we just made a date. Is offering to tour-guide a man you'd love to kiss cheating?

"Wonderful."

He smiles at me and I smile at him, and the sudden silence threatens to ruin our vibe.

"You know, when you used the word college before, it occurred to me that in England, college is usually what I think you call high school here. Well, except in Oxbridge. Oh *sorry,* you probably wouldn't know that term. It means—"

"So did you go to Oxford or Cambridge?"

After an amused glance he says, "Cambridge."

"Which college?"

"You know the colleges?"

"A few of them. Try me."

"Trinity."

"Where Isaac Newton was a student, right?"

"Indeed, the very one."

"Indeed," I mimic his accent, this time out loud.

"Next!" The combination of the cashier's blond hair, large lips and huge torso make him look quite a bit like a bodybuilder duck.

"What can I get my new friend here?" the Brit asks me.

"Oh, thank you. Hot chocolate. That's all I want."

"And for *youse?*" says the ducky cashier to the Cambridge grad.

"Sugar donut, thank you. And make that two cocoas."

"Youse?" my "new friend" discreetly parrots to me while our paper cups of cocoa are being filled several feet away. "What has your country done to my poor language?"

"We corrected a few things, too. Calling a fight a *wobbly* is outlawed in every state of the Union."

"I'm amazed you even know that term." He studies my face and gives me the verdict: "You're charming, by the way."

"And so are you," I rally back.

"Well then, we might as well be introduced. What's your name, Miss S.? Susan? Sabrina?"

"Shari."

"Sherri? Is that short for Sheridan?"

"No, Shari, not Sherri."

"Oh. Right. That sounds so—American. Is that short for Sharon, then?"

I bristle at his question. Like Debbie and Tammy, plain old Shari is a pretty damn common name among lower and middle-class Jews of New York. There are at least five Shari Diamonds in Manhattan alone; I saw us listed on a computer screen when my Citibank manager brought up my account on his computer the day my checkbook was stolen. As the manager double-checked my address, I noted a Shari Diamond in Stuyvesant Town complex on Fourteenth Street, and two of us on Avenue A.

When I was around sixteen my mother huffed when I asked her why she had to choose such a tacky name: "I can't believe I've given birth to such a snob."

I'm still not crazy about my first name, but my mother would never let me get away with a legal name change like the one my Binghamton friend Rain Alexander fixed for herself just before our college graduation—Rain changed her name to Mary so that she wouldn't come off sounding like the upstate New York hippie kid she was in her post MBA interviews. I use

Shari socially but for professional publication I always use S. Roberta Diamond, uglier, sure, but far more respectable looking.

I cram all these thoughts down almost as quickly as they well up. Who needs a North American class and demographic lesson with a sugar donut? I answer with, "No, just Shari. It's pretty common as a full name in New York City."

"Right. Well, my friends call me Kit."

"That a nickname?"

"Yes. Short for Christopher."

Oh, good God. Gary is *not* going to believe this.

Suddenly it really does feel like cheating. *I am not hooking up with this Chris,* I sell myself again. "Myself" is not buying. It's awfully hard to think of Kevin Bernstein now, but I have to try and think of him if I'm any sort of decent human being. I endeavor to do just that, but only my half-committed relationship doubts seep through. Even if Kevin is appealing at first, the more time you spend with him you realize how nebbishy he truly is. He does, however, have endearing brown cowlicks, and an exceedingly warm body temperature—which makes sleeping with him a pleasure since I'm practically an amphibian. I would hate to think a body in the bed is the only reason I've stayed with him.

"You look alarmed." He studies my face again: "I'm sorry, have I offended you somehow?"

"No. I'm just a little worried."

"For heavens' sake, what about?"

I wave off his concern and we talk some more. In another scarily pleasant surprise, it turns out that "after business" in Chicago, Kit is scheduled for my very flight from Chicago to New York's LaGuardia Airport.

"Now you'll absolutely have to be my guide to the Big Apple. Do New Yorkers really say the Big Apple by the way?"

"Surprisingly, yes. Do the British really drink a lot of tea?"

"Well, I have a fair bit," he says congenially. He tacks on, "By the way, have I asked you already, what is your work here exactly? Are you in a conference in Chicago?"

"Yes."

"I heard every room in the city is booked. My bellhop told me there's an ephemera conference going on in my hotel, as well as a convention of *M*★*A*★*S*★*H* enthusiasts."

Before I can tell him which group *I'm* booked for—there's at least three in my hotel, too, including a chemists meet-up—our hot steaming order is finally ready in the take-out bag. There is a further distraction when Gary arrives back by our side with a news report on his sorority president seduction.

"What's taking so long, you two?" Gary asks.

I raise my eyebrows in exaggerated frustration. "We just got our order. There was a donut hole holdup. How are you faring over there with your *chick?*"

"She loves me, my friends, but she wants to walk."

"As in outside?" After Kit hands me the paper cup of cocoa, I gratefully wrap my frozen fingers around it. "Sweetheart, Gary, we came here for the warmth."

"Run with me, *sweetheart*. We have to tootle outside

or the little lady will get pissed off not to mention frostbitten."

Kit nods okay. The cheeky British bastard's hand is practically on my ass as he guides me out the door.

I catch Kit's eye and smile ever so slightly. Given the tiny go-ahead he actually shocks the slut in me when he pinches my butt right through my coat. Most self-respecting American women would give the guy a miss right there. But in my reading of the moment, I'm going with raffish over chauvinist, and I pinch his flat Anglo butt right back.

When Kit opens the door, it's even colder than when we ditched the tour. "Oh damn. I've lost one of my new gloves," I mutter out loud before we introduce ourselves to Gary's gal.

"Put this on," Kit says as he slips one of his soft brown leather gloves off and offers it to my gloveless palm. My hand has never had it so good. "I'll go back in the shop and check for you."

"Shari this is Sally," Gary introduces me to his quarry.

"Hi!" she says pertly.

"Hey."

"I haven't seen her in seventeen years, since college graduation."

"Really?"

I nod. "But we write sometimes, and e-mail."

"And now she's blessing me with her presence because the Volachuks are in town."

Sally looks confused, so I take over Gary's mangled explanation. "I'm writing my dissertation on a language called *Volapük*. I'm presenting at a conference tomorrow."

"Oh," she says, without an ounce of interest.

"You know how we became good friends?" Gary says, rescuing us both. "I kidnapped her my freshman year."

"Excuse me?" Sally says a bit prissily.

"Our junior year," I say. "The year we got our own apartments off campus. Gary tricked me by saying we should stock our fridges before the storm."

"The central New York storms are brutal," Gary says, smirking.

"He knew that I didn't have a car, and that I would jump at the chance for a lift to Wegman's, which is a mammoth New York state supermarket chain where you can pick up anything edible in bulk."

"Anything! Frosted Mini-Wheats, Tootsie Rolls, spinach pasta shells—" Gary puts in.

I nod. "We zipped past the supermarket as Gary so solemnly explained that yes, well, he lied and we were in actuality going on an eighteen-hour road trip."

As proven by Kit's reaction just minutes ago, *everybody* loves this story.

"That's terrible," Sally says. "You never told her she'd be away for a day? That's just *mean*."

"Truth is," I say, surprised, and a bit desperately, "I ended up having tons of fun. We were bound for South Bend, Indiana for a big football game at Notre Dame."

"I went there," Sally says matter-of-factly.

Gary is ecstatic. "You went to ND? For a visit? Isn't it effing great there?"

"Yes, and I wasn't visiting. I went to school there. My father and grandfather went, too. I was a legacy."

You'd think that legacy tidbit would hurt, but I can

tell Gary is even more interested than before. Gary wants in the country club, too. He may taunt me about my proclivities, but he's just as much a sucker for the upper classes, the All-American kind.

The Woman in White speaks again: "Since your friend from England is still looking for your glove, I'm going to race inside and freshen up. I should have done that before."

Gary and I are alone. He sighs loudly. "She's gorgeous. I'm not out yet."

"What about the bitter girl you're dating?"

"This from a girl pinching someone's ass while her boyfriend waits by the phone?"

"Shit, you actually saw that?"

"That's what I like about you. Used the big words in school, but push comes to shove, you're just as loose as the townies. Worse." We share a vice-ridden laugh. "So, what are you going to do with him?"

"Do? He pinched my ass, he didn't ask me out. It's tour sex. A dead end after the flirtation."

"You sound like you've had it before."

"When you go to conferences a lot, it happens."

"Bullshit, I've never had tour sex. You have?"

"Two conferences ago I had a great touchy-feely conversation about Gorgonzola cheese with a man from Milan at Niagara Falls, and then the boat docked and he introduced me to his stunning fiancée."

Gary snorts, and I do too—I've never told that anecdote out loud before.

"I actually think Lord Faggot really likes you."

"I'm having a big flirt, that's all. To be honest, I'm

thinking you should give up on Doris Day's niece. I'm not sure about her—"

"You spoke to her for two seconds. And I'm supposed to listen to you? You who hates all women who are naturally blond?"

I laugh. Gary has a point.

"So you don't want these then?" Gary fans the Bulls tickets in front of my face.

Has hell frozen over? "*You're* not going?"

"I live here. I work with them. I'll see them again. And no bullshit, this girl might be the one."

"One little kitty chicken pock and the other poor girl is completely out of your running?"

"Three dates, that's all we've had. Hailey is a nutjob anyway."

Who am I to make a value judgment? Even Gary sees the mutual charge I have going with Kit. Am I about to cheat on Kevin? I'm not sure that I'm not.

"The master plan is you have to say you're going back to the hotel unexpectedly so I can drive her home. You can use those tickets for your own bait."

"I have a boyfriend in New York, remember?"

"You look pretty interested in the man to me."

Sally pushes open the Dunkin' Donuts door.

"Hi!" Sally says cheerily. Maybe she is liking Gary. Her full lips are even pinker than before. Why is this woman possibly the one? Is it her nose, the exact button nose shared by so many of the one-night stands Gary had paraded down our dorm floor?

"Hi again!" Gary says.

"Hi!" I say with extra perk, and Gary shoots me a

quick frown to let me know my condescending tone is not appreciated.

Kit emerges a few seconds later. "I searched everywhere. Your glove is missing in action."

I shake my head sympathetically. "Don't worry, please. It was so nice of you to look."

Gary can now introduce Kit to Sally.

"How long are you here?" Sally says.

"A week. Than I'm off to New York."

Gary inconspicuously kicks the back of my ankle in delight. "I can't believe I have to give up my ticket to the Bulls," he says. "They're mind-blowingly close to the court."

Kit's face brightens enough to notice, but he seems careful not to pitch his hopes too high. "Why can't you go?"

"I have an early morning meeting I have to prepare for."

I zoom in for the kill. "Kit, you think you might want to come on the extra ticket?"

A big American-sized grin from Kit. "Bloody hell I will."

Gary's prey is next, although I'm not giving him good odds.

"Can I drive you home?" Gary says to Sally. "If you live near Lincoln Park, that's where I'm going. And I'm parked a block away. Will you keep me company? It's one cold, windy block."

Sally's apology rambles: "I can't. I told my boyfriend I'd meet him back on South Michigan. I hope I didn't give you the wrong message. I told my mother I would finally take the tour, but it was just too cold, that's all. I'll have to do it again when the city warms up."

Despite her awkward *Oh-did-I-lead-you-on?* delivery, I'm surprised Gary hasn't snatched the tickets back.

"You have a boyfriend?" he says to Sally. "You're breaking my heart."

Sally sways her head with another guilty grin. She's a good girl with a voice of conscience. Unlike the New York floozy standing a few feet from her.

While we all say our goodbyes Guy says in an extremely low voice, "Go for it, I'll go next week." Then, loud enough for Kit to hear he says, "You need me to draw you a map back to your hotel? If I was you I'd hop a cab."

"I'll find it. Don't worry." I give Gary a forehead kiss. "But let's have a drink before I leave. What's the name of that bar you wanted to go to again?"

"There's a place you'd like more. The Red Lion. Very British. Right up your alley." Gary shambles away with one last cry behind him, "Call me when the conference is settling down!"

"British pub, eh?" Kit says, when Gary is partway down the block. "So you make a habit of hanging out with the likes of me?"

I improvise: "He means because as an undergraduate I majored in English Literature. He grabbed my study notes once and couldn't believe I knew what *machicolations* were."

"What are they?"

"Medieval openings in the floor for attacking enemies."

"Well, that's new to me. But I read English at Trinity. So feel at home here."

I bob my head in appreciation. He *read* English at *Trinity.* I last heard that phrase during a documentary about Salman Rushdie.

"How many hours to the Bulls game?" Kit reaches in his pocket and removes his tobacco and rolling papers.

I look at one of the tickets I'd shoved in my bag as he rolls his own cigarette in the cold air. "Five," I say.

Cigarette in mouth, he reaches for a shiny gray lighter with red jewels on the engraved snake's eye. Once his tobacco is lit, out pops a cell phone and a business card he must have requested from a previous taxi ride in Chicago. "How shall we kill that time? Or should we meet later?"

"Would you like to come back to my hotel for a drink?"

He holds my gaze. "Where's that?"

"The Hyatt."

"You got a room there? I couldn't get a room there. As I said, so many bloody conferences going."

"It was booked for me two months ago. It's busy, but they have lots of restaurants. We could get a nosh."

"A *nosh?* You use that word, too? That's rather English of you."

It is? I laugh a little, confused. I thought nosh was a Yiddishism. "Everyone says nosh in New York."

"*Really?* They say *nosh* in New York City? *Nosh?* I can't believe that. A nosh, then. Shall we?"

★ ★ ★

"Did you know that Tony Blair will be here next week?"

"Where did you hear that?" Kit says after he's refused any cab money from me, even the tip.

"On the way to my hotel from O'Hare. He's staying here—"

"In the Presidential Suite," our driver pipes up.

Feet on the curb, Kit tightens his argyle as another brutal prairie wind gushes through to our bones. I point out the fluttering Union Jack on one of the hotel flagpoles. He frowns. "They have the flag upside down."

"They couldn't—"

"A major insult to the crown, unless one is signaling distress."

After a nervous laugh I say, "Well then, you'd better talk to the concierge before Blair gets here."

"You think so?"

"I'm sure anyone you talk to will be appreciative for the heads-up."

The young woman serving as the lunch-break concierge noisily shuffles through papers and brochures, giving us no heed until Kit coughs politely.

She shrugs her shoulders at the bad news. "I'm sure our hotel knows what it is doing."

"Maybe not," I say emphatically.

She hates me already. "Does it really concern you? Do you have a specific problem about your room?"

"Ma'am, doesn't it concern you if your hotel is reflected badly?" Kit says more diplomatically.

She huffs and gets the older Indian manager with a pale brown face and bushy eyebrows. He's apparently been clued in to the problem couple—after a raced hello he says, "Sir, I am well aware of how the British flag should fly. My father lived in England for some time."

"Sir, I really think this is not a matter of pride. You have a head-of-state coming, and I think perhaps you should fix your mistake."

"*Sir,* I have not made a mistake, *sir.*"

Kit pulls out his flag-emblazoned passport holder and shows the manager where he's gone wrong. The manager's nose wrinkles as his error sinks in. He angrily hits a pylon next to the check-in desk; his punch causes a particularly ugly piece of corporate art, a lithograph of green and blue rotary telephones, to bounce a bit on the wall.

"I'll leave you a diagram," Kit says. The manager remains silent as Kit tears a bit of paper out of his spiral memo book. Out comes the expensive silver pen from the architectural tour. "The United Kingdom flag isn't symmetrical. When you are facing the flag, you have to look at the white diagonals. On the left-hand, the hoist side, the white bands *above* the red diagonals are wider. On the right-hand side, the fly side, the wider white bands sit *below* the red diagonal."

"Thank you, sir," the manager says coldly. "We'll fix it right away, sir."

"It was the right thing to do," I say comfortably from my new seated position in a plush lobby armchair.

Kit takes the seat opposite. "But I knew he was mad as hell, and I felt badly about his resentment."

I felt a little badly, too, but I'm impressed how Kit kept to an unpleasant task until it was done. "Yes, an uncomfortable moment there, but you had to do it, *sir.* You might have saved his job. I'd speak up if the American flag was flying wrong."

It's hard not to compare what Kevin would have done—that is, nothing, as much from timidity as from a sense of *for godsakes, give the small guys a break.* Like my mother, Kevin does not like to offend anyone, which makes him well liked by men, but gives him that nice-guy whiff that turns a good number of women off even considering his boyish good looks.

I can barely hear what Kit says next—a swarm of soccer players have entered the Hyatt lobby bar high-fiving and screaming at each other in Portuguese. Kit smiles in frustration. As far as this man's looks go, I suspect he is the kind of guy who needs softening bar light to really look good to the rest of womankind, save the Anglophiles. He desperately needs a tan, and while his teeth aren't stereotypically nasty, they could use a good cleaning. Smoking isn't helping him in that department. My roommate back in New York would cringe; Cathy has been trying to land a nice Jewish boy with nice white teeth since I've known her. Call this a Gary stereotype if you will, but I agree with her that American Jewish men take amazing care of their teeth. But what can I say? Kit and his slightly discolored incisors and cuspids just do it for me.

And sadly, Kevin with the bright whites back home just doesn't.

I sigh to myself. I haven't had sex with Kevin for a month. I hate faking it. I can come with Kevin, if he's patient, and especially if I'm on top. But these days I just don't have the energy to spend thirty minutes on anything with a high activity level.

True, my listlessness is not entirely Kevin's fault.

I have recently arranged an appointment back in New York City with a thyroid specialist. I got the name of the doctor from Velma, the Jamaican secretary for my graduate department. She tapped me on my hand before handing over the American Airlines tickets and the check advance for my conference. "Listen, mon. You are tired, too tired for a young girl. You see a doctor. It's your thyroid, mon. I was conking out everywhere but now I take Synthroid." She claimed her visits and medicine were covered in the student and clerical staff plans, and that some of the most respected doctors at New York University gallantly do student and faculty clinic work once a week.

I think Kit is talking to me again through the clamor. I scootch over even closer.

When I'm half an inch from his ear, he has a question for me. "Are you peckish? Because I'd really fancy a crumpet about now."

I nod and shout, "What actually is a crumpet?"

His voice is raised, too. "It looks like a hockey puck. You melt cheese on it or butter."

"It sounds like an English muffin."

"No, I had one of those in my hotel today. There's nothing English about an English muffin. A crumpet is—it's a crumpet." He smiles for a brief second and says even louder and more coyly, "Oh, it also means sex, but that would be rude now to use it like that, wouldn't it?"

I smile big in response because, even shouting, I cannot vocally compete with the soccer team.

We mime to each other to move away from the fray.

When we can hear again we investigate our options. All Seasons Café in the lobby is closed for renovation, and at the concierge's suggestion we move shop to Knuckles Sports Bar, which wouldn't normally be my first choice for an intimate chat. A college basketball game is on that appears to be very important to not one but two men with bright red W. C. Fields noses. Both of their angry yells are directed toward the projected image that dominates the room.

"Asshole!" screams yet another fan at the screen. He's minus the gin blossom, but just as drunk.

Kit grins at me over the din, yet he manages a peek at the TV screen. I'm not insulted—even though he said he doesn't know much about college basketball, he has confessed his love of the sport.

My next question is solely to aid my nervousness. My family unanimously disapproves of my habit of filling silences with chitchat. "Do you know what hijiki is?"

"Not really," he half-yells after a perplexed look. "Can you use it in context?"

"A Japanese man on my flight was hyper-concerned about the arsenic levels in hijiki."

"Seaweed?"

"Of course," I yell. "Seaweed."

"Shari, I can hardly hear myself. Can you hear me at all?"

Now the whole room goes berserk. "Bring it home!" a chunky woman in a Mickey Mouse sweatshirt yells at the screen.

"We could go to my room," I say uncomfortably, but thrilled with myself for the big push.

Kit agrees with a neutral up and down dip of his chin.

CHAPTER 3

My Mensch

After I push seventeen, a linguist I have a nodding relationship with enters the elevator. He nods hi. I nod hi. I have no need for embarrassment. You'd never know the man at my side was headed to my room. Kit's face is dignified, with a certain sexy-as-hell arrogance.

When Kevin is in the elevator he pushes me up against the corner and imprisons me under the stinky hollows of his surprisingly fleshy armpits. I've had doubts about him, but never this harsh. Why am I thinking of him as a total horror, a too-nice loser? Even if I've had my reservations, others want him. My roommate for one, and she's an attractive, smart woman. "Okay," I say to myself as therapist, "so if Kevin doesn't do it for you, why haven't you broken up with him yet? Is it fear, or guilt that his mother has died earlier in the year?"

"Actually," I answer myself, "I suspect Kevin really

does love me as much as he says he does, and with all of my dissertation stress, right now I couldn't bear the wounded seal pup look I'm sure will come when I pull the cord."

I've lost a parent and I know how painful it is. He has years of grieving left to do and even that won't numb it all: it's a cruel line of dominoes, memory. But I do not love Kevin, and I have never said I do.

Kevin and I met six months ago at a film aficionado costume party thrown in honor of my longtime friend Tom Cohen's successful Cinema Studies dissertation.

Tom, the Man of the Hour, was outlandishly dressed as the "King of the Rumba," i.e., Xavier Cugat. He'd grown a thin moustache for the occasion, bought a South American hat and borrowed a chihuahua to carry in his arms. I had thought Cugat wasn't an actor, just a famous Spanish bandleader, but Tom then cited three Esther Williams's films that Cugat appeared in playing himself. Tom had obviously spent hours thinking out what would floor a roomful of Ph.D. students. His dickhead brother Doug took the piss out of Tom's earnestness by wearing a $5.99 Rite Aid Batman plastic Halloween outfit—he mocked Tom by walking around the room saying he was "citing *Batman Forever*"—a funny joke any day except the day someone's ten years of academic sweat and labor is being celebrated, his brother's, for God's sake.

Doug had one redeeming thing going for him though, at least as the single ladies in the room saw it. He had brought along a cute friend all of us were checking out—Kevin with wavy brown hair and big almond-shaped brown eyes. I privately gave Kevin's costume an "A for effort"—his adorable Sherlock Holmes getup was built around the expected houndstooth detective hat with earflaps tied together at the top. I smiled at his plastic pipe, and he said hello.

I could tell off the bat that Kevin was taken with my racy forties dress that was lined with flesh-colored silk, and my black peep-toe three inch mules. (I didn't have to spend a dime on my costume as everything was culled from my thrift store vintage wear.) I happily explained to cute Kevin that it was a tribute to Vivien Leigh's role in *Waterloo Bridge*—I was Myra Lester, the ballet dancer who falls in love with handsome Roy Cronin, a First World War British army officer, who has been called to duty. When she mistakenly thinks he's dead, scandal mushrooms around her as she turns to prostitution. "I'm sure I'm boring you to death here," I remember apologizing.

"Not at all. I love how you talk."

I could tell he was trying really hard to follow. He picked up on the word British, and the conversation drifted to Kevin's obscure Kinks and Stranglers record collection.

That Anglophile in me knew all the tracks on the Kinks' *Village Green Preservation Society*. Kevin was *amazed*. Doug, Tom's brother, drunkenly interrupted us: "Yo, Kev, Batman has to drop the Batkids off at the pool, hold my beer." Doug cracked himself up, and left our vicinity.

Mortified, holding a beer, Kevin said, "I know him well, but right now I wish he'd just leave."

I whispered nicely, "It's okay, really," and then to make

Kevin feel better I brought up my fondness for "Always the Sun," the only Stranglers song I know the lyrics for.

"I am your slave now, you realize that," Kevin cracked.

Soon after that Doug left Tom's apartment altogether with my friend Marni, a shocking exit—Marni is an academic lady if there ever was one, a year or two away from finishing her dissertation on courtly love in *The Canterbury Tales*.

Free of his embarrassing buddy, Kevin, as per his promise, stuck to me like glue. It was cute at first, but eventually he got on my nerves even if in appearance, he was the adorable catch of the party. About that I was proud.

At least I'd thought he was the catch. My weak fidelity halted abruptly when a new guest, a handsome English biology Ph.D. candidate at Columbia University, introduced himself on the three-person line for the bathroom. I beamed like a girl on the hunt when the scientist said he'd christened his new orange-ringed kitten Helix the Cat.

Kevin hovered nearby as I admired the party Brit's Hamlet costume. "Are you Olivier tonight?"

"Nay. Richard Burton's Hamlet."

When I offered up that I was a linguist with training wheels on, he said politely, "What was the first language you learned outside of English?"

"Ubba Bubba, from *Zoom*."

"Pardon?"

"It's an American kids' show. Ubba Bubba was *Zoom*'s version of pig latin. To be or not to be becomes *'Tubbo bubbe ubbor nubbot tubbo bubbe.'"*

I cribbed that example off a fellow linguist's blog, but

it was still pretty funny flirting if you ask me. The scientist, however, only looked mildly amused.

As I emerged from the bathroom after my own pee and a careful check for mascara smudges, another very single woman greeted Hamlet by saying, "my friend Annette claims you are Columbia's brightest young star."

I looked over this gal's amazing figure, shown off in a costume even raunchier than mine. I was outrivaled and literally outdazzled: at first glance my competition looked almost nude. But she was wearing *something*—her boobs sparkled and glowed with swirls of dark and light gold. I bitchily noted that her obviously flat-ironed hair had enough spray wax on it to look like high gloss on a car, and that her pimple, colored over by brown eyeliner to look like a birthmark, looked more like a wet Cocoa Puff. But Hamlet was obviously taken with his beautiful fan of the Genome Project. As I silently sipped the particularly strong vodka gimlet Tom had poured me—it never left my hands, even in the bathroom—I overheard her say "Don't worry about the religious right. I have a ten-year-old cousin with rheumatoid arthritis and damn straight I want you to explore what stem cells can do. Nobody should live a shitty life because her DNA is not good."

Hamlet nodded enthusiastically. "Science saves lives. Ignorance doesn't." He whispered something else in her ear, and then she said much more seductively, but loud enough for me to step out of her sandbox, "That's very flattering, I was nervous about the costume but many of the risqué Ziegfeld girls wore bodystockings."

"Can I ask you something important?" Sherlock Kevin wondered. How long had he been standing there, waiting for me to look at him? Defeated, I turned and smiled at him.

He took a deep breath: "I have to get your number. You're gorgeous and brilliant. That English guy you were talking to is really a complete asshole."

On any other night I might have realized that after the initial attraction wore off, Kevin was, in the end analysis, a bit pathetic. But he said some magic words there. Gorgeous and brilliant? Me? Did he know that was the exact flattery that would get me in a moment of vulnerability? Kevin of America was receptive to everything I had to say. Within ten minutes I was passionately kissing him in the kitchen next to a sink full of iced beer.

We walked the nine blocks to my apartment during which time Kevin explained that he was the first in his family to go to college and that his parents back in Michigan were working-class good eggs in a factory midmanagement life.

I admitted that I was working-class Jewish, too, but mostly just listened to him talk. I was drunk and I wanted to get laid.

Cathy smiled jealously when I brought Kevin inside and introduced him. We'd only yesterday talked about how desperate we were for any half-decent male companionship. I offered Kevin all we had to drink, cold club soda. My party pickup was loudly amused by how many bottles of salad dressing were in the refrigerator when I opened it up—fifteen in all including ranch, Italian, green goddess, Caesar and tarragon.

Cathy explained that we were both following a new *Glamour* diet of nibbles instead of full meals, and needed whatever flavoring we could get.

I coughed loudly when enough was enough; this girl can talk as much as me. Cathy flashed a knowing grin at me and retired to her room.

"How do you say, 'You're so amazingly hot?' in Ubba Bubba?" Kevin said, just before he kissed me again.

Kevin's first *I Love You* came quickly, at the Fourth of July outing on Roosevelt Island two weeks after the party smooch. We were with his friends, and he seemed five years younger, and not in a good way. Kevin's face was covered with gooey melted chocolate hazelnut gelato. He was also plenty smashed—buddy Doug saw to that, personally handing Kevin Bud after Bud, trying to pry him away from me. He wanted Kevin to see how he'd mastered "Stairway to Heaven" on a toy pineapple-shaped ukulele his parents had bought in Hawaii.

I was taken aback by Kevin's drunken holiday announcement, but since I hadn't heard a sexual *I Love You* said for several years, secretly I was a little moved. I playfully tugged at the bendy green glowstick around his wrist that we'd each bought for a buck from a Puerto Rican street vendor turning his own holiday hibachi chicken. I told Kevin that it was early for me but I was "really digging him"—which was true—and he waved over another holiday peddler darting through the crowd, chancing for a quick sale to the newly in love.

The red rose was rather sweet. But the next day as we nursed his hangover I'm not even sure he'd remembered buying the rose, let alone what he'd said.

The next *I Love You* came in mid-September right after I had decided three months was enough of a go. He was sweet and sex was okay, but I knew in my heart of hearts that this wasn't a match. I had what I was going to say all worked out. I would lead off with what a catch he is. "I mean seriously," I practiced out loud before Kevin's arrival, "how many women in New York are looking for a handsome and kind Jewish guy? You'll forget about me in a millisecond." But just before my letting-him-off-easy speech, Kevin fractured his wrist. In a New York scene the writers from *Friends* might have written, I rushed him to the emergency room in a pedicab: we couldn't get a taxi and he was too embarrassed for me to call an ambulance because he'd apparently brought this injury upon himself after he'd heard that his mother in Michigan was diagnosed with cancer. Nick, our cyclist, deserved a medal for pretending he couldn't hear a thing Kevin was saying and for that record time he made a mile and a half to St. Luke's Hospital in the Village.

Not the day to break up.

His mother died in November, and then before I knew it, it was New Year's Eve.

I know, I know. How could I let this continue? But he was having such a terrible year.

We were dining at Roberto's in the "real" Little Italy of New York City, Arthur Avenue in the Bronx. Kevin had made reservations after I'd casually mentioned that I had just finished the "Best of New York City" issue of *The Village Voice:* Robert Sietsema, the notoriously persnickety and adventurous food critic for the *Voice* thought Roberto's modern Italian was ten times better than the dime-a-dozen red-sauce joints on the strip.

"I love you more every moment," Kevin said with a teeny bit of mozzarella sticking to his tongue. I was already a bit nauseous from the texture of the tomatoey mussels in my mouth. I decided right then to drop the bomb sooner than later; it was just not right spending the New Year deceiving someone in mourning. He deserved real love back.

I smiled uneasily. Why ruin his day during an expensive dinner? At coffee, that's when I'd do it.

We shifted over to one of the coffee houses whose windows brimmed with cookies and cannolis, and we dug our spoons into the icy rock-hard chocolate and strawberry spumoni he'd ordered for dessert.

"So no *I love you* from you?"

"Kevin—" I really was going to answer him this time, but after one look at my face he quickly brought up how his mother gasped for words as she neared death. He squeezed my hand as he said, "She was calling out her kids' names, and bits of recipes, and Blade, the name of her first dog. She was staving off death, Shari—"

And just like at the party, he'd said the exact right thing to get me to do what he wanted. I'd tell him tomorrow…honest.

CHAPTER 4

Crumpet, Anyone?

I sit on the corner of the double bed in my hotel room, its tan-and-plum quilt still neat, I banish all thoughts of Kevin.

Kit sits down on one of the two plum polka-dotted armchairs.

"Are you still *peckish?*" I ask.

"I am, a bit. I could order up some room service. I'll put it on my card, of course."

"Well, sure then." I'm all for that. I'm an academic with an unfinished dissertation; I feel amazed but guilty as hell that NYU has sprung for a hotel as deluxe as this one. The conference is here, sure, but they could've easily stashed me in some faraway Econolodge. I think Dr. Cox, my Ph.D. advisor, was being kind to me when he saw I had nothing new to report at the start of year four. He made me swear that I'd do some cultural vacationing on my time off. "Go early and take in some blues," he'd ordered, "or bundle up and walk along the beach."

I owe it to Dr. Cox to be careful about charging the university a double meal, as the departmental financial auditor will be going over my expenses with a magnifying glass.

Kit grabs the hotel folder off the desk and pulls out the menu. "Beef stir-fry wrapper? Or shall it be the fresh fruit plate? Or maybe a bacon, lettuce and tomato sandwich?"

"Do they have any chicken?"

To-mah-to, I echo in my head. *Tomato, Tomahto.*

Kit checks the room service menu. "Chicken Caesar."

"Oh, I'll have that."

Kit places my salad order, and his order for a vegetable omelet. I'm silently thrilled that he also asks for a pot of Earl Grey.

The bright afternoon light floods my eyes and reveals every pore on my guest's pinkish-pale complexion. I'm guessing he's around my age, thirty-five, no more than forty.

My basketball date retrieves his cool lighter from his pocket again.

I extend my palm for a better look. "I noticed that before."

He hands it over. "Do you smoke, too?"

"No, I just wanted to see it."

"It is a Zippo. This model is called The Viper."

"My uncle once told me that all of the Royal Air Force pilots used to carry only Zippos in the Second World War."

Kit nods. "Your uncle must be an old man if he was in that war."

"He's fifteen years older than my mother. She was an accident." I give it back. "Um, by the way this is a no-smoking floor."

"Do you care?"

I'm not about to give him a sermon about my father's early death, but I did go to the trouble of requesting a non-smoking floor. I glance up. "I do."

"Very well," he says with a small, pained smile. He puts away the lighter.

"I appreciate it." Suddenly I feel at a loss for words. "Do you mind if I close the shade? The light is blinding."

"Be my guest," he says nicely, although he looks antsy now that cigarettes have been given the kibosh.

Goodbye view facing a gorgeous slice of the skyline of Chicago.

"Can I ask why you have a cot in your room?"

"I'm guessing there was a family here before me. The maid probably forgot to take it away."

"That's probably it."

I have to fill holes of silence. I am a Jewess, and genetically programmed to do this.

"I can remember when my nursery school cots were rolled out and the nap record went on."

"You can?"

"Most likely I remember many days rolled into one. It was always the same record, the soundtrack to the movie *Born Free*."

"That's the lion film?"

"Yes."

"Very melancholic if I recall?"

"'Pretend you are Elsa, the poor little orphaned lion cub,' our liberated braless teacher would say as the music filtered through the room: 'Born free...'"

"'As free as the wind blows,'" Kit finishes the lyric line.

"I can still see the shadows racing along the ceiling as I listened, pushing away my thoughts of sleep."

"You know of course that you have a wonderful way with description."

A Cambridge grad thinks that? "Thank you."

There is the sound of a vacuum cleaner in use down the hall.

Okay, enough. What happened to the randy ass-pinching? His renewed "good breeding" is taxing my patience. I'm thinking maybe Gary is right and this bloke could even be gay until, perhaps emboldened by the industrial soundtrack, he stands up, sits next to me, and kisses me gently on my lips.

I breathe out. "I really hoped you would do that."

"I would have been more of a gentleman but with no smokes, see, I needed to speed up the action."

I hold up his hand and examine it in front of him. "Tough fingertips." He smiles as I chew on one. We buss and nuzzle but we don't get any further carried away; we're both well aware that there will soon be a room service door-knock. When it comes in the form of an earnest rat-tat-tat, Kit unbolts the door, and in scuttles a twenty-something room service attendant, a young man with a perceptive smile.

After Kit is back in his chair I reach toward the teapot but he puts a hand on mine and says, "Let me be mother."

"Excuse me?"

He pours for us. "That one *is* a British expression. It just means *let me serve.*"

"New to me. I like it. Men don't mind saying it?"

He stops to mull over the question. "I never thought about it too much."

I watch him eat, and admit that I'm afraid to eat in front of him after reading in a passage in a British novel about Americans spearing our food like barbarians. He is balancing everything on the back of his fork, and without even a pea tottering, gets the sliver of folded egg and its contents to his mouth.

"Would you like me to show you how to do this?"

I nod, amused.

Kit flips my wrist over, and tells me to put a bit of everything on the upside down fork. When the bits of chicken, tomato and lettuce fall off, he holds my hand until I get the precious cargo into my mouth. I never knew having someone hold my wrist could be so erotic.

Before our meal is halfway through, I joke, "I'm glad you don't have a briefcase with you." You idiot, Shari! Did you actually say that out loud?

"Pardon?"

I can't curb the nervous rant. "Uh, what I mean is, this is the part of the film when you chain me to the bed, and that's not for me."

Kit whistles. "Not in this film. My kinks are much more harmless than that."

"Oh, man, I've heard about those British kinks. Are you going to put on my makeup?"

"No I am not!"

"Is it ice? Do you like ice rubbed all over you? Wasn't there a duke who liked ice?"

"Maybe. Maybe not."

Happily, he doesn't seem to mind the excessive New York verbiage. He's still smiling at me like he's undressing me.

"I'll find out."

"Oh, you will, will you?"

I remove his loafer and black sock and reach for the ice water.

"Eh, what's your game?" he cries out in a mock Cockney accent.

"Your heels?" I rub a slightly melted cube along the arch of his foot. His toenails are squarish like Kevin's, but his second toe is longer than his big toe, and Kevin's go down in neat order, stubby little Matryoshka dolls. I push Kevin's face out of my thought clouds. "Ice on your heels?"

"Ooh, that's quite lovely really."

I remove his other loafer and sock.

"Keep that ice coming. This is much better than a smoke."

We move over to the bed and Kit lies on his back as I rub three more ice cubes into his heel. "That would kill me. You are an iron man."

Kit wrestles loose and pulls his black rollneck sweater back over his belly button. With all the G-rated bed action going on, a good number of gold pound coins and American quarters have fallen out of his pants pocket. He leans down to scoop them all up and plops them on a side table.

I chokehold him with my legs and he wrestles again until we find ourselves both back down next to each other in our clothes. We're laughing our heads off.

"Recite!" I demand as I lie next to him.

Hesitation. "Recite what?"

"Any British poet."

"What makes you think I know any poetry?"

"You read English at Cambridge for fucksake!"

"I know a little verse—"

"Then recite!"

"I know a little of—will Christopher Marlowe do?"

"Indeed! Recite! Stand on the bed!"

"What is this, *A Fish Called Wanda?*"

Only one of my favorite movies. "Recite!" I say, excited to be connected to those beloved characters even in a moment of inadvertent umbrage.

He rises in his bare feet, stands on the mattress, and even if only to humor me, pretends to be swept over with an ungovernable passion. *"Was this the face that launch'd a thousand ships/And burnt the topless towers of Ilium? Sweet Helen, make me immortal with a kiss!/Her lips suck forth my soul—* I've forgotten the rest."

I laugh and tackle him to a reclining position. He has the gathering-dignity face of a nude male model about to remove his loincloth. Kit unhooks my new "Wanton" Wonderbra and leans over the bed for his belt that I have just thrown to the floor. From my prone position, I'm amused to see a little zipper on the back of the belt leather.

"You have handcuffs in there?"

"A Frenchie." He adds with a little laugh, "I guess it's a condom to you."

The name of the package catches my eye. I'm finding this entire encounter a bit filthy, yet I like myself placed squarely in this scene. I'm wide awake for one, and for me that's a rare state lately. Then again should I worry about a man who has a condom belt zipper? Is he the optimistic type who has random sex all the time? But you have to think at least he's using a condom. I laugh a little at the thought of a British condom, and idiotically say out loud: "One-hundred-eighty pounds-worth of Durex, please."

"Pardon?"

"*The Young Ones.* The 'Sick' episode when Mike the band manager asks the drugstore lady for condoms while Vyvyan is hammering a nail into Mike's head."

"Right, I saw that," Kit says with a bit of exasperation.

"Sorry about that. I need to pick my timing better."

"Don't worry. I'm just surprised you got that program here."

"On video. I'm a complete Anglophile. You can test me on anything by A. A. Milne. Monty Python, too."

He takes a finger and puts it on my mouth to shut me up. This is a sexual strategy the men I've slept with have probably wanted to take but dared not risk.

He takes off his glasses, looks at me a little fuzzily and says, "Am I just a fetish to you then?"

"Keep your glasses on!" I beg. "You won't look British without your glasses."

Kit shoves the corner of the pillow in my mouth. "Now I'm really going to shut you up."

His face is so convincing that I'm actually nervous for a few seconds that I'm going to get hurt, but am quickly relieved to see he is just playing along.

"So, fancy a bit of crumpet?" he whispers into my ear.

The many room lights we left on have rehued Kit's pink face a blanched and yellowy color, but he still looks mighty good to me having, as Austin Powers would put it, "Shagged the Yank rotten, baby."

Can I be this content? Me, the sourpuss? Has Kevin been a forced hibernation on my happiness quotient? I breathe in Kit's pleasant musky scent impregnated into my skin from the missionary position.

Kevin's boxy body bathes me with his perspiration during sex—he's soaking wet even when he performs like a wind-up circus acrobat whose might wanes out after two or three tumbles. *Kevin's sweat repulses me.* There, now I've officially thought that mean thought, too. But this man lying next to me is not Kevin, and I readily lick my wrist to taste his delicious salt again.

Although silent with postorgasmic fatigue, Kit holds my gaze. He scratches my thigh and stomach with his fingers. Is this the silent British version of afterplay? At least he's not rudely asleep. I play with a reddish strand of sweaty hair clinging to his cheek and coo into his pale white ear, "Help, Chris Robin, I'm stuck in the tree!"

"Christopher Robin!" Kit says in a jokey indignant way before he pecks the tip of my nose.

"I'm so glad Gary had that meeting," I say.

And then he mysteriously sits with a start.

"What is it?"

"Of course, you know, I wasn't planning on being in your hotel for so long. I mean this little rendezvous just happened—"

Rendezvous is it? "And?"

"And I have my own presentation tomorrow in this hotel. I don't want you to think me rude, but I do have to look my papers over before we go to the game. I'm going to shatter my competition. I could get them and come back if you like before we go to the game."

I sit up. As I adjust my limbs, I notice that my body is covered in long colorless scratch marks that I sure as hell hope heal before I see Kevin. "Your conference is *here?*" What did he do again, or did we never get around to that? "Oh, are you with the chemists?"

"I'm on the soccer team."

"Ha." His comment was a little weird, come to think of it. What kind of academic really sets out to shatter competitors? Not the ones I know; we know each other's foibles too well. Like most academic disciplines, we're an incestuous little circle. A bit of spite is as harsh as it gets.

He smiles. "Actually, I'm with the linguistics conference."

I gape at him. "Me, too."

Who have I just screwed? There are eight hundred people in our linguistics conference. Christopher who? I wish I could reach into my night table for the conference catalogue and quickly check.

"Oh, jolly good. What is your area of expertise?"

I cough slightly in embarrassment. There's a pecking order of importance in my greater field. And Volapük sure as hell is near the bottom rung. "You first," I practically squeak.

"Volapük," he says. When I don't say anything back, he adds, "You know what that is?"

"Of course," I begin. I can't finish my sentence as my heart is pounding so fast.

"I didn't mean to insult your linguistics knowledge, but not everybody"—he picks up my limp hand with a worried look. "Hey, are you that disappointed in my specialty?"

While there are academics whose research overlaps with mine, many with papers that reference Volapük and Johann Scheleyer, the Catholic priest in Baden who invented it, there are only three of us in the world dimwitted enough to make this kook's language a full-time calling card.

Columbia Professor Dr. David Mitchell is the big name in the field. He put this obscure topic on the academic map in the early seventies, when he wrote the first formal articles for journals. He specializes in over seven obscure languages. Despite all of his degrees, he demands everyone call him Dave. The younger academics in the constructed language field love this eccentric dearly; this is a man who knows all the lyrics to *every* psychedelic sixties song, even the more obscure ones like "I Had Too Much to Dream Last Night" by Strawberry Alarm Clock.

The only other Volapük authority that I've ever come across—and only by reading his very occasional journal publications—is the mysterious Christopher T. Brown. The last one, which has nothing shocking in its content, was published without any academic affiliation listed under his name.

This is just great for whatever bit of academic reputation I have. "So," I say as calmly as possible, "how are you going to shatter your competition? What is your presentation about?"

He looks at me like I'm an insane woman, which admittedly, at this moment, I am.

"I'm just curious. I mean, why would you *shatter* your competition? Who says that about their colleagues at a conference."

Nothing follows except for Kit's decision to pat me on the head as if to say don't get all neurotic on me, you crazy little American.

My face radiates disgust. I stand up, nude and mad at his blasé response. I take a deep breath. "I'd like you to leave."

"What just happened here? What have I said that's so offensive to you?"

I can't answer him.

"What about the Bulls game?" Kit says desperately.

I grab my leather knapsack and open the front pouch.

"This is ridiculous," he sputters as I shove the tickets into his hand.

"Please, Kit. Just go," I say in a clear and irate voice.

Eventually my bloody fling gets the message. He eyes his wristwatch like a losing coach checking the clock.

"Go," I say.

He quietly exits with the tickets.

A few minutes later, I wing a purple go-go boot against the door.

CHAPTER 5

The Presentation

There's a steady stream of instrumental defunked funk in the elevator ride down from the seventeenth floor to the conference room level. I'm not looking forward to seeing anyone, let alone speaking. I'm saddled with a thumping headache and the stinging, looping memories of yesterday's abrupt turnabout from romantic to tragic.

My cell phone rings as I step onto the plum corporate carpet outside the elevator. I'm so busy obsessing about what went awry that I don't even bother to check the caller ID. Was I wrong to kick Kit out? Should I have told him who I am? I know I should have, but I froze. Getting him out of my room seemed like the best course of action at the time.

"Hey, cutie! Everything cool with you?"

"Yeah," I say with a start. Kevin. I'd never called him.

I take a seat on a black leather couch in the foyer. "What's new on your end?"

"Same old cyber shit, but hey I saw Dave Grohl this morning coming out of the Thirty-fourth Street Station. Just an average schmo getting off the E train."

"I forget who he is."

"You're about to be embarrassed here. Dave Grohl like in the Foo Fighters? Like in Nirvana?"

"Sorry. Of course."

"He had headphones on, headed to Madison Square Garden. I'm pretty sure his band is playing there next week. I wished I were going where he was going. Maybe things are more interesting in your part of the country?"

"Nah."

"Are you jet-lagged?"

"Not really. I'm just going over my material for my presentation."

"So what did you do last night?"

I gulp and think.

"Are you there?"

One of the linguists I just barely know waves to me. He's a prematurely graying wiseass that my closer "friends" on the conference circuit have nicknamed Palindrome for his insistence on inserting a palindrome whenever possible in conversation. "Did you say your name is Stella? *Stella won no wallets!*"

I nod hello to Palindrome, and then as coolly as possible say to Kevin, "I saw an old college buddy and then I hung around the hotel with one of the Volapükists." I'm not going to fib a night of Solitary Boggle and mini-bar M&M's. I'm not that righteous about lying, but I'm just not a very good bullshit artist. I'd rather withhold information than lie.

"Damn. You're so high-falutin'. How many Volapük-ists are there?"

"Enough," I say honestly. "So what about you?"

"Are you kidding? With you out of town? The mouse is away—the cat shall play."

"Excuse me?" I say after another small start. Who's confessing what here?

"Poker night with the Three Musketeers. I even got a spot outside Josh's building thanks to Doug's radar. Takes a drunkard in search of a beer to tell you where the best parking spots are."

I force a reply: "Is that so?" A long chat with Kevin right now would be akin to voluntarily hooking myself up to thumbscrews. "Well, I have to get going. My presentation is in a few minutes."

"Good luck. Afterwards, eat a slice of deep dish for me."

"Will do."

I have to break up with him in person. He'd probably never know I cheated, so why even tell him? I was going to break up with him anyway, wasn't I? I will away the mangy thoughts of infidelity. I'm way too anxious about Kit's presentation to deal with my mounting guilt. As I rise from the couch, I hear, "Shari Diamond!"

Bethany Klein is an elegant Esperantist with a perfectly pressed pantsuit and a henna-pack black bob.

"Looking forward to your talk?" Bethany says with a warm smile.

"It'll be fun," I manage. "How was the flight in from Seattle?"

"Perfect. Come, let's walk together. I want to show you pictures of the newest rogue in my life."

I'm grateful for those pictures of nine-month-old Caleb Gerald Klein-Moskowitz. Another sixty seconds delaying doom.

The sorry story on the dissertation: five years ago, I naively put all my dissertation eggs into the Volapük basket. As I finished up my full-scholarship English literature masters at NYU, I intended to continue there with a Ph.D. dissertation on Sir Thomas Malory's background as a knight, and the influence his profession held over his great work, *The Death of Arthur.*

That all changed when I met a fellow coffee drinker in a Dodgers cap at the East Village Starbucks. He had an amazing face, with expressive sunken eyes and white lashes. If he didn't have a strong Brooklyn accent, I'd describe him as an Orkney Pict, those ancient Brits who inspired the Scottish legends of Fairy Folk.

He had spotted me reading a book about the literature of Middle English, and leaned over to ask me a question.

"You ever heard of a language called Volapük?" he said in a higher pitched voice than I expected.

I hadn't.

He told me he was an amateur linguist, and then he told me all about this universal language I'd never heard of that, at the height of popularity, had three million businessmen fluent in it for international trade. My elf was certain that there was an elderly farmer in upstate New York who'd learned the language from his father.

Like Doctor Doolittle, the farmer was rumored to talk in Volapük to his animals, but in his case merely to keep what he remembered of this language alive. His children apparently weren't interested, so the animals would have to do. As our Starbucks swizzle sticks swizzled, the caffeinated tale continued: "This was not a language he learned from a textbook. It was passed on to him the same way second generation Americans learned Italian or Yiddish. Every day the Volapük farmer supposedly took a cane and walked around naming his animals in Volapük, and parts of the landscape."

Every time he said Volapük, a little gob of saliva fell on his crotch. But he was quite convincing.

After he left abruptly, I sat and thought.

Earlier that week, after depleting most of my savings with one month's worth of bill-paying, I had read a *New York Magazine* article on young academics that tilled their dissertation subject and wrote lighter user-friendly nonfiction books that got extraordinary advances, and sometimes even film deals.

While I sipped my second double latte a crazy life strategy gelled in my head: I'd drop my King Arthur dissertation plans and find this secluded Volapük farmer. Even though my advisor, Dr. Cox, was a well-known sweetie, he was also a professor in linguistics; he'd never go for it, would he? How would I go about finding the farmer? Cox would ask me right away.

But if I could…

I allowed myself another flight of imagination: I'd get my doctorate, a childhood dream, yet I'd make hay of my degree with a mainstream memoir about my search that would sell to a big publishing house. I'd never have to ask my brother Gene for a wad of money to keep me afloat. (Not that I ever had. Before true poverty I've always managed to get a mind-numblingly boring temp secretarial job.)

The more I thought about my plan, the more in love with it I was. I'd have some rare adventures to boot.

Later that week, I gingerly brought up my encounter with the Starbucks linguist to Dr. Cox. Instead of laughing at me, or barking sense into me, he nodded enthusiastically: "A treasure hunt. You obviously have passion for this subject, and those with passion finish what they start." He felt my new Ph.D. idea could still fall under his official guidance precisely because he was one of the few faculty members whose expertise straddled literature and linguistics. "I'll get this through," he said unreservedly.

Only after departmental approval did I realize I'd forgotten to ask the man where the farmer lived upstate. How would I ever find him? I've never seen the Starbucks guy there again; he just seemed to pop up from the Earth's crust and disappear again. But I sold myself on the romance of this career turn, and I was certain that all of the details would fall in place.

They haven't.

I do know that there are over eighteen-thousand dairy farms in New York State. Since that fateful day in Starbucks, I've been to three upstate cattle sales, and three different New York agriculture fairs, including one where I gained more than passing knowledge of poultry, and where I was taken to lunch by a poultry farmer with an *Ask me about my cock!* belt buckle who said he knew exactly who I was asking about, but in the end knew absolutely nothing about Volapük at all.

My last attempt to find the Volapük farmer turned into a comfort session for a distraught rancher whose population of prize-winning cows had been reduced by severe cattle tick fever over the previous week.

Underwhelmed by my lack of success, I contacted the amateur Volapük association, full of enthusiasts stricken with linguistic curiosity after reading about real universal languages. This mainly encompassed the hardcore science fiction and fantasy fans that actually have bothered to learn *Star Trek* scriptwriter Marc Okrand's Klingon and J.R.R. Tolkein's Orcish and Quenya.

After four years, I'm supposed to be the pro linguist, but how am I any more informed than the Hobbit readers? I'm marooned in an academic hell of my own making.

I've replayed those fifteen minutes in Starbucks a thousand times in my head. The man with the story was about seventy-five, much older than your typical Starbucks customer. Could I have been duped? He could have been mistaken, or even worse, a chronic liar.

But what would the man have gained by spinning what either one of my long-deceased Yiddish-speaking grandmothers would have called a *bubbemeister,* a tall tale? Nothing. Surely nothing. He just looked caffeinated, and eager to share his amateur linguistic knowledge.

So part of me holds out hope that I just haven't

found the farmer yet. Did Stanley stop looking when told that his quest for Dr. Livingstone was folly?

"Maybe you'll get a clue about the farmer at the conference," Dr. Cox said when I awkwardly asked him about funding to go to Chicago. He was well aware of my impending use-by date for NYU subsidy.

Noam Chomsky, the rock star of libertarian socialism, is concurrently the rock star of linguistic theory. Years ago he famously floated the theory that language has a universal way of developing in children. His star participation in this conference was one of the reasons I wanted to go in the first place, and I was peeved when I realized my pod of presenters—participating in what most linguists deride as the "dead language" panel—was a meager alternative to the keynote morning lecture in the Grand Salon ballroom. Because of Chomsky's talk, details of which have not been revealed in the catalogue, there is a skeletal audience of only thirteen people in the Frank Lloyd Wright Conference Room where Kit and myself are to give our dueling Volapük presentations. With Kit's pledge to "shatter his competition," I wonder if the lackluster crowd disappoints him. I steal a glance over to his side of the long dais table, and he sneaks a quick look back.

I give him a lackluster wave.

He waits a few seconds to return it. He must be shocked to see me on the dais with him. He grabs the program and mouths, "S. Roberta?"

I nod.

His mouth forms a little O.

I shrug.

He must sense my telepathic message: *Let's talk later.*

He's still pretty damn attractive in that wool jacket; I'll give him that. I'd hoped in the toxic afterglow of last night's catastrophe my silly lust would wear off. It's the man that counts, not the tweed.

I glance to see who else is in the room besides Kit, myself, Palindrome and Bethany Klein. Dave Mitchell is here of course, Mr. Casual, unshaven and dressed up for his Volapük lecture in a T-shirt that bears a vulture and the words Dead End—one-upping last year's crowd-pleaser T-shirt that read, I Bring Nothing to the Table. There is a smattering of the other Esperantists I'd met at the last linguistics conference in Ithaca and have a big smile relationship with.

I wipe the puddle of cola someone's knocked over on my presentation seat and sip from my own can of Diet Coke. The audio man asks me to test my mic.

"Hello, hello," I say. *Help, help.*

Kit looks at me like he can hear me think. He removes his glasses as he tests his mic, blowing into it like it's an empty bottle.

"Words please," the audio man barks. "You're going to kill the mic!"

"Allo, allo." Kit's cheeks turn pink as he speaks, and with his genetic makeup, he's pretty pink-cheeked already.

"Hey, Mr. Tambourine man," Dave sings into his mic. There is a small giggle from the people seated in the room as he continues halfway through the song.

When the soundcheck is all done, Dave whispers in his crusty voice (almost certainly modeled on Bob

Dylan's): "Mystery solved. Christopher T. Brown is British."

"Yes," I say numbly.

"Sounds Cambridge to me, though there's something else in there, too, I think."

I choose my words carefully. "You're on the money. I spoke to him earlier."

Dave Mitchell nods, pleased with himself.

Recognizing accents also comes easily to me. I think I have all significant American regional accents down. Sometimes, like when I'm on the F Train, I take pity on classical composer Glenn Gould who suffered a world of sounds no one else around him could hear. My ear is not in that league, not by a mile. But Dave's may be; he can almost always pin more specifics than me on any talking English voice. Last conference I heard him nail linguists' accents to Tottenville, Staten Island; Adelaide, South Australia; Vancouver Island, Canada, as well as recognizing San Franciscan American-born Chinese.

As Kit reads to himself the paper he's scheduled to present after me, I see an additional parcel in front of him. What could that be? I glance again at what he has listed in the program. "New developments in the research of Volapük." Again his academic affiliation is unlisted. Who could afford such a low-paying career? What sort of a pampered life does he live beyond being a Cambridge grad?

The head panelist is Sadiqa Fawzi, an Arabic woman who has published an extremely well-received article on the vestiges of Ancient Sumerian spoken in contemporary marshland Iraq. She acknowledges the room and begins the panel. "Our first speaker is Bethany Klein, whose paper is entitled 'Reexamining Orkan: Esperanto as an influence on *Mork and Mindy.*'"

A scattered tittering ensues as Sadiqa continues Bethany's short biography, but I'm not surprised. Unlike me, Bethany genuinely gets a kick out of those creepy fantasy meets. At the last linguistics conference in Albuquerque, during our tongue-in-cheek group outing to the legendary New Mexican truckstop, The Iron Skillet, Bethany surprised me with her intricate knowledge of *Star Wars,* describing—in great detail—the deck levels of Khetanna, Jabba the Hutt's Ubrikkian luxury sail barge.

Bethany's voice is assured despite her hokey thesis: "Were the writers of seventies television series *Mork and Mindy* familiar with constructed language before they began their show, or was Juilliard-educated Robin Williams the driving force for the ingenuity of this language? Part of Esperanto's appeal is that you can guess the meaning from the root or the onomatopoeic sound of it. I ask you to examine some words from Mork's lexicon. Do you remember these? *Shatzbot!* The only legal Orkan swearword. *Yek* is a daytime yes, while *yug* is an accepted daytime yes. *Nap-nap* is the nicest no, *boo-boo* is the businesslike no and *nin-nin* is a philosophical no. And the strongest no is a *nox-nox.*"

I tune out at her analysis of *cez-gekup,* the Orkan word for indigestion.

I like Bethany a lot, but, man, this is truly the pits as far as presentations go. I'm scrambling for nice things to say to her later.

There is weak applause when she is done.

Sadiqa will now introduce me, another low-rung academic with nothing really new to present. "Ms. S. Roberta Diamond, a fourth year Ph.D. student at NYU, will address her research methodology for the growing Volapük online community...."

"Good morning," I say when she is finished. My stomach rumbles as I miserably look down to my paper. You would think I could memorize the first two sentences for maximum impact, but I need those typed words to keep me going. The crippling combination of my own pathetic paper and the presence of the man I've accidentally gone to bed with isn't helping my public speaking phobia.

I swallow before I continue, "I have been intrigued with the growing usage of Volapük on the Internet. I wanted to explore exactly how many of these new layperson enthusiasts were out there. Five? Ten? I think many in the room today will be startled by my findings."

Once I get talking my voice stops wavering. But who am I kidding? Like Bethany, everything I go on to say is a meatless pronouncement. So I add thirty names to the list of amateur enthusiasts. Whoop-de-do. Volapük has been mined. It's a dead language. Nothing exciting will happen. No fevered rebuttals. The most curious thing in this room today is the face behind Christopher T. Brown.

"Thank you, Roberta."

"Shari," Dave Mitchell says authoritatively into his microphone. "For those in the know."

"Which do you prefer?" Sadiqa says into her mic.

Slightly off-mic I say, "Shari, please."

I wish I had the courage to watch Kit's facial reaction to my name said out loud. But I have a chance to watch his pale lips soon enough as he is before us all a minute or so after Sadiqa's short introduction acknowledging that Kit is an independent linguist. There are jealous looks on the floor. Who can afford independence in this profession? Or maybe they are pitying looks for not having a major university's clout.

Kit acknowledges the panel chair and peeks at me quickly with a tight face. I stare at my presentation paper as he begins, dramatically: "This is *lain*."

I know the word. Wool in Volapük.

"It comes from a *jip*. *Lain* is wool, and *jip* is a sheep. These were among the most popular words in Volapük a hundred years ago. As Ms. Diamond so eloquently pointed out, Volapük is alive today because of enthusiasts, individuals more used to seeing a computer mouse than a field mouse."

Where is this presentation going?

"But what if we could time-travel back to when Volapük was not a novelty, but a viable means of communication for millions of businessmen, many of who ran farms? Many of who had sheep and cattle they could get the best price for abroad. In lieu of time travel, the next best thing for Volapük research would be to find a man who remembers the heyday of farming. A man who at eighty-seven years of age, is still farming, and for whom Volapük is no novelty."

I look up in horror.

"I have found what every linguist of a lost constructed

language longs for. A subject of study who has learned the language from his parents, and not from a book—" he pauses dramatically as he glances over to me "—or the Internet."

Dave watches me as he takes a sip of his melted ice water.

Who the hell could he be talking about? What upstate farming convention did I leave unvisited?

"Robert Royden is a farmer outside York who has been dismissed by family and friends as a crackpot. Until I interviewed him two months ago, he had no idea that he is the last man on earth who has spoken some Volapük from infancy."

York? I could strangle that old guy from Starbucks. The Volapük-fluent farmer he'd heard about wasn't in New York. He was in frigging York, or let's make that Fucking York!

I feel like sobbing as Kit plows on: "Royden's father, who engaged in agricultural business around the world, providing wool for several countries, taught him how to speak in the businessman's language from his toddler days. Today's families teach their children a second language so they will have a financial edge in the world. Yesterday's families taught them Volapük. Robert Royden told me he sometimes dreams in Volapük.

"Are there any questions before I move on?"

There is loud chatter for a minute and Dave Mitchell says loudly: "How did you find him? How have you authenticated his claim? Perhaps he is an enthusiast from another era, a man who picked up Volapük as an odd hobby in the fifties?"

In 1998, in the rush to discover the missing link between dinosaurs and modern birds, a curious fossil was
bought at a fair with no field notes. Despite some initial eyebrows raising over this perfect find that popped
up magically, the National Geographic Society paraded
it as the real deal.

An elaborate hoax. The humiliation that followed for
the reckless paleontologists was a brutal lesson that has
trickled down through all of academics.

With the audio/visual section of his presentation, Kit
has prepared a counterblow for every doubt. He has re-
produced yellowed photographs from the turn of the
nineteenth century including a staggering one of the
farmer as a young boy with his father at a Volapük convention. It is staggering because I have never once seen
a photo of a Volapük convention.

Kit rolls down a screen, and motions to the audio/vi-
sual assistant. A video plays.

He has interviewed neighbors from farms adjoining
Royden's home who apparently had no idea how
unique their otherwise unremarkable farming neighbor
was, and how important to the world.

And then the farmer appears on screen. The man I
have been looking for in the wrong continent is tall,
lean, broad-shouldered and beardless. As painful as it is
to watch any further, I do. He's got a signature shock of
white hair. His old-fashioned glasses rest on a large and
aged nose. He saunters around a lush moor landscape
that the Brontës would have been most at home with.

The farmer ambles silently in front of the camera, and
then stops to point out everything in his walk, theatri-

cal one-syllable declarations like an Australian aborigine interpreting landscape to a documentary film crew would make.

"Kun," he announces as he points to a cow. He rips a small piece of bark off an enormous oak tree, and after a smile, says, *"Jal."*

With Kit's evidence and this film clip, I am convinced that this farmer is the real deal. And my psyche is in shambles.

"Are you aware of the Volapük society that exists on the Internet?" a voice asks off-camera. Kit's smooth and controlled voice.

"I don't have a computer," comes the answer.

When the lights go up, Kit summarizes his finding and then adds: "Through my fieldwork, I have also compiled over three hundred new words that were used by his father in business dealings, mostly farming terminology that is not in any lexicon of this intriguing language."

At the end of his very impressive speech, the baker's dozen of academics in the room applauds wildly. The antisocial linguist who never introduces himself at any conference, the one who always clutches his red overflowing looseleaf binder as he crouches on a chair against the wall, is also on his feet. My distraught head is disconnected from my clapping hands.

Kit takes his seat to even more loud applause.

"We will take a five-minute break," says the moderator Sadiqa. "And then we will hear from Professor David Mitchell of Columbia University."

"Bravo, Mr. Christopher Brown," Dave says from his

mic. "I think those were such extraordinary findings that I will pass on my presentation. Honestly, I have nothing new to say. This is Mr. Brown's day."

I swallow. Nothing I said even registered with the real academic here, the gatekeeper of what counts. I never told Dave of my search for this farmer, in case he would stumble onto the guy himself. With an endorsement like that—Dave is a whale, and I am merely a pilot fish in terms of importance to this self-contained world of constructed language—Kit's "find" will be written up as the highlight of our division.

Should I call Dr. Cox? Tell him my academic raison d'être is kaput?

Kit rises from his chair and once off the dais is surrounded by well-wishers.

There is a loud eruption of noise as the doors to the Grand Ballroom open.

Palindrome's buddy for the last two conferences I've attended was Ned Jenkins, a Vulcan and Klingon expert who has told me he attends both science fiction and linguistic conferences. Ned has a staggering resemblance to chubster Spanky McFarland from the *Little Rascals*. You want to like him for that, but even if I wasn't still stinging from Kit's sucker punch, I'd stay clear: Ned has a warm persona in his journal articles, but whenever I talk to him with new expectation he is as nasty as ever.

"Chomsky was amazing. I didn't miss anything right? Same old, same old, right?"

Palindrome lights up. *"Now Ned, I am a maiden nun: Ned, I am a maiden won!"*

"Have you been waiting all year for that?" Ned wonders with a laugh.

Palindrome's smile reveals his jagged teeth. "Yes."

Dave removes a loose eyelash and says, "You missed more than you think. We had a breakthrough in the Volapük arena. Chris Brown found a man who learned the language from his father as a small boy."

"Dreams in Volapük," Palindrome says.

"Who is Chris Brown?" Ned asks.

"I am," says Kit. "Christopher."

"Kit," I correct.

"That's just for my friends," Kit says without looking up. "Professionally I prefer Christopher."

Dave glances at me. He looks at me a bit suspiciously, and then looks again at Kit. "Remarkable. You should write that up for the journal, Christopher Brown."

"T. Brown," I say. "Don't forget the T."

Once again Dave squints at me. He hooks his thumbs under his trim waistband as he finally addresses me. "That's all we hear from you? Besides me, you're the one who should be giddy with interest."

"Unless Shari's jealous," Ned says, and then the prick looks at me with a pukey grin to gauge my reaction.

Inside I'm as angry as a pit bull straining on a leash. "Not at all."

Ned sneaks another quick gleeful look at me before he licks the expert's boots: "I've never heard of an academic giving up his spot, Dave. You must be really blown away."

I catch Kit's unsteady smile. He is not gloating, I'm sure of that. I think he just doesn't want to lose Dave's all-important support.

"I am, but I have a real reason for shortening my time. I've arranged to go to an Otis Rush rehearsal."

Ned shakes his head after the elder statesman bids goodbye to the "young ones." "That Dave."

A temporary worker announces that my panel session must leave the room so the panel session on French dialects can set up.

"So how are you this morning?" Kit says to me as we walk toward the door.

I wait until Ned and Palindrome are farther down the hall. "How was the game?"

He stares at me and finally says, "Superb. Thank you, Miss S. Roberta Diamond."

"Congratulations," I say meekly. "You really deserve it."

"So that was one big bit of missing information. We could've talked about it. You could have stopped me from blithering on last night like a fool—"

"Yes," I say.

"Well, I didn't really kill you. You're still standing."

I laugh harshly as I fight back tears. "Yes, you did."

"How's that?"

"I was looking for that farmer."

"Pardon?"

"You achieved your goal, Kit."

"What goal is that?"

"You wanted to shatter your competition, and you have."

"You're taking my words far too seriously. Your presentation was very—"

"My presentation was very nothing, you know that. And I've been looking for that man for four years."

At first Kit's face is unreadable. Then, with everyone looking on, he picks up a hand of mine and strokes it.

"I'm sorry for how I behaved yesterday," I say. "But..."

Tears flow as I burst out with everything: my search, my impending bankruptcy, my research and my sense of self. With the considerable emotion even the worst lip reader wouldn't miss—far away Ned looks delighted every time he looks over at us—Kit swiftly steers me to the corner by my elbow. I'm talking through my gasps of air. "I thought he lived in upstate New York," I add, lest he should think I had the good sense to search in England.

"Oh, good God." He wipes a tear with considerable grace and pity like a British reconnaissance soldier who has come across the sole bloodied survivor of an overrun platoon. "Would you like to meet him?"

It takes a long while to answer this time. "What, go to England?"

"Yes, that's what I'm saying. Maybe there is something good to come from this."

He waits as my brain talks out this bizarre opportunity. Don't I owe it to myself to follow this to the end? Kevin and I were planning a little trip to the Smoky Mountains in a month, his treat. And regardless of that additional relationship betrayal (tack it on the list), how would I ever go on my diminished student stipend? "I'm not budgeted for that in my research, just this conference. I've been doing this academic thing too long. My funding is about to run out. I can hardly get to New Jersey on our miniscule budget."

"You shall be my guest then."

"This is crazy. Right now there is no one on earth I hate more than you."

"Why not? I'm not on an academic schedule. I'll whirl you around London. Then we can drive up the moors to see—"

"Another time, Kit. I can't even afford a little of that. I don't know about you, but I can barely pay my rent. A plane ticket is definitely beyond my means."

"I'll buy you the ticket. We'll go to a travel clerk immediately, shall we? Meeting Robert will give you closure. There's a little inn about ten kilometers out I stayed in." He flips open his cell phone. "I can ring the inn from here—"

"Who *are* you? Enough with the International Man of Mystery already."

He laughs loudly. "No one famous, don't worry. I just can do this for you if you want. Free. One hundred percent free. A gift."

"Don't you mean a consolation prize?"

"Listen, I could take a page out of that awful Ned's book and offer the trip to Dave. It would get me in the right journals, but honestly he's not nearly as sexy."

I sit.

He waits again. "I really like you."

"You drive a hard bargain," I say finally. "Free?"

"Free."

"Free?" I check once more.

"Gratis. Every second of your stay."

"You could stay in my apartment while you're in New York this week. It's not fancy but it would even things out a little. Make me feel like less of a harlot."

"Do you think I'm buying you?"

"No, I think you really mean to soothe me—"

"Thank you," Kit says firmly.

"My roommate is in Los Angeles until next week."

"If that's a concern for you, fine. I'd love to stay with you."

"Did you have any plans?"

"No, just a look around after the conference."

After a moment I say, "Are you a Sir then?"

He glances at his watch, ignoring me. "Shall we?"

"Tea time?" I say with a sorrowful little laugh.

"How about vodka time?"

He smiles. Ned and Palindrome peek around the corner as he kisses me apologetically on the cheek.

Three Skyy vodka martinis later, I've temporarily expunged the unofficial end of my career out of my mind.

"And people in Europe don't think American vodka is any good," Kit says, marveling at their mistake.

"I think Skyy is brewed around here. It's made out of something weird, I can't remember what it is—"

"I can't remember anything right now," Kit admits just as woozily.

When the final tab comes, Kit's in the men's room. I mentally calculate my share. I reach in my pocketbook for two of the very few twenties I have left.

On Kit's return he waves away my money with great ceremony. "Let's go to the rest of the conference together," he adds. "It's not you against me. Let everyone think we are a force to be reckoned with."

CHAPTER 6

Noo Yawk

If you've ever lived in New York you know the look of disappointment that first-time visitors have when they step into a taxi and drive a mile or so. Our two airports are in rather unflattering sections of my childhood-home borough of Queens. But I always resist telling guests to hold onto their hats because I know as soon as we are near the BQE—especially on a clear blue day like today—the magnificent Manhattan skyline will zoom into view across the East River from Brooklyn and Queens. Even without the two towers, it still takes my breath away.

These days I live in Manhattan's East Village, a neighborhood of historical note where there thunders an imposing herd numbered in the thousands: the artists, musicians, writers and social activists, and savvy young executives down-dressing to pass as cool. The prime "grazing" ground for this easy-to-spot mass is the unofficial heart of the neighborhood, Tompkins Square Park, a cube of three short city blocks between two longer avenues that was once a salt marsh belonging to peg-legged Dutch governor Peter Stuyvesant. My small rent-controlled apartment over Tompkins Park Laundromat was "inherited" through my roommate's way-older brother who was an NYU student before the East Village real estate boom. It overlooks Tompkins Square's Hare Krishna Elm, the tree on the southern end of the square that is revered by Krishna converts as the site where their religion was introduced to the west in 1966. We have but two windows that face the southern end of Tompkins Square Park; it can get very noisy because just a few feet over on Avenue A there are nine bars with heavy traffic even for Manhattan.

My roommate Cathy Loeb, a Ph.D. candidate in Asian studies, has filled every inch of our groovy (i.e., cheap and small) apartment with her many bonsai and other Asian curios like her miniature jasper "Tang dynasty-style" horse, and a hilarious costume jewelry charm bracelet with Plasticine *tamago, ebi, maguro* and *ikura* that hangs on her doorknob.

"I can't believe I'm in the real East Village," Kit says as he parks himself and his coffee cup on Cathy's mother's old couch slip-covered with a remnant blue poplin score we actually found on the street. He peers out the window. "So where are the famous beatniks?"

"Dead or in a nursing home."

He takes his first sip from the take-out coffee we bought before we went upstairs to my place, almost undrinkable brew from *coffee.dot.com* a late-nineties cyber boom relic two blocks down Avenue A. "No offense, but this is bloody atrocious." In stating his horror he almost knocks over an inch-high Chinese mudman from the Guangdong Province that Cathy claims protects her favorite oak bonsai and gives her good feng shui. She is so worried about her plants that I was shocked that she was spending ten days away. I rush to the oak—the mudman teeters but lands on his feet.

"Yeah, coffee pretty much sucks in New York."

"What is it?" Kit asks when I'm encased in thought. What's troubling me is that the soil in one of the bigger bonsai pots looks freshly wet. When did Cathy leave again? I was sure that she left the day after I left for Chicago almost a week ago. But I let it go and keep up my share of banter:

"Nothing. Just thinking to myself." Where was I? "Oh, I read that Lavazza sent over their espresso expert from Italy but he threw his hands up in disgust."

Kit laughs. "The BBC picked up that story. The press is always up for an American bash."

"My roommate makes good coffee but I don't. I'm afraid you'll have to suffer."

"So where is your roommate again?"

"At a giftware convention in L.A. She makes these Jewish origami ornaments."

"Pardon?"

I laugh. "An ironic Jewish thing."

"Oh, is she Jewish? We had a lot of Jewish Americans at Cambridge."

The tone of that statement troubles me. "Do you know that I'm Jewish?"

"Really? Diamond? Is that a Jewish name? I didn't pick it. Do you avoid eating—"

"Pig?" I answer for him.

"Yes." Is he too afraid of offending me to continue?

"I'm not Kosher, but I'm definitely Jewish."

He says nothing.

I study his face. "Do you care?"

"No, of course not. It's just that—are you okay with me? I'm Church of England, you know."

"Of course I'm okay with that." Now is not the time to bring up Aunt Dot. Or for that matter, her back-up agent—my traveling roommate with her additional lecturing on Jewish self-loathing. Once, a month or so before I met Kevin, Cathy tried to get me hooked up with her humorless single cousin with a fat face and a twirly mustache who sold scaffolding brackets to construction companies. He may be a Cohen, a descendent of Moses's brother, but I sure as hell didn't want to help him continue his five-thousand-year-old line. Her reaction to my refusal to go on a date was so predictable: "Your birthright is a gift, not a curse. Why do you hate yourself so much?"

Hate myself? I almost moved out that night, and later when she apologized for the cranky rant, and begged me to watch the third-to-last-ever episode of *Sex in the City* with her, she admitted that Kevin is her ideal of the perfect man. "Could I borrow him?" she asked.

"What, for sex?" I laughed nervously.

No, Cathy likes Kevin's comical "deep" radio voice he could summon at the drop of a hat so much that she's had him narrate her two videos: *Folding Your Heritage* and *Folding Your Heritage Two* that have upon release been big hits with the *Heeb Magazine* and *Jew-cy* T-shirt crowd.

Kevin needed no coaxing—and just before the record button was pressed he admitted that he had five rabid townie fans when he hosted the *Ode to Grunge* hour during his undergraduate years at Michigan State.

"*Oy*, three more folds to get you a Chanukah *dreidel*," he articulated into the mic with a boyish grin in the shoebox NYU recording studio we'd secured through another one of Cathy's NYU friends. Cathy was laughing hysterically when he told us during a coffee break about the time his henpecked father overdramatically stormed to the bottom deli drawer in the refrigerator with a hole-punch "to fix things" after Kevin's mother Dee Dee scolded him for buying Munster cheese and not Swiss like she had written on the list.

Cathy later said I was incredibly lucky for finding myself "one of the nice ones," and I have to say I nearly loved him that day, squeezed in so close to his vocal adorableness.

Kit's managed to finish his awful coffee. "So how much origami does she have to make to pay the rent? How much is tuition?"

"The cost, the whole degree will reach—actually I can't think about it, suffice it to say that current tuition is around thirty thousand a year."

"That's a joke, right?'

"No, unfortunately that's the figure."

"That's sickening! What kind of bloody country is this?"

"Usually you can get that covered in grad school, but I'm still recovering from my undergrad bills, and it's been ten years already. We're pretty lucky—our rent here is only thirteen hundred a month for this matchbox, and that's pretty damn good."

"Thirteen hundred dollars is pretty damn good? That's over eight hundred quid if you do the converting—"

"That's a great deal for this neighborhood."

"Matchbox. I never heard that word used for an apartment before."

"Really? In New York it is the second most common word after rip-off."

"Did you have Matchbox toy cars here?"

I look at him, confused, and then say, "Oh, you've changed topics. Yes, they sold them here."

"My favorite was the fire engine and the combine harvester."

"*Ah,* the combine harvester."

He shoves me a little after the mild mocking. "I was trying to remember what happened to them."

"My brother had a Matchbox collection, too."

"You have a sibling, then?"

"Two. Both brothers."

"Do they live in New York?"

"One's out in Queens, in Forest Hills, in a nice place."

"So which queen was Queens named for?"

I smile. "I happen to know this."

"I didn't doubt for a second that you would."

"It was chartered in 1683 for Queen Catherine, although I don't know much about her."

"She was the wife of Edward Charles the Second, I believe," he says in academic tit-for-tat.

"So if I ever go on *Who Wants to Be a Millionaire,* you're my number one lifeline."

"You have that show, too? A child could answer those questions. 'Jack and *who* went up the hill—'"

I do a little raspberry with my tongue. "That's the warm-up level for a hundred dollars. It gets harder."

Kit shrugs with continued game-show contempt. "So where is the town of Queens anyway?"

"No, Queens is a borough. We passed through it when we landed at LaGuardia."

"Oh was that it? It throws you off, doesn't it? Queens sounds so royal."

"A definite no to that, but a few neighborhoods are upmarket, like Forest Hills."

"Where your brother lives?"

"Yes."

"Tennis area, right?"

"Yes. The U.S. Open used to be held there."

"You know, my brother lives next door to my mum."

"Do they live in an apartment in London?"

He pauses a second as if he is measuring how much he should reveal. "No, they're in the country alongside a stream."

"That sounds pretty amazing."

"It is. Nigel lives in a gristmill that was abandoned in the next lot. It still has an original sawmill and granary—

it was a real fixer-upper across from some unkempt medieval watercress beds."

"You're just saying all that to turn me on, right?"

"Pardon?"

"Gristmill? Medieval watercress beds? Do you have any idea how exotic that sounds?"

"It's lovely, I must confess."

"What does your brother do for a living?"

Kit smirks. "Do?"

"What? Doesn't anyone in your family work?"

"Ah, not really, since I don't make much money from what I've written for the journals. Nigel collects things though. He's a bit of an oddball."

"Not as odd as my family."

"Try me."

I really don't want to go into too much detail with a man whose mother lives across from medieval watercress beds. The most sophisticated possession in my extended barely middle-class family is the photo my uncle made us all copies of since he joined a World War II veterans social group. It's a photo he took in 1945 of horses pulling a wagon loaded with a massive cask of wine down the cobbles of a small French town. After that we're talking mom's and Aunt Dot's historical romance novels and Gene's vast library of World Wrestling Federation DVDs.

And what about Dot's skunks? My brothers and I have pooled our memory, talked over plausible explanations, and have continually come to the conclusion that there simply is no sane explanation. And there's much more insanity to Dot than her skunks. There's Eric, her six-foot-three life partner who Dot met seven years ago on-line at Skunk Chat, the skunk lovers' Web site.

"C'mon, I'm waiting," Kit says, arms crossed.

I offer Kit the more palatable insanity of my mother's significantly older sister, Fay.

"My aunt Fay's the World's Greatest Talker who constantly carps on about her neighbor Delores who wouldn't shut up."

"That's all? Weak. I need better than that."

I'm not ready to broach Dot yet. It may make a good story, but I want this man in my life.

I tell him about Fay's enormous soap frog collection, and that she makes everyone collect bagfuls of orange peels she reincarnates as vile orange-peel chocolate bark that she neatly repacks in cookie tins hand-painted by her, cookie tin beach scenes of waves, angelfish and albatross. "Oh and Fay has bought up America's supply of watermelon tea candles that no one has the heart to tell her really smell like nail polish remover."

Kit sneers. "Sorry, your auntie Fay doesn't have a patch on my brother—hoof trimmers."

"What?"

"That's what Nigel collects. Vintage hoof trimmers."

"Okay that's pretty damn odd," I concede with a laugh. "What's the prize in his collection?"

"I don't know. I think he has some eighteenth-century duke's hoof trimmers. He buys them on—on eBay, like you."

"Another sucker 'cross the pond."

"What does your brother do?" Kit asks.

"The older one has something to do with a bank. But

I'm throwing my other brother in the ring here, he lives in a commune on Staten Island that supports itself making environmentally-sound sandals that involve no animal slaughter or pollutants."

Now why am I telling him that?

Kit is unfazed. "Pretty good, but I'm sure I can ante you. Did I tell you about Uncle Frederic with his gong collection?"

I laugh so hard my coffee jiggles in its take-out cup.

"That's it? No more after that sentence?"

"End of story. Frederic goes to church and at night he collects gongs via mail correspondence with gong collectors across the globe. Good lord did he get 'a boot out of' the gong exhibit last year at Christie's. Made his year."

In the past ten minutes Kit's speech has quickened to that of a nutty Queens passenger telling the weary bus driver in the front seat all about his winning pick at Belmont. Is it the pace of Manhattan that has him going, or the foul caffeine?

I nudge him. "Hey listen, chatty, since you're obviously not jet-lagged, do you want to take a little walk around the Big Apple now?"

"Love one."

"Hungry?"

"Starved."

"Over in the West Village there's Corner Bistro—it's been voted the best hamburger in the city for about ten years running. It's a bit of a hike, but—"

"Take me there immediately please. I haven't eaten a hamburger since Mad Cow broke."

While Kit's in my *loo,* Kevin calls on my cell.

"When are you coming home?"

Kit and I moved our flights up by two days—we'd heard all we wanted to hear at the conference, and maybe I'm a coward, but I'm grateful for a bit of time to plan the kindest goodbye I can come up with. I never said anything to Kevin about calling in every day. I'll face my fate later.

"In two days." I grit my teeth as I hang up, not even nearly ready to deal with my not-exactly watertight lies.

On the pavement, Kit slips his arm into mine, and under the midday sun our combined body-form is a double-headed midget. His midget head is higher than mine though, for in our real dimensions, I'm five foot four and he's about six foot.

After those days in Chicago together as teammates, there is no question that we are on our way to being a couple. It took us all of three hours after Kit's meteoric rise in linguistics for me to sleep with him again.

Yes there is that major hitch to this fabulous, pinch-myself-to-believe-it union (other than the small fact that my dissertation is in ruins)—I haven't broken up with Kevin yet.

"What are you grinning at now?" I say to Kit.

Kit nudges me. There's a stray tabby on a brownstone stoop awakening with a hilarious look on his face. "Churchill."

"Huh? I don't get what you mean."

"There's a well-known photo of Churchill looking maniacal. The photographer yelled at the old bastard to get the perfect shot. Everything else on the roll was a real dud."

During the next three hundred yards, a fish tackle sign in a vintage collectibles store inspires Kit to tell me how to catch trout using a lead sinker. "Rod fishing for trout is very calming," he said. "You can sit there for hours. When you throw a lead-weighted line into the water it travels a long way. On a quiet day only the current in the water drags your lines to one side, and then they go taut—"

I've never listened this hard to Kevin. Am I a snob for wanting sharper banter than: "Check this out, Shari. I have finally found the secret for perfect oatmeal. None of that one-minute, five-minute crap. You have to buy the long-cooking kind and cook for at least ten minutes, and then instead of sugar you put in four packets of Equal."

Am I a snob for hating the minutia Kevin insists on telling me about his *Manga* collection? My thirteen-year-old neighbor—an eighth grader at the Earth School—collects those Japanese comics, too. I've wanted to yell at Kevin all last month: Listen up. I really cannot give a rat's ass about *Marmalade Boy!*

There is a luxurious depth to our conversations. We could talk all the way into the early hours, and we do. Kit knows about so many different things that I'm intimidated. I've never met a man who could utter a sentence like, "The reason so many Americans collect stoneware was that it was a truly indigenous art form; sending for dishes from England was a costly endeavor," and then cough and explain that, "Of course, salt-glazed stoneware was the Tupperware for the early nineteenth century."

"Of course," I laugh, and he winces a bit.

"I'm being terribly pompous, aren't I?"

"Not at all. I love hearing you talk."

He seems positively relieved, a fact that thrills a bit. "No, I love hearing *you* talk."

"The mutual admiration society," I say, and he squeezes my hand.

The only area that seems off limits is his personal life. For once in my life I don't probe.

As the sun rouses me from sleep I give my new lover's sleeping lips a quick peck. I sneak some more marvelous looks of him from the sink as I brush my teeth and remove the traces of eye makeup never removed the previous night. Even though he's out like a light I gabble on about how he is as handsome in slumber as an RAF test pilot played by Leslie Howard or David Niven during World War II, power-napping after extraordinary figure-eights in the feathery white cirrus clouds over Europe.

"Where are we going today?" he says when he awakens a half hour later.

"*You* are going to the Empire State Building. I think tourists should do those things by themselves."

"And you?"

"I have an appointment with a doctor."

"Something wrong?"

"I've been feeling sluggish."

"You could've fooled me."

"Thanks, but really, I am not myself. The doctor's a

thyroid specialist. I'll make you breakfast and a map. It's always good to plunge into a new town. I'll meet you here at five."

With a hand feeling my throat Dr. Zuckerman repeats, "Shari Diamond," as if he's heard my name before. "Are you from Queens originally?"

I answer him once my neck is released. "Yes."

He has piercing grayish-blue eyes that give him that aging-Paul Newman appeal. He checks my ears. He temporarily puts down the probe and says, "Oh, I got it. You went to my son's bar mitzvah. Do you remember Owen Zuckerman?"

"Yes, of course," I say, as he shines his little flashlight in my eye. "Wow. Owen. How is he?"

"He's fine, fine. A very accomplished young man."

I haven't thought of fellow bookworm Owen Z. for years, except once right before I started grad school I had an out-of-the-blue erotic dream about him.

Owen was a cute and painfully quiet boy and my dream had him acting so out of character that I still remember it. (I find erotic dreams starring rarely-thought-of persons of your past the sexiest dreams you can have.)

My dream took place a few miles away from my apartment complex in Owen's house in Jamaica Estates.

In real life, Owen had a birthday party there once and he almost became popular overnight, as no one knew he lived there before the invite went out. It was a *serious* mansion, landscaped with exotic greenery quite the anomaly to Archie Bunker Queens, and patrolled by an Alaskan husky named Tiny. Owen admitted to the gathered teens that Donald Trump's dad lived a few doors down, this during Trump's first prereality TV waltz with fame. But with his severe shyness nothing could save Owen.

Dream Owen was bright red and shy as he was in real life. Dream Owen started kissing me. He ravaged me with his piercing eyes, the same ones his father has—then came his embracing arms.

Dr. Zuckerman opens my paper robe and swirls my breasts to the right and gives them a little squeeze. Since the medical student observing this session from a stool in the corner seems unfazed, I assume the fondling is a legit part of a thyroid check and not malpractice.

"What do you do now?" he asks.

"I am a linguist."

"What languages do you specialize in?"

"Volapük. It preceded Esperanto as a universal language."

"Outside my area of expertise, I must admit, but that sounds right up Owen's alley."

"What does he do?"

"After Cambridge he toured around the world, but he's settled in at Columbia now as a historian. He did his doctoral thesis on the Battle of Pinkie. No one ever knows that either but it's—"

"The Battle of Pinkie Cleugh."

Dr. Zuckerman clucks in surprise.

"I'm good with British and Scottish history."

"Now he's changed centuries and is looking at the alliance between America and Britain in the Second

World War. Goes back and forth a lot. He just got a book deal with Oxford."

"Impressive," I say sincerely. "That's the place you want to be in as an academic." I continue: "I have a friend who was at Cambridge, too. Do you know which college Owen was in?"

His nurse interrupts us and the answer never comes. "Okay, Ms. Diamond, you can get dressed, and come into my office to discuss your thyroid."

He waves off the student doctor.

Dr. Zuckerman's office is dominated by a huge 1960s 7-Up poster with the slogan *Thirst Goes Thataway Rightaway*.

He smiles and checks his folder, and looks up again. "Right now, your hypothyroidism is not a serious case. But it is, I'm afraid, there. Something to watch. I suspect a bit of Synthroid wouldn't hurt, but I'll need to look at our results to be sure."

"Synthroid?" Ever since I spent a few miserable months on the Pill in college, I haven't been a fan of daily medication. "Are there any side effects?"

"Not really. If you take it the way you're supposed to take it you should have more energy. And oh, you might even lose five or ten pounds without any dieting, not that you need to—"

"What woman doesn't want to lose five to ten pounds?" The Good Doctor is being kind: my tummy is a little much these days. My size eight jeans have been on the far right of the closet for three years now.

"Call me in a week to discuss the results. It's a

good thing you're taking care of this sooner than later."

"Actually, I might be in England by next week, if I can rush through my passport."

(Kit and I took one look at the emergency line by the International Building, and decided to use a passport service firm, which promises you a passport in three days.)

"What's the problem? Expired?"

I pause and say, "Actually, I've never been abroad before."

"Really? I thought all of you kids took that junior year abroad."

I bite the inside of my cheek before I speak. "Not me."

"Well you'll love England. We visited Owen in Cambridge often. We even rented a castle one weekend."

"Wow—"

"It was called Eastnor. Somewhere near the Cotswolds. *Gorgeous,* as my daughter Wendy would say. That was the loveliest weekend. Just the four of us. My son. My daughter. My wife was alive then."

I smile respectfully, dolefully. I know from personal experience that an understanding smile is appreciated more than a false thought about a dead person you barely remember. Owen's mother was so quiet that I can't even picture her. She was at the party for sure, peeling and quartering oranges for his friends to eat. Her hair was dark, but no, her face is not coming.

As I put his card into my jeans pocket he says, "Would you like to hear from Owen? He's been single for a year and he's so shy that I'm afraid he won't go out again."

"I kind of already have a boyfriend," I say. (Or two.)

"Well, maybe you can touch base with him. He is really quite a brilliant young man now. I've been doing the matchmaking for the family. A regular *Schadchen*. My wife would be proud. I was in our lunchroom and found a nice pediatric endocrinologist for my daughter Wendy. She's been dating him for two months now."

I laugh. This man does not need a history of my sordid love life—I can let Owen know where I stand lovewise if I ever meet up with him. "I'd enjoy hearing from Owen; I'm sure we'll have lots to talk about." I fiddle with one of the beautiful marbles that are in a candy dish on his desk. "An onionskin. Nice."

"You collect them, too? Amazing. I've never met a woman who collects marbles."

"And you still haven't," I smile sadly. "My father collected them. My brother Gene has his collection now."

My father has been dead for twenty-five years and I still tear up whenever I let that relevant information out.

Dr. Zuckerman picks up on my own mood shift and says, "I'm sure Owen would love to hear from you." He smiles kindly and writes out his son's phone number. There's a "212" area code on the piece of paper. Owen is in Manhattan, currently on this side of the Atlantic.

"Oh, Ms. Diamond, before I forget, after the blood test eat some meat. You look pale."

"I promise I will."

"Good. And I do really think you'll get on with Owen. I hope you don't remember him as unsociable. Many mistake his shyness for aloofness."

"No, not at all. I always enjoyed Owen. He was quiet, but going places, and everyone knew it. I really will give him a call."

CHAPTER 7

The Roast

"How was your day?" I say after Kit opens the door with my spare keys.

"The Empire State Building was amazing. Much nicer than the Sears Tower. Amazing art deco details, and the view from the eighty-sixth floor truly is splendid. How was your doctor's appointment?"

"He's probably putting me on thyroid pills. It should pep me up a little."

"I told you this morning. You're plenty peppy."

"And I told you, I'm peppier with you around."

He blows me a kiss. "Are you cooking?"

"I bought some food. I'd thought I'd make you a little dinner."

"Thought I smelled something."

"Well, it's a roast. I stopped by the supermarket for a big shopping spree in your honor."

"A roast?"

"My doctor wanted me to eat some meat today. Don't you British people like a lamb roast?"

"On the odd Sunday." Kit looks at his watch. "Midday though. And truthfully, I think more people eat curry these days than a joint."

"A joint? Who's eating a joint?"

"That's what we Brits call a roast, my poor innocent. When you spend time in England you'll see."

"So after the condescension is over, are you going to eat it?"

He grins. "The joint? If you've cooked it—"

I laugh myself as I point to the table Cathy and I bought in Kmart, formally set for the first time in its poor little particleboard life. Every inch of me is having fun. Did I really need that coming Synthroid?

"Very sweet." Kit lights my dollar-fifty white supermarket candlesticks with his Viper Zippo.

"I even found a recipe for Yorkshire Pudding on the Internet. This is my week's allowance."

"Can I pay for the bill?"

"No, not in New York. This is my town. Remember, this is to make me feel better? So I'm not so much of a moochie whore."

"You are anything but a moochie whore. You are a very gracious host. I'm looking forward to dinner." He thumps his chest, a hungry gorilla. "Meat." When I grin he adds, "What's the side dish? You have to make sure the potatoes are overcooked and the peas are mushy."

"Kohlrabi."

"If you're going for authenticity, that's far too sophisticated for my country's palate."

"Let's pretend we're on a manor estate."

"I've been on them. Trust me, the potatoes are overboiled there, too."

"I love your shirt by the way." I peek at the label. As I suspected: Thomas Pink, from Jermyn Street. "Oh, we have Pink in New York now, on Fifth Avenue."

"You're too much. I didn't even know what label was on. This was a Christmas gift from my mum."

"It's one of the important British labels."

"Oh, is that so?" He shakes his head. "This British thing you got going is a bit daft, really." But even as he scoffs at me he looks as genuinely happy as I am.

Kit looks over the kitchen oven, a gleaming brushed stainless GE Profile, and clucks. "That's some stove on a budget."

"Cathy's mother is a chef. She gave it to her as a gift—hey, hey! Kit! Don't touch that button!"

"What button!"

"Oh no, Kit, you've locked the self-cleaning button. Cathy had to show me how to open that up."

The culprit doesn't look worried. "I'll unlock it. Tell me what to do."

"I don't know how to unlock it!"

He sees my face and I explain: "This happened to me once before and I spent an hour trying to figure out how to fix it until Cathy came home to the rescue."

"We can figure this out. We have to. Otherwise we don't eat."

After ten minutes of farce, Kit has a brainstorm. "Let's call the oven people."

"They probably do have a toll-free number," I concede.

We find it through Yahoo.

"Oh, hello, GE, this is Christopher Jones here in New York. My dining companion and I have a problem with a button on one of your products—yes, the cleaning—yes, oh, thank you. We have our dinner inside of it, you see—a saddle of lamb—lamb is lovely, yes—jolly good…"

Kit opens the oven according to his phone directions, but to keep cooking would mean eating far later than we expected to.

"Spaghetti?" I ask.

"I think we can salvage some of the meat that did get cooked." As he carves off any done bits I shake my head in dismay.

"We can make do with this," he insists politely.

I laugh. Which makes him laugh. Then we sit and eat, adoring each other.

After a second glass of wine he asks, "If money was no object, where would you want to go in England?"

I smile as I put down my glass. "There are a few musts. But money *is* an object."

"Imagine a minute. Forget your worries. Where would you go?"

"Surely you jest."

"Hit me with them."

We sit back at the table, and I hand him a notepad by the telephone and a pencil with a goat marionette eraser topper, a weird souvenir that a fellow NYU linguistics

Ph.D. candidate brought me back from her recent Old German fact-finding trip to Salzburg.

Kit twirls the goat's head and smiles as I take a long sip of the bargain basement red wine I got. "Most of them aren't incredibly exotic locations, just meaningful ones. Like Jane Austen's house, and Cambridge of course, and I heard it's pretty near the town Dr. Doolittle was filmed in and the Millennium Wheel—"

"The London Eye," he corrects.

Venturesomeness flares up inside me. "And the alley where Jack the Ripper was from, and Wimbledon, and the big tourist spots—Big Ben, and Buckingham Palace—and Abbey Road, and if we get to the Cavern in Liverpool, and of course we have to see John's and Paul's childhood homes, and Westminster Abbey, and Bath, and the Cornwall Coast, and the White Cliffs of Dover, and Sherwood Forest, and—"

"Diamond, you are too bloody much. You're a bigger Anglophile than the Queen." He picks up my Knead-a-Pet pig, the isometric toy Kevin bought me to ease my pain after typing academic papers. Kit's thumb squishes the part with the snout. He smiles. "Where can I buy myself one of these?"

"Brookstone. A tourist trap, but men love that store. We can stop in there tomorrow."

"Oh, don't forget the farmer in York," Kit remembers.

I wince. "Oh, God—I forgot you are my enemy. Why'd you have to go and pop my balloon?"

He pokes me. "It hasn't been so dreadful now, has it?"

I ignore the question. "Don't forget Stonehenge."

"I was afraid you were going to say that. Talk about bloody tourist traps. We're not going there."

I seize his pigless hand. "I'll pay for the daytrip. Can you imagine going to New York and not seeing the Empire State Building?"

"But one is good and one is crap."

"Where is it?"

Kit shakes his head in defeat. "In Salisbury, county Wilshire. Don't worry, we'll go if it means that much to you."

"Hello?" a familiar voice says. "Is that you, Shari?"

I freeze in my seat. How to explain to my boyfriend the half-cooked roast dinner and the tray of mint peas? And how the hell did he get inside? I never gave him a key.

"Shari?"

I'm still mute, but then I've never been good at poker.

"Who's he?" Kevin asks with great suspicion.

"This is a fellow academic from the conference," I say hastily.

"Kit Brown," says my mannered dinner guest after I falter the rest of the introduction. For all Kit knows this could be my neighbor down the hall checking in.

"How did you get in?" I ask dumbly.

Kevin lasers in on my eyes. "Your door was open. And I have a key. Cathy was afraid that her bonsai would die and had me pick the keys up so I could water the plants. I thought you were coming back tomorrow."

"I shortened my stay a bit."

Now Kevin's expression straddles suspicion and dismay. "So you flew in after I spoke to you?"

"Would you care for some dessert?" I stammer. How will this encounter end? "I made it."

"Since when do you cook?" he murmurs loud enough for me to hear.

"Well, considering what we're eating, I'm not sure that I do."

Kit is still painfully unaware of the true scenario. "No, *I* ruined the roast," he says congenially.

Kevin's delayed response is tipped with considerable poison. "What's for dessert?"

"Rice and raisin pudding," I answer meekly.

With all of his brains Kit misses the story here. He thinks he's being helpful with: "Oh, lovely, you made spotted dick."

Seconds seem like millennia, and I can almost hear Kit's brain processing the scene.

"Are you a friend of Shari's?" Kit says suddenly.

"I'm Shari's boyfriend."

Kit looks at me and quietly says, "I see."

I take a deep breath. "We need to talk, but not now. Why don't you come over tomorrow? I'm going to England next week—"

"You're going to *England?*"

"Yes, Kit has located a farmer who speaks Volapük."

Kevin's voice strains in his attempt to sound unaffected. "Isn't that the man you were looking for?"

"Well, yes."

He resumes his cross-examination. "You look pretty happy about it. If it was me I'd be crushed."

"We're not competition anymore." I look over to Kit for backup. I feel even sicker when I see he's fuming, himself. "Can we meet for breakfast tomorrow?" I say desperately.

It was tomorrow that I had planned to sit him down and tell him, "You are a lovely person, but you are not the one. Please come to accept that this relationship sagged and twisted to its own death."

Kevin heads toward the door. "So I'll leave you two fucking liars alone, okay?"

What can I say? I cop it.

But Kit doesn't. "I don't appreciate being addressed like that," he says from his chair. "I have no idea who you are and I've never lied to you."

"I don't believe you assholes."

Kit rises to follow Kevin out of the door. "I need a smoke."

"Wait, Kit."

"Yeah, I see where your loyalty lies," Kevin snarls as he twists the doorknob.

"May I be afforded an explanation as well?" Kit says with his own backward glance.

That elevator that is such a luxury in the East Village, even if it breaks down at a drop of a hat? I'm stuck in it. With Kit. And Kevin.

Is this Divine punishment meted out? What further castigation do the fidelity gods have in store for me?

I press the alarm button.

Kevin crushes a foam-packing peanut littered in the corner of the elevator with his hiking boot. "Listen, Shari, no more baloney, please. Can you at least tell me what is really fucking going on here?"

Hatred is really spooky in surround sound.

"Can we just speak privately, please?"

"I want to know the truth now!"

Kit looks intently at the ceiling.

"She didn't tell you about me?" Kevin says.

"No."

Now Kevin glares at me, face scarlet-red. He's holding back tears the best he can. "That's even more insulting."

I look at Kevin directly for the first time of the day. "I like you to pieces, but I've never been in love with you. And I never said I have. Circumstances have made it difficult to call this whole thing off, but even if I hadn't met Kit it was going to happen. I just hate that it's happening this way."

Kevin puckers.

The door opens. We've been rescued by Max, the six foot Vietnam veteran handyman of Avenue A, a man who's been on the cover of at least three tattoo magazines for his almost completely tattooed face.

He greets us with a fat grin. "Ehhhh—it's the linguist. Where's your friend with the bonsai?"

Between Cathy and myself, we've been stuck four times in the past two years, and that's on the low side for residents of this building. Even though it's chilly outside, the fix-it man has on a white undershirt. He once told me that ever since Vietnam he feels the seasons differently than the rest of us; he claims autumn in New York feels like a hot rotten summer, while summer is "Max's inferno."

I give him a thumbs-up. "You're the best," I say feebly.

Kit and Kevin step out.

"No problem." Max jokingly pops his left bicep, the one with a photorealistic tattoo of Robert DeNiro in *The Deer Hunter*. "Your janitor called me. He was too sleepy to do it himself."

After killing people, everything, according to Max, is "No problem."

Locked bathroom door? No problem. Kid wedged salami down the sink drain? No problem. Love triangle stuck in elevator? No problem.

"You're lucky I wasn't at my girlfriend's, kids. I've had it to here with sleeping at her place. Today there was another holdup on the number five, a robbery. I had customers in the morning, floor tiling, and they were fit to be tied. I lost a hefty tip they usually give. Everyone from the zoo stop was late again today."

"The zoo stop?" Kit says, the first words he's uttered since Kevin's tirade in the elevator.

"Just across from The Bronx Zoo. When the gorillas urinate, I know it, and when the giraffes move their bowels. That scent just floats over."

Despite our own shit going down, Kit opens his wallet fat with money. "Here's to make up for the gorilla piss delay." He slips Max twenty and Max appreciatively slaps Kit on the back.

Kevin takes this in, glances at me and heads for the glass door.

"Wait, Kevin."

"Just get the hell away from me." He turns the knob and is ready to flee.

I won't let the door slam and I hold him by the arm.

"Get the HELL away from me."

"What's happening here, man?" a Goth teen asks from atop a parked purple Volvo. His voice croaks either from all-night drinking or puberty.

Kevin is sure of his sympathy. "My girlfriend's screwing me over, that's what's fucking happening." He looks at me once more, eyes full of hatred, and then stomps away toward the horizon.

Kit, cigarette quickly rolled and lit, mulls over this unseemly development. He drags deeply on his cigarette before his verdict. "I didn't want that." It's hard to hear his incensed voice with all of the traffic. "I'm a bloody tosspot for—"

I'm not thinking straight, but I also didn't pick him as a man to instantly flee my side, even in this mess. "You weren't so angry a second ago when you were doling out gentleman's tips for gorilla piss stories."

"Don't give me that tone. You had a serious bloke in New York and you kept that from me."

"Please. We didn't discuss anything. For all I know you have a wife."

He takes a few seconds to answer. "Well, I don't."

Kit scurries ahead of me to the park, to a bench near the Hare Krishna elm.

"Wait! Wait, Kit, please," I say to the winter air. He's across the street and sitting down on a bench, head in his hands. I notice my feet for the first time, when Kevin entered the room I was in the yellow furry duck slippers with orange beaks he bought me as a gag gift since my feet are always cold.

"Won't you let me talk?" I say a minute later after I waddle across Tompkins Square Park to sit down next to him. I can feel a few pebbles wedged into the synthetic nonslip soles of my slippers.

He's staring straight ahead as I begin to sob.

"His mother died. It's not an easy story." Even if Kit's not going to listen, I'm telling. The saga of the unwanted *I love yous* tumbles out of me. "Add that stress on to my missteps with my master's—I'm sorry, Kit. It wasn't working with Kevin, but I wasn't strong enough to break up with him."

He's still not biting. It would be easier to draw emotion from a medieval knight in armor.

I clutch his arm as I plead. "Haven't you ever stayed with someone out of guilt?"

Kit stares at my hand. "Is there anything else you're keeping from me?" he says finally.

"No. What about you? Is there someone back home?"

Kit doesn't answer. We sit in silence. I pluck a leaf from a bush next to my bench and strip it along its veins.

An elderly white man across from us brushes his bald scalp to relieve an itch. He violently spits. Pleased with his creation, the man lowers his glance to consider it.

A pigeon picks at half of a sandwich thrown out by a young woman with frizzy hair.

Another old-timer calls to the pigeon. But the bird has other things on his agenda, like eating, for one.

Kit surprises me with a quiet question. "Did you ever go to fairgrounds in the country?"

I'm very confused by his first choice of words. But if this is his olive branch, I'll take it. "Not really. Am I missing out?"

"This is a sad story."

Has he forgiven me? "Yes?" I say cautiously.

"I was seventeen. I would not lose my virginity for another six months."

"To who?"

There's the faintest smile on his lips. "All you need to know here is that I am a seventeen-year-old virgin, and that the ultimate embarrassment at a carnival is to be one of two seventeen-year-old virgins tagging along with a carload of couples. You're trapped, as a carnival is built for couples. Young teen couples. Everything you do you do with your girlfriend. Everything a man does in a proper working teen couple is designed to lead up to possible sex. Everything an unattached straight male did, just leads to humiliation."

"This does sound sad already."

"Ian, the other virgin, was my de facto date. We went on the Ferris wheel, the swinging pirate ship—actually I got some relief with that one, that one seated a lot of people in the row. Then the water flume, which has a machine that actually took an instant souvenir picture of you when you went down, which for some stupid reason Ian paid five quid for. I told him to destroy it."

I laugh. It really feels good to laugh.

"But it was the bloody Zipper which ruined me."

"Not the Zipper!"

"You've heard of it?'

"They had that ride at Coney Island once, but from the look of it I steered clear."

"Good thing that." He stares at me with a fixed grin. "More story?" he says finally.

"More story," I say softly.

He tamps down a bit of unearthed soil at the base of our park bench before he continues. "To compound the humiliation, he screamed. I actually thought he was going to try and hold my hand as our basket started to rise over the air. The basket goes upside down and you think, okay this is pretty bloody scary, because there's another basket of upside-down terrified people you can see clearly in front of you if you can stand to look. I quickly grabbed hold of the bars in front of me, and pressed my face against them, and tensed my whole body, I said nothing as it was running on its track."

"Does this get worse?"

"The individual carriages start to swing—"

"Oh, God—"

"You're feeling like you'll lose your lunch, it can't get any worse—"

"It does?"

"It does. Everyone on the thing is spun as fast as socks in a spin dryer."

"What happened next?"

"Ian blubbers out that he is gay and in love with me. That was a bit of crimp in my afternoon, as I was already nauseous. I'm a straight virgin spending all day on stomach-churning rides with a gay virgin. I'm nauseous. I'm humiliated."

I bravely reach for his hand and he allows me to take it. "Why are you telling me this?"

"It's not funny?"

"It's very funny, but—"

"Humiliation. That's the theme here."

"Aha."

At least we're inching toward some form of resolution. We sit in silence again as an overjoyed squirrel feasts on the goodies at our feet, a rotting apple core and half of a blueberry bagel.

The sparse clouds a few blocks away drift over to right above our heads and promptly veil the silver three-quarter moon.

Kit extends his other hand. I turn it over and I rest my chin in his palm like it's an optician's chin rest. He tilts my face up and gives me a long look. He doesn't have to tell me that we're still together. I have to admit, I feel sorry for Kevin, and I'm swollen with guilt. But when I thought I'd lost Kit, my heart almost stopped. I run a finger along the weathered crags of his face.

He rises. "Let's go back to your flat."

"Yes." I can feel my pulse again.

How will Kevin ever expunge his hatred caused by my betrayal? I will try to call him in the morning, and if he doesn't pick up, I'll send him an e-mail. I will plead with him to forgive me, it took me three decades, but *I'm finally falling in love.* That has to be what I'm experiencing. Well maybe I won't say that exactly. I will, however, explain once again how dear Kevin is to me, and that circumstance and deep "like" stretched our commitment out, not love. I know Kevin cannot not read his e-mail; he is of that generation, my generation.

Did I want to drop a boyfriend so carelessly? Never. But I've finally stepped inside the decompression chamber, and the relief I feel is monumental.

CHAPTER 8

Uncle Sam

Apparently Kevin *can* not read his e-mail: since we are both America On Line subscribers I can tell his AOL e-mail has not been opened yet. He won't answer his phone, or his door, despite my pounding for half an hour.

When I return home from Kevin's building, defeated, Kit rubs my back. "You're so tense. You have a huge knot."

"Oh, man, that feels great."

"What else can I do for you?"

Kevin may be shunning me as if I were the plague, but at least Kit has forgiven me. Kit and I were supposed to leave for England tomorrow, but there's no sign of my expedited passport. "Terrorism delay," was all our issuing service would say. "No one's speeding through unless there's a family death."

Kit and I need to discuss options on how to pass the days until the passport arrives.

"This might sound weird, but we can go to my uncle's Second World War meeting," is my first suggestion. "He's getting an award from his group in Westchester. My mom's been pleading for me to go since she has a doctor's appointment she can't break. I was going to take a train there—"

"That actually sounds quite interesting. What unit?"

"The Ninth. He was a ski-trooper or something"

"Ski-trooper. You have to mean The Tenth Mountain Division. They're legendary worldwide."

"They are?"

"I just finished reading a book about them. They were the elite force. They were all Harvard or Yale ski bums, adventure hounds. After the war a bunch of them launched the U.S. ski industry, and I'm pretty sure one of them went on to start Nike."

"Are you sure? The last I checked, my uncle never went to college."

Kit looks genuinely surprised at that fact.

"Does your uncle have a wife I need to remember?" Kit says, as I drive our rented Chevy down the F.D.R. I've never owned a car, but I'd take my sorry driving over someone used to the other side of the road. Kris, the third of my Chrisses in Binghamton taught me, and I've kept up the license for ID.

I shake my head. "Divorced years ago. No kids."

"Are you close to your uncle?"

"I never ask him that much, but he gives me hugs, we get along fine. He invited me to this event after all."

"I bet he has superb stories to tell. The Tenth

Mountain! Do you even understand what that means?"

"No," I say truthfully. "Just what you told me yesterday."

"They are supposed to have the highest IQ of any group of soldiers ever."

"Really? I told you—I don't think my uncle ever went to college."

"There's a story right there. If your uncle wasn't Ivy League, he must have been frightfully talented in some arena to gain admission to their ranks."

"I'm not sure. I've never really asked. He's street-smart, but we vote differently every presidential election. I'm scared of engaging him in conversation."

"Ask. Before it's too late." He hesitates a second. "There is so much I would ask my father if I had the chance."

I wish I could look at him instead of the road. "I'm sorry he's gone."

"We didn't talk much, but my mother loved him. He was a good old British stodge."

"What does that mean?"

"He was a very private man."

"Like someone else I know?" I tease as carefully as possible.

"It didn't help that at school I was the squib on the line, the little guy 'til forever. He was born with a defined torso. He didn't really have compassion for what I was going through, and I resented him for that and hardly conversed with him."

"I cannot imagine you short, ever."

"Before my growth spurt I was Piggy from *Lord of the Flies.*"

There's a backup before the Willis Avenue Bridge that crosses Harlem River, connecting uppermost Manhattan to the Bronx. I touch Kit's smooth-shaven chin during a red light. "I've seen your belly button. You're naturally cut."

"Hardly. I was short and fat for one year but it seriously ruined me. I had to get into rowing to get my self-esteem back. I worked out in private for a year."

"What about Nigel?"

But this private man with a quick leak of emotion has morphed back to unreadable. My question is left hanging as a teenage driver passes us with a subwoofer so loud that neither of us can speak.

"My ears are still ringing from that bloody car," Kit says when we are safely on the Interstate Eighty-seven towards Nyack.

"Nothing like that in London?"

"No," Kit says.

"That's a thing here."

"What's a thing? A bass that reverberates to Jupiter is a thing?"

"I think there are guys who genuinely get a kick out of setting off car alarms."

"Sometimes your country is harebrained."

"Do you want to talk about your father?"

"When the time is right. All right?"

"Kit, of course that's all right."

Apparently I have to go gentle here.

★ ★ ★

When we enter the Best Western Hotel in Tarrytown seeking out my uncle Sam's meeting, there's no one behind the reception desk. We call out to no avail, do some exploring past an indoor fountain with water gurgling over rocks, and find ourselves in front of a mural of a headless horseman.

"Is this something to do with The Headless Horseman?"

"We're in Tarrytown."

"The Ichabod Crane Headless Horseman? Set in this town?"

"Is there another Headless Horseman?"

"But wasn't it in—" he struggles for a second or two "—Sleepy Hollow?"

"Next town over. They named it that to get some tourist dollars. But this is the place."

"How bloody amazing! That was Nigel's favorite story. He used to scare the bejesus out of me running around the house—"

Even before he takes a photo, and writes in his pad, I can tell he's not being sarcastic. I've been to Tarrytown a zillion times to visit Sam but I never thought much of it. I guess it would be kind of cool to see a town a favorite novel from childhood was set in. I'd pinch myself if I were ever ambling around the real secret garden.

"By the way, how hilarious is it that you have an Uncle Sam who was in the military?"

I look around the corner, smile and point my thumb. Kit stops his commentary when he has a look: there's a roomful of octogenarians chatting up a storm. Sure enough, there is an easel set up with plastic event letters. Tenth Mountain Veterans. I catch sight of my uncle in full uniform; he's thin like my mother, but much shorter. He looks weighted down by his impressive slew of badges and medals. I've never seen Sam in uniform before. He gives me a big bear hug, and I introduce him to Kit.

"I thought his name was Kevin," Sam says gruffly.

"No, that was—Kevin and I broke up," I say uncomfortably. "Kit and I are a recent development."

"It's an honor to meet you, sir," Kit says quickly. "You were part of a legendary outfit."

Sam beams. "We have some boys in Afghanistan now. So the tradition continues."

A seventy-year-old man with a full head of it's-got-to-be-dyed black hair slaps Sam on his back. "Who are these young things?"

"My niece. Shari, this is the infamous Frank Alvarez from Yonkers."

"Sam's niece, what do you do?" says Frank Alvarez from Yonkers.

"I'm a linguist."

"Hear that, Gladys?" he says to a woman with long white hair standing a few feet away with an open makeup case to her eye. He beckons her over with a finger and a yell. "Sam's niece!"

She obliges.

"This is Gladys. Seventy-five years old. Doesn't she look great? A former professional tap-dancer."

"You're giving away my age, Frank? Thanks a lot."

"Hi," I say. "I'm Shari."

"She's a linguist."

"Very nice to meet you," Gladys says. Then, to Kit: "And you. Who are you?"

"I'm Shari's friend Kit. I'm a linguist, too, I'm afraid."

Frank calls out to Uncle Sam, "So you got some intellectualism in your genes, Blum?" He turns to us. "Me, I'm still in gutters. Someone has to sell them."

"No shame there," Kit says. "My uncle made his name in dung. Lives well."

"Buys a lot of gongs," I say. Kit secretly pinches my hip.

Franks smiles broadly. "So you know the value of a niche. Why retire? My job plus these meetings keeps the old noggin cooking."

"Tell him about the mushrooms, Frank," Gladys pipes in.

"I'm not going to bother this young fellow about that. We just met a second ago."

"I'd love to hear about the mushrooms," Kit says.

"Just that some fellow talked me into buying cheap carpet for my van—with all the moisture after a rainy day, before you knew it a big long spindly toadstool and three little mushrooms were growing back there."

"The creepiest thing I have ever seen," Gladys says.

The food will be served momentarily; we've inadvertently timed our entrance well. The president of the chapter pleads with the chatting veterans to find their seat.

Uncle Sam makes sure we sit next to him. He hands me a large gift in purple tissue paper to unwrap. Sam is very, very big on giving gifts. (He scored a wholesalers card years ago and goes to the Seventh Avenue stores and buys "fun" things by the dozen.) I open it up: a George Foreman four-hamburger minigrill.

"Hey, thanks," I say sincerely. I can actually use his present this time.

"Knocks the fat out," Gladys imitates the infomercial pitch as she takes her seat next to Frank. "I don't even cook in my regular oven anymore."

"You got the George Foreman?" a soldier at a neighboring table asks. "That's one of the better things Sam has in the duffel. He must love you."

"I have a gift for you, too," Sam says to Kit.

"Me? But you don't know me—"

"The nut has backup gifts for every occasion," Frank says. "Take it, it might be a watch. The one he gave me last year is still working."

Kit opens a small gift wrapped in red tissue paper that Sam hands him from a small duffel bag full of tissue-wrapped gifts.

It's a two-inch plastic bird.

"Thank you," Kit says with notable confusion.

"It balances on your finger," Gladys says. "I got one from Sam the first time I met him, too." She places the beak of the bird on Kit's forefinger, and whaddaya know, it balances and the rest of its body flies above his hand.

Kit grins at the physics show.

"Grab one of the big ones, too," Sam demands.

Kit opens a square box wrapped in blue tissue paper. "A Yankees wall clock," he announces to the table.

Sam smiles, and addresses me: "I invited your brothers, but they didn't call back."

"Gene never comes to anything, and Alan is… well—"

"Alan," Uncle Sam answers for me. Since Alan never listens to anything Gene says anymore, Sam was the one my mother sent to try to talk Alan off the sandal commune. He failed just as miserably as the rest of us.

Sam was indignant when he called my mother. "Alan wants us to understand that anarchy is the only way to gain back our country."

"Maybe you shouldn't have reached out to Alan through a Second World War veteran," I'd said when Mom relayed the pitiful report to me.

She had cried. "I was desperate. I want my son back."

The outlook has not improved in the year that's passed. Alan only occasionally takes my calls to make sure everyone is still alive.

The lunch orders for the meeting arrive.

"Who had the medium beef?"

"You did," I say to Kit.

"Oh, you did, too, Frank," Gladys says.

"Go ahead and take it," Kit says emphatically. "I think veterans should get their beef before me."

"Listen to this fellow. This is how American youth should be. Respectful. None of this government bashing."

I poke at the not-so-nice mushrooms on my salad as Kit says to Frank, "How long have you and Gladys been together?"

"Oh, we're not together."

"I'm his event buddy, but this cat's got a young girlfriend." Gladys speaks after a bit of her lunch goes down her hatch. "His wife didn't cook. That doesn't fly with

Puerto Ricans. If you don't cook for your man, all the women in your husband's family talk about you."

"My ex said the hell with *Love* and *Obey*," Frank says after a nod.

"How did you get to serve in the American military if you're Puerto Rican?" Kit asks.

I quickly interject, "Puerto Ricans are American."

"Puerto Ricans got the vote in 1917—" Frank says.

"I thought you weren't a commonwealth until 1952," Uncle Sam says.

"But we have a relationship with the mainland back to the Spanish Civil War, Sam."

"So Puerto Rico is rather like Australia to Britain?" Kit asks Frank.

"No kangaroos, though," Gladys says kindly. She steers the conversation back to the previous subject. "His girlfriend is a young one, darling."

Frank shrugs. "I wouldn't bring her here. I know these dogs from the war. I don't want them drooling over my little lady."

Uncle Sam laughs knowingly.

"How young can she be?" Kit says.

"You don't want to know," Gladys assures him.

"All I'll tell you is I go dancing with her every week at the Pittsburgh Center in Yonkers. Boy does she come from *moonyan*." He rubs his fingers together. "Yeesh, yeah, big money. No need to get married. I'm happy. She's happy. All she wants to do is sleep, eat, fuck and dance."

"Hey, curb the potty mouth," an ex-soldier calls out from across the table. "My wife is here."

"You two married yet?" Frank says to Kit.

"No," Kit says, quite shocked.

He honks in approval. "As long as you get married by Exit Thirty."

"He's got a ways to go," my uncle calls out. "Must be about Shari's age, twenty-five—"

"Sam," I stop him. "I'm *thirty-five.*"

Sam stares at me in disbelief. "How the hell did *that* happen?"

"Thirty-six," is Kit's delayed response to Frank.

Well thanks to Frank, now I know my new boyfriend's age.

"You look good for an old geezer," Franks says.

Kit grins. "I stay out of the sun. Bad for the Brits." He takes a drink of water, and asks, "So, what's your dance?"

"Jitterbug," Franks declares. "There's still a few places old-timers can jitterbug in the Bronx. You should talk to Shari's uncle about it. Sam was the jitterbug king."

He was? "Tell me more," I say to Sam.

My uncle smiles. "They saw me dance in Colorado. Most of us knew each other in Aspen. The Tenth trained in an ad hoc military hut in the Telluride area. Forget about my dancing—I bet you didn't know that the ski industry started because of our fellows. Pfeifer built Aspen of course, he's a good man, and Pete Seibert created Vail. You know Nike sneakers?"

"Sure," Kit says politely.

"Bill Bowerman. Founded the damn thing, and one of ours. And Bob Dole is Tenth Mountain, too. A real joker. I trained with him in the Rockies. Sent me a postcard recently. He's the one who convinced me to switch parties."

Even if he knew some of this information already from his recent reading, Kit is entranced. Me, too, although I'm embarrassed it took a foreigner's accompaniment to have heard any of these stories. *My* uncle knows these people? Really?

Another soldier runs over to our table. "Anyone have a clean glass? I'm looking for a clean glass."

He takes the empty one from our table, and as soon as he is seated back at his table, Frank pokes Kit and says, "That fellow was a hypochondriac back in the war, too. Just what you need in the Alps. We're worried who's still alive after the battle at Lake Garda, and he's worried if his finger is frostbitten."

After the meal, the president of the chapter calls us to order, and after a pledge of allegiance to the American flag and a moment of silence for the new crop of Tenth Mountain reps in Afghanistan and Iraq, he proceeds with his order of business before the awards.

Another former soldier interrupts: "Why are we having this meeting on a Wednesday? If we want the descendants to be part of this why don't we have it on a weekend? I frankly think you've made a hash of it, Ed. Time for Harry to run for president."

"I can hardly even get to the meetings," someone, who I assume is Harry, says. "Now you want me to grow an extra pair of testicles and run for president?"

President Ed is indignant: "Honestly, Phil, I haven't made a hash of it. I rang the head of the descendants to give us a date. No answer. There's only one descendant eager to help us however she can, a woman named Kay Kay."

"What kind of name is that?" calls out an amused voice from the back, rickety with age.

"Kay Kay?" says another decorated soldier. "It's people like that make me feel like I'm living in a giant cartoon where I'm the punch line."

"That's her name. She lives in Manhattan on Fifth Avenue and Fifty-eighth Street—does all our labels for us—I send her a hundred names and she has them back to me in a week."

"Sam's niece, do you know Kay Kay?" a man way down the table asks me.

Sam waves an exasperated palm in the air. "Murray, don't be silly. New York is a big place."

"It's an unusual name, Sammy."

"No, I don't know her," I answer back with a smile.

"Son of a gun, all of you," Frank hisses says with an exaggerated pained expression. "Mr. President is speaking, have some respect."

"Yes, well, where was I as far as the descendants go?"

"Kay Kay," Uncle Sam calls out.

"Yes, Kay's not the problem. She's lovely. About the others, I said to my wife, what the dickens. Let's have a meeting when it's convenient to us. If anyone wants to go after them again, be my guest. You can look at their Internet site—"

"Can I have that Internet number?"

A woman at the front table says, "Address, Pete. Internet address. And it's in the *Blizzard,* Pete, read the new issue of the *Blizzard.*"

"A smart lady," the president says to the woman. "You're a dynamo for pulling together that latest *Blizzard,* honey."

Kit beams at me. I can tell he loves these characters and their unselfconsciousness that comes from living through experiences worse than anything either of us could even conjure up in our heads.

Another hand goes up, and the veteran is called upon: "I want to ask that we send the mementos to my house."

"Son of a gun," says another without permission to talk. "I brought that up five years ago."

More voices:

"Let the guy speak, Murray."

"He's an officer."

"Yeah, Quartermaster, you had to talk from the back and now you can talk from the front."

Then it's time for my uncle's award. The chapter president nods to an official photographer and says, "I now call upon Sam Blum, who finely and bravely served our country from 1941 to '45."

There is loud applause and hooting.

I never knew my uncle was such a natural ham when handed a microphone. "Who's just cheering because he wants a George Foreman grill?"

Even louder hooting. Sam bows with a grin, and I can tell here in this room, he is greatly loved.

"Twelve days in combat and I got my *kishkes* blown out at Riva Ridge—many of you know I had amnesia, so everything I've learned about my time there I learned from rehooking up with you fellows."

After the award ceremony is over, and Sam is reseated,

I give him a kiss and reveal more of my embarrassing family ignorance: "I didn't know you had amnesia."

My uncle looks at me, deciding what to say. "My legs were pinned by the shrapnel—the military used the New York Jews and Italians as pack rats."

Several soldiers, mid-dessert, look up in surprise.

"Let's save this for another time," Sam says dramatically.

I hold my uncle's eye. "I'd love that. How about when I get back from England?"

Sam smiles again. His teeth are suspiciously white, very possibly he was just fitted for a new set of dentures. "Good for you. I knew you'd get there. When are you going?"

"In two days, with Kit."

"I love the place myself."

"You've been to England?" This is insane. How did I miss this tid-bit, too? There is not a chance I wouldn't have heard about a relative's trip to England.

"I was there with your grandmother in 1974. We saw London, and Stonehenge, although that was a real tour-ist trap."

Kit nudges me.

"Grandma Sadie went to England?" I'm beyond surprised now, I'm gobsmacked.

"Your mother never told you that?"

"No." And why wouldn't she? Does she still think my family embarrasses me? Do they? C'mon, I tell myself. I'm being a bit paranoid here. Even my mother has other things going on in her life than to be my family almanac. So a remarkable detail or three finally got re-vealed.

Kit smiles as I sting. "I'd love to ask you more questions one day, too, Sam. I've read two books on the Tenth."

"I'm on e-mail." Sam writes down his new Earthlink account details on the program in his spidery old handwriting, and I wonder what else my mother hasn't told me.

CHAPTER 9

The Pill

I'm stepping out of the shower as the phone rings. I call for Kit to answer it—it could be the passport agency.

Kit brings me the phone and whispers, "A woman with a masculine voice."

That's either Aunt Dot or Dr. Zuckerman's nurse calling back with the results of the blood test.

"Ms. Diamond, I have Dr. Zuckerman waiting to speak with you."

"You're still in America," Dr. Zuckerman says two minutes later. "Good. I thought I was going to have to leave a message."

"Passport mess."

"Maybe you can use one of those services."

"I did. They're not going any faster."

"Well, at least your doctor has delivered. You are hypothyroidmatic as I suspected, a strong candidate for Hashimoto's disease."

I clench my jaw before I speak. "How bad is that?"

"If you're going to have a disease, it's certainly not the worst. Lethargy is one of the main symptoms, which explains your energy level the past few months. And you can gain a lot of weight with a loss of metabolism. Count yourself lucky there."

"I know I was joking about my weight in your office, but I was thinking about what you said—and realized I've mysteriously gained about ten pounds the past two years." Disease? That word lingers in my head as I nervously ramble on. "Not that I'm normally a stick, but I've never had a weight battle before—"

"Sssh. Calm, calm, you'll probably lose it just with Synthroid. This is a disease that's easy to control with a daily pill. But it is a pill you'll be taking for life I'm afraid." He pauses dramatically and adds, "I am going to put you on .75 milligrams to start. I think you'll feel an improvement right away, and when you get back, we'll test your blood levels again. It takes a while to level off."

"Okay." If he's not too worried, I'm not going to shit myself either.

"So, what's your pharmacy's number? I'll call in the prescription."

"Hold on."

As I reach for the Yellow Pages to find Avenue A Drug and Beauty, a beloved mom-and-pop holdout among the billions of New York Duane Reades and Rite Aids, he tells me they'll probably fill my prescription with a generic version of Synthroid—Leve something. I make like I was listening carefully and tell him whatever's cheap and effective works for me.

"So, bon voyage," Dr. Zuckerman says warmly after I give him the number. "Maybe you can look up Owen in England."

"Is he in England? I thought he was here."

"I told you, he's back and forth all the time. He's leaving sometime this week. He'll be based in the British Museum scholar room. They know him there if you ask. He's trying to arrange for an international cell phone, but no word on that yet or where he's staying."

"You know, you *are* a wonderful *Schadchen.* You've got yourself a second career if you want it."

Dr. Zuckerman laughs and after a final goodbye hangs up.

"What's a *Schadchen?*" Kit says as he pours me a second cup of coffee. (Our brew has improved, as late last night we stopped in Porto Rico Importing on East Ninth Street for fresh ground French Roast Colombian.)

"Yiddish for matchmaker. My thyroid doctor is trying to set me up with his son."

"And you are going on that date?"

"No. I told him I was taken but he didn't seem to listen. I don't have the energy to repeat myself. I knew his son as a child, so I would like to look him up, platonically. I'll explain my current rap to him."

"Well maybe you'll have the energy for his son when his medication kicks in."

"Hey, listen. One handsome man in my life is enough!"

"His son is handsome? Maybe the doctor's making a good match—"

"When he was twelve. And hey, I just called you handsome—" I wave my hand to dismiss this bit of silly conversation. Kit grins as I give him a playful squeeze on his elbow. "Anyway, how is this ambrosia coming out of my dinky coffeemaker?"

"I made it differently. I boiled it in a pot, and then drained it. You don't get enough caffeine in those makers."

"I'm impressed. You can make me coffee every day of my life. I can't touch this."

We sip and comfortably stare into each other's eyes.

Is he as wonderstruck as I am by how everything except a timely passport has just magically worked out for us? "A penny for your thoughts," I say.

"I'm a very happy man." I kiss him again on his nose. "A pence for yours."

I smile guiltily. "I was thinking about how this is the smug coupledom Bridget Jones hated so."

He double-checks my eyes, surprised. "You read that kind of fluff?"

"Um. Yeah. To relax."

He scrunches his nose.

I hit him on his arm. "Hey, snob! Look at me, Kit! Lay off Bridget Jones. A woman is fighting for two British men's affections. You think I'm not going to like it?"

"I just thought you were more selective."

"Excuse me, Cambridge snob. And by the way Helen Fielding is very smart. She 'read English' at Oxford."

"Whatever."

"Oh, you picked up that obnoxious phrase from my little shitty America."

He sniggers. "You're the one with class consciousness, not me."

"I'm not asking you to be my therapist, *arse*-hole. I'm just saying, you leave off Helen Fielding and furthermore, if you ever, ever say a word against *The Secret Garden* I'll wring your neck."

"That's a kid's book. Apples and oranges."

"Sure, but it's my all-time favorite book. I'm just giving you a heads-up."

"What is it with women and *The Secret Garden?* Every girl I've ever gone out with talks about this book."

"It's sexy."

"It's a kids' book. How sexy can it be?"

I think for a second as he smirks at me. "There's this tradition of treacly American TV specials called *Hallmark Hall of Fame.* They aired their version of *The Secret Garden* in the late eighties."

"So naturally, you watched it."

"Of course I did. And the girls I liked best on my dorm floor *had* to watch, too. That was one of the first times I saw my man Colin Firth, as the grown-up Colin passionately kissing Mary."

"Your man," Kit laughs to himself.

"Yes, my man," I say defensively. "We cheered from the couch. The writer and director simply rewrote them as family friends, because they knew what girls *really* wanted from those characters, and finally had them go for it."

"Should I reread *Rin Tin Tin* for the sex scenes?"

"Is there anything else you want to deride me about?"

Kit sips and then says, "Yes, as a matter of fact. Did you ever have a conversation before about how you sleep?"

"Why, how do I sleep?"

"You're like an arrow spearing me in the side. You twist sideways, and you're constantly jabbing your feet into me."

"Whoa. That's specific."

"Well, if we're going to sleep together some more, and I assume we are, we need to figure out a solution."

"Yeah, well talk to me as soon as you trim your toenails, Kit. It's like nuzzling up to a horned stag."

Kit coughs indignantly, but the ringing phone halts the littlest of duels.

"Two more days," another woman from the passport service insists after a loud sneeze. "There's nothing I can do."

"There's a backup due to terrorism," I preempt her. Her coworker is probably avoiding me after I called her on her expedition skills.

"Exactly. So you've been keeping tabs on the…"

I grunt toward the receiver when I hang up. "We have to change our tickets again. There's no way British Airways is having this."

"Drink your coffee, I'll call."

"Oh God, thank you. I don't think I can listen to this." I choose Cathy's bedroom with its softer light and thick new mattress perfect for reading the paper. I lie across her expensive down quilt. I must remember to neaten it before we leave for the day; she'll be back tomorrow.

Kit calls me out again.

"That's fixed. So what are we going to do with still more extra days in New York?"

"British Airways went for it? No crazy fee?"

"We're going four days later than our original plans. That should give us time for that bloody passport."

"You're my hero. How did you do it?"

"Charm school," Kit says between chews. After his success on the phone, he's finally trying out the bubble gum tape I bought him in a Korean deli.

I blow out air in envy and awe. "Cambridge is one damn expensive charm school."

Kit laughs and says, "Maybe with the extra time I can meet your brothers or your mother."

"My mother is easy," I say. "Gene and Alan, that'll take a bit of finagling."

"Finagle then. Can't we do it in one hit? How about a dinner party? We can host it here."

Our lot is decided by a phone call later that afternoon from my banker brother Gene.

"Hey, stranger, what's new?"

"Not much," I lie.

What would Gene be telephoning about? Even if we're not exceptionally close anymore, we're on okay terms. But he *never* calls.

"Were you planning on calling me this century?"

"Of course, but you can call, too." I swallow guiltily. As a matter of fact, I was very close to ringing him this morning after facing facts: even though asking for a handout is just not done in my family, I'm going to need a loan as I sort out my botched dissertation. A trip through England is a luxury, but what then? I have to do it. My stomach tenses. Do I have to do this now?

"You hear about the funeral? I got the call from Eric."

"Wait—what—Dot died?" Sure, I complain about Dot's incessant nagging to my mom, but I don't want my aunt dead. In one instant I realize I love(d) her.

"No. The skunk."

I breathe out. "Oh, my God! Dot's okay?"

"You thought Dot died, idiot? You really think I'd be jabbering away when I said hello?"

"It's been a rough week. Don't fight me today."

"Who's fighting? I'm just the messenger. We have to go to the funeral. It's tomorrow. They need to bury him in twenty-four hours."

"Why? Because he is going to decompose after that and stink up the place?"

"No, because he's a Jewish skunk."

"What?"

"You have to bury a Jew in twenty-four hours."

"He's a skunk."

"This is Dot we're talking about. It's going to be at an animal cemetery in Westchester tomorrow."

"She lives in the Catskills though."

"Apparently this is the best resting place a skunk can go to rot. It's where Judy Garland's dog is. That was a big drawing card."

"Can't you or Mom represent?"

"Represent? Who am I, Snoop Dog?"

"Listen, I have a friend from England in town. I'm touring him around."

"*Listen,* then you have to take him. Mom says Galoot—"

"Galoot," I repeat with considerable sarcasm.

"Galoot," he picks up after a little laugh. "Yeah, Galoot was like a son to Dot. Mom'll never hear the end of it if we don't go."

Uncle Sam, as quirky as he is with the chronic gift-giving, is from my mother's side, the Blums. I can't think of one Blum that is really off his or her rocker. But I cannot subject Kit to the full-blown Diamond madness. Can Kit spend another day on his own? Maybe he can take in the Guggenheim or the re-vamped MoMA.

"I'm not promising anything. Give me the details," I say to my brother as Kit looks at me inquisitively.

"Alan's coming."

"Alan? Our Alan?"

"I do not lie."

Alan Andrew Diamond has always been the most difficult for my mother to wrangle, especially when we were kids. In the morning he'd go through all of evolution before he could fully function as a human being. He has the strongest will of anyone I know, in a negative way, and even to this day he leads the pack of everyone I know for most phobic.

"If Alan can leave the sandals behind and come, you can get your ass out there, too. Do it for Mom. Surrender now. You can fight her for an hour, but she's going to make sure you do the right thing."

"The Catskills is so convenient."

"No, I told you, pay attention. The funeral is closer than that. In Hartsdale, next to Scarsdale. Galoot's getting the royal burial at a famous pet cemetery."

"Dot." My single word sentence is loaded with disapproval.

"She's your flesh and blood, and she loves you."

"You're working for your mother now?"

"You're going to cave. Let's get it over with."

"We just returned the car rental."

"What's your roommate's name? Cathy?"

"Yeah?"

"Cathy and you don't have the kind of money to be renting cars. Use the subway. Isn't that the point of living in Manhattan?"

"Pay attention. I told you, I have a visitor from England in town. A guy. We've been sightseeing."

"Then bring him along. If he's a visitor here, he might even enjoy it."

"A cemetery? C'mon."

"This place sounds kind of insane. Mom was reading to me from the brochure she picked up with Dot when they made the arrangements."

"What, they picked out a skunk casket?"

"Rosewood. Cost Dot five hundred bucks."

"Um, I was joking."

"And there's lots of famous dead dogs. You can come to my house and I'll drive you."

"Let me talk to my friend and I'll call you back."

When I click the receiver down, Kit say, "Oh, goodie. A skunk funeral."

"You don't want to go to this."

"Are you kidding?"

"Seriously."

"Seriously. And why are you so shocked about Alan coming? Did he have a fight with Dot?"

"You picked all of this up?"

"My conversations with my family last four seconds. Americans are very expressive."

I throw my crumbled napkin at him. "Alan is a handful."

"How's that? You haven't really talked about your brothers too much."

I list just some of Alan's countless phobias over the years: green olives stuffed with pimiento, vomiting, plungers, a postcard of the Hieronymous Bosch's *Garden of Earthly Delights* a neighbor once sent to my mother from Madrid, undercooked egg, sharp whistle blasts, and the sharp-toothed boar in the We Serve Only Boar's Head meat products sign in the window of our local deli.

"Is that all?"

"And barber chairs."

"And melty chocolate?"

"No, he loves chocolate. Who doesn't love chocolate?"

"Call Gene back. Tell him we're coming."

I do, and agree to bring Kit to Gene's apartment via the F Train. From there he will give us a lift.

CHAPTER 10

Car Pool

Gene's two-bedroom spread is in Parker Towers, one of the more enviable apartment buildings in Forest Hills. In the ride up to the nineteenth floor I explain to Kit that my older brother's interiors will look professionally done because they were designed by his old girlfriend Jill—a woman with two facial features exactly like a stock Dr. Seuss character: a short upturned nose, and a vertically distended upper lip.

"When did they break up?"

"Six weeks ago. He's being predictably secretive about the relationship demise."

Gene ushers us in. I'm surprised how he's aged even in the six months since I've seen him last. His hair has thinned, his forehead has prematurely pleated, and I'm a little worried about a possible double chin emerging.

But his killer smile is there, the one that the ladies in the Forest Hills bar scene love.

After a sibling kiss, Gene says "How-d'ye-do?" to Kit and shakes his hand firmly.

"Nice to meet you," Kit says.

As we turn from the foyer into the living room I see that his interior has been redone once again. Jill's gone, and there's no way his unseasoned eye could have ever pulled this together so expertly. It briefly occurs to me that my brother's digs bursting with expensive furniture and mail-order baubles may be off-putting to a man offering an overseas freebie vacation out of pity.

"So when did you get this decorated again?"

"New girlfriend," he says to me. "Also an interior designer. Didn't want Jill's stamp on it."

"Are you dating one of Jill's friends? What's her name?"

"Cannot divulge," he says robotically. "Must break three-month mark."

"Nice place," Kit says.

"Thank you. It's the ultra in fake American Colonial, or so I'm told."

"Oh," Kit says.

There's an awkward silence.

"Kit is also a Volapük specialist," I say to fill the void.

Gene is relieved at the sound of spoken word. "There's two of you doing that?"

"Three. There's also a man at Columbia." I keep to myself: Dave Mitchell's prolific praise of my competition, and how that stung me so. I marvel at fate. There's the very enemy himself, fingering a wooden Mancala tray.

Kit picks it up. "I like your Mancala board. Very old. A bit of African Colonial mingling in I see."

"Since when do you play Mancala?" I ask Gene. "My old roommate played it. I might even give you a go."

"This thing's for a game?"

I can see Kit is hesitating with a ready response. It looks as if he doesn't want to come off as a know-it-all. His overstuffed mind can't help itself: "It's an African strategy game. Mancala is one of the oldest games in history, you know. Yours is from the Congo, I'm pretty sure."

Gene shrugs. "I've been using it as a candy dish. Jill made me buy it at an estate sale. She thought I needed something old for this place."

After more brief niceties, we get ready to go to his car parked in the building's in-house garage. Gene loves his car and he hates hassle. An assigned parking space is the main reason Gene chose Forest Hills over the Upper East Side when looking around for a good place to buy. It's by no means the sole reason he bought here. Gene's a dime-a-dozen go-getting guy in Manhattan, but in this borough with a nice place and a banking job and a BMW X5, he is a big fish. In Queens he gets laid.

Gene hits the elevator button for Lower Level. "So did my sister tell you what a whackjob our aunt Dot is?"

"I didn't go there," I say preemptively.

"You said she was big on candles," Kit reminds me.

"No," Gene laughs. "That's another crazy one-syllable aunt, on our mother's side. Fay's a lightweight. Dot is a class unto herself. For starters there's her body."

I throw my hands up. He is such a jerk sometimes.

"God. Pick on the skunk, but not her fat. Fat doesn't equate insanity, Gene. Lots of people have weight issues."

"I'm not talking about her fat, Shari. Her toes are disgusting. Did you ever see Dot's hammertoes when she wears sandals?"

"Are the sandals environmentally sound?" Kit says dryly.

Gene laughs, surprised that his guest already knows that insider joke, and I shoot Kit a look to shut up. Later, I'll laugh, too, after I take Gene to task. "She only has one left hammertoe now, so you can cross that off your list. Mom said they cut the tendons on seven of her toes, but the one that is left was full of arthritis."

"How do you get seven hammertoes?" Kit asks with an interested but slightly sickened face.

"She wore stilettos all her life," I say to Kit and then I look intently at Gene. "Let's leave poor grieving Dot alone."

"Well you said Kit didn't hear any evidence of insanity in our family."

"No, I actually still haven't," Kit says.

"Okay, than what's with the skunks as pets?" Gene demands of him.

I jump in: "I'm surprised to hear how attached she was to this one. I don't know anything about this particular skunk other than its untimely demise."

Gene addresses me back and Kit rolls up a cigarette before we get into the car. I catch Gene's frown at the smoking. "Have you really ever bought their childlessness? Dot couldn't adopt?"

"Gene, *enough,* okay? Leave her alone. You're just being mean. If you remember, before Eric, she had no partner. It wasn't easy to adopt as a single parent twenty years ago."

"You're playing innocent, Shari, like you don't rag on Dot twenty-four/seven—"

"Gene!" I knew introducing Kit to my family was a dumb idea. Going to see Sam in Headless Horseman territory was a surprisingly nice experience, but it looks like when it comes to introducing the rest of my eccentric family, it's all downhill from here.

"Nice car, by the way," Kits says, after we've climbed into Gene's beloved BMW.

"Thank you," Gene says proudly.

I say nothing.

Gene starts the ignition. "Well, one last thing then, Shari, and then we can talk about the weather."

"What?" I spit out.

"I don't buy it."

"Buy what?"

"That she couldn't have a kid. Mom thinks that, too, by the way, that Dot didn't want a kid, that she never wanted the emotional responsibility of children. She never wanted anyone who would talk back to her."

I'm ready to smack him.

Kit looks politely out the window at the moving cars as we pull out onto Queens Boulevard toward the Long Island Expressway, but I'm sure his distraction is partly due to distaste.

"Oh," Gene says a few blocks into our journey. "We have to also warn you not to laugh when you meet Eric."

"Look, no more vitriol, please, really. Save it for a phone conversation."

Kit coughs uncomfortably, but Gene has no shame: "Eric looks like your worst nightmare of Gene Wilder, and then toss in that he's hard of hearing."

I'm peeved at him for blatantly ignoring my warning, but the thought of Eric as Gene Wilder's doppelganger makes me laugh out loud, and Gene sneaks me a triumphant grin. "All right, you get one point for funny," I allow.

"Gene Wilder," Kit says. "Do I know him?"

"C'mon, of course you do," I say. "You know about regional African Mancala styling but not Gene Wilder?"

"I'm not sure I do."

"Really? You never saw *Blazing Saddles?*" Gene says loudly.

"No."

"Producers?" he tries again.

"Never saw that."

"You never saw *The Producers!*" This comes in a shriek; even before the Broadway hit, *The Producers* was Gene's favorite movie. He has been known to hum "Springtime for Hitler" in his sleep.

"Don't get carried away here," I say. "Everyone has to watch the movies you watch?"

"What about *The Frisco Kid? Sherlock Holmes' Smarter Brother?*"

"You're a big fan of this bloke, I see," Kit replies tartly.

"Sharing a name with him has made him a buff." *Stop it, Gene,* I say to myself. Even though my brother has an overall sunny disposition, he's so pigheaded sometimes, with his cruel women's body comments. And what I also didn't prewarn Kit about Gene is how he relentlessly teases; he almost destroyed Alan's sense of self when he decreed that Little Brother was definitely homosexual because he couldn't climb the rope in gym. Our mother never figured out why Alan went into another of his terrifying dark funks that week—but before she sought professional help a noticeable swagger miraculously replaced his despondency. Gene told me everything Alan had that very day confided to him—and made me swear it was "in the vault." Alan lost his virginity bonking a Roosevelt Mall rat named Robyn whom he'd previously avoided when she swanned up to him at school dances in skintight jeans and obscenely low-cut shirts.

"C'mon," Gene persists. "Who didn't see *The Producers?* That's the greatest movie of the twentieth century!"

"What does he look like?" Kit says. "Maybe I'll know his face."

"Check out Eric when you meet him and you'll know."

"How is Alan coming to the cemetery?" I say tensely.

"His new girlfriend at the commune is driving in."

"Yes, I meant to ask you about that commune, Shari," Kit says.

And I was so relieved when you didn't.

We pause the conversation when Gene decides he better stop to pee at Burger King now or he'll be in trouble in fifteen minutes. Kit's out for a smoke as fast as Gene stops the car. Time to fret about what family inferno lies ahead.

The last time I saw Alan was the week he had gone to the extraordinary step of inviting me to dinner at the sandal commune, and met me at the Staten Island ferry so we could take a bus there. It wasn't a formal commune per se, as a San Franciscan might expect, but rather a series of houses on the same block bought up by the collective. They wore normal clothes, if a little thrift-storish. It's established that I'm big on thrift store finds, but these were the dreg clothes you see after the sitcom stylists have already picked over goodies like the seventies dresses with kimono sleeves. A P.A. system wired between the houses called everybody into the communal dining room for dinner. The food served was nominally health food; each member brought a dish from his or her home kitchen, beet-colored macaroni, and some sort of dessert with wheatgrass. Instead of soda, they served Juicy Juice, for that lovely canned juice taste, and used off-brand ketchup that looked to be sitting in someone's refrigerator so long that a dark maroon crust manifested around the bottom of the bottle. Alan leaned toward my ear and admitted that only half of the commune residents were there; the rest were out and about; I assume he told me this to quell my fears that he lived in a cult. During the meal they talked about group experience and conflict resolution. Someone had bought a used car, not from a friend, and as it turned out it was not in very good running condition. He was trying to figure out what he should do. Should he get some of the money back, or all of it? This discussion was led by an elderly man I assumed was the spiritual leader, a man with a beard named Xander. The thing that actually freaked me out most of all was that there was a member of the group who spontaneously got up and started rubbing Xander's old callused feet. Nobody said anything, not even Alan, so apparently this was normal.

When we went back to Alan's house, he said, nervously, "Pretty great, huh?"

Mom pumped me hard after my visit, but I didn't want to break her heart. Alan would never go back to live with her in Queens, and although I didn't think the place was a cult, it was a life choice that appalled me. Besides, if he left, where would he live? He never finished school, and his long list of phobias now included applying for a job.

"Aren't you excited that Alan has a girlfriend?" Gene says as he climbs back in the car.

"Why?"

"That's pretty fucking exciting. All he wanted to talk about the last time I saw him were drapes."

"Curb it. You know he's had other girlfriends."

He waits to answer until Kit has his seat belt on. "Are you so sure? Have you met any?"

"No, but stop telling Alan he is gay. Maybe he's just not as showy as you—"

"Showy? Is that what you call heterosexuality?"

"There's new drapes on a commune?" Kit slips in.

"Oh, c'mon, drapes?" Gene turns to Kit: "What do you think, Mancala Man? This guy is sharp, sis, he'll tell you like it is."

Kit shrugs with a guilty smile, and Gene laughs in response. I'm a little mad for the mateship betrayal.

Gene turns his focus to his printout from MapQuest. "We need to take the I-87 North toward White Plains. But I want to stop for gas."

"Oh," says Kit. "We took that road to see Sam and the Tenth Mountain chaps."

Gene crinkles his face in confusion. "You've met my uncle Sam?"

"Great guy. Amazing life. By the way, I'll pay for the petrol."

Gene waves him off. "It wasn't your idea to get dragged to a skunk funeral. You're not paying anything."

"Actually he insisted on tagging along," I say.

"Gene," Kit speaks for himself, "is there a person alive who wouldn't want to go to a skunk funeral?"

Gene chuckles. I think Kit is finally winning him over. He stops at the no-name gas station inside the boundary of the Bronx. "Bargain unleaded," he explains. "What New Yorker can't stop for a deal?" Gene wasn't lying; he won't let Kit pay. After a polite fight, Kit heads inside to the minimart to search out a can of Red Bull, or at the very least a Coke.

"You must be serious about this guy," Gene says through my open window as he pumps. "He knows about Alan and the sandals, and man, he's already met Uncle Sam?"

"Yes, I like him *a lot*. So maybe we should keep the dirty family laundry locked inside the den, whatever's left of it."

"I didn't say anything *that* bad."

"Let's go to the videotape."

"Ragging on your family is accepted the world over. Get over it, priss."

The exit numbers Gene's printout from MapQuest says we're supposed to see coming up are not matching *in the least.* We're miserably lost. I'm betting we went wrong somewhere earlier on the Bronx River Parkway, and say so.

"We're lost," Gene barks, "that's what I think."

Kit tries his best to be invisible in his seat.

This does not bode well for our afternoon drive. Gene does not like to be lost, ever. "This can't be fucking right," he says a minute after his last outburst. "This is making me very nervous. Fuck. Christ." He pulls out at the nearest exit and asks a young gas station attendant for directions.

"He said we're too far. We have to take the Taconic back to Exit Fifteen. Shari, keep your eyes peeled for the first left."

We soon find ourselves once again aimlessly driving down a long stretch of highway.

"I think that little turn out of the petrol station was to the left," Kit says quietly.

We take another desperate exit and there's not a business to be found. We're maneuvering up and down hilly roads in a residential neighborhood, town unknown. I have a charley horse going on my left leg, but who would complain in this environment? I quietly shake it out.

"Okay, that's it," Gene says testily. "We're going in that diner and someone is going with me if we are getting to Dot and her skunk on time."

"I'll go," says Kit.

"No, the someone is Shari. And then, when Shari has written down the instructions, this time we'll all be looking for the right signs."

"C'mon, Gene. I'm the worst person for navigation, you know that."

"All you have to say to yourself is 'I am not pathetic' ten times and you'll be okay."

I take the punch again. I hate him so much when he gets road rage, but he needs to calm down if we're not going to let Aunt Dot and my mom down.

We enter a local eatery with a lonely, forlorn-looking exterior. The sad look continues inside. The only visible staff is a world-weary cashier with an orange-hued tanning salon tan; she's mid-discussion with an elderly female customer.

"Is that really the right amount?" the customer asks suspiciously.

"It is."

"I'm not blaming you. It's the machine. It cheated me twice already. The machine. Not you. Please check. Yesterday the other cashier charged me for two muffins. I'm not saying it was his fault. It was the machine. I'm not blaming you. Can you check?" Next she turns to Gene and says, "I'm not blaming the cashier, you know. It's the machine. Twice it cheated me."

Gene says nothing. He points her back to the exasperated cashier who's looking over the bill.

"Sorry, ma'am, that's how much it is for coffee and poached eggs," she says. She shakes her head angrily as the old woman gives up and walks away murmuring.

I watch outside of the window where the customer is walking past the parking spaces and toward the open road. Gene pokes me. "Your job here is to listen!"

I see the anger management course Jill the Ex insisted he enroll in didn't do much.

The cashier assures Gene that she can get him to where we need to be. I borrow a Bic propped up against the cash register and write everything down on the back of a catering flyer.

"How did it go?" Kit says when we're back in the car.

I answer for the both of us. "Well, this lady sounded like she knew more of what she was talking about." I carefully read my notes out. "Down to the bottom of the hill, past the train tressle."

"Trestle," Kit corrects with a sharp letter *t*.

I glare at him. "Not the time for an English lesson."

Kit and Gene look at each other conspiratorially.

"There's the tress-*t*-le," I say pointedly a minute later. "Okay, make a left to Taconic South."

"Aha! So it's not so impossible for you," Gene says. "This is the year Shari is going to stop looking at the world in autofocus."

When we're safely on the highway I respond. "This is rather empowering."

After a silent tense stretch of road the whiff of a road-kill skunk overwhelms us.

Kit zings a perfectly timed tension buster: "We must be near Galoot now."

Gene breaks into a smile before me. "Maybe we can scoop him up and chuck him in Galoot's grave for a be-reavement buddy."

After I laugh, too, Gene says, "So what do you do in England for fun?"

"The usual," Kit says. "Drink a bit, watch a bit of telly."

"Sounds like me," he laughs. "You like to fish? I've been getting into fishing lately."

The only fish Gene knew about last time I checked was gefilte fish, Nova lox and herring.

"I'm an angler," Kit says.

"Me, too," my brother says.

"Angling?" I say to Gene, with an amused look. "Is that so?"

"Hey, you, fuck off again. Don't insult the driver." He then directs his voice toward Kit, "And you, listen good, there's some of the best fishing in the world two hours away in the Catskills Mountains."

Kit listens attentively. "Really? Two hours outside of Manhattan? What town?"

"The best is in Roscoe." Kit writes the town name in his memo book. "You planning to go?" Gene follows up, amused.

"No, no, I just keep a travel journal."

"Yeah, well good thing as it's the wrong season of course."

"But still, angling two hours from Manhattan. Brilliant."

Gene turns around and smiles at me. "Told you I was brilliant. And everyone said it was you with the clever head."

"Don't get too excited. Every word out of his mouth is *brilliant*."

"Look at the arrogance I put up with here," Gene says to Kit. After a momentary slide of conversation, he adds, "You like music, Kit?"

"Of course."

"What're you into? What's on the special compilation?"

Kit thinks. "Wagner is my favorite composer. Vivaldi. Special? I guess Bach's Minuet in G deserves a spot on the list. What about you?"

I nervously await Gene's response. Classical was never played in our house, and I imagine this answer will threaten him as much as it threatens me.

Gene simply asks, "You like the Beach Boys? I heard they were incredibly popular in England."

"They are. They still tour all the time. But I just know a few songs."

"They're my boys. The Beatles are Shari's boys."

"I thought Colin Firth was her boy," he says, and leans back toward me to check on my smile.

"Who?" Gene doesn't wait for a reply. "Did my sister tell you she is the biggest Beatles freak in New York City?"

"I'm pretty far gone," I say, "but there are Beatles fans who know what minute John's mother went to the hospital for labor. I'm freak-lite."

"I never got the buzz off them," Gene says. "I saw some documentary on cable of when they were young. I couldn't understand a word of what they were saying."

"Liverpudlian is hard," Kit says, matter-of-factly. "First time I ever heard George talk—when I saw *A Hard Day's Night*—I thought he was saying 'Can I have a jam butty?' but I wasn't sure at all."

"What's that?" Gene clucks.

"It's a jelly sandwich," I say to Kit. "Jam on buttered bread? Correct?"

"Yes, that's it."

"You knew that?" Gene says with glee in his voice. "What did I tell you about her? The whole earth likes 'Yesterday,' and, well, what is the name of that crazy Beatles song you said is your favorite?"

"I just said I like it, I've never said it's my favorite."

"What was it?" Kit asks.

I hate when Gene goads like this. I hesitatingly lick a back tooth. "Blue Jay Way."

"What?" Kit asks. "I didn't hear you."

"Blue Jay Way," I say, louder. "Even you might not know it," I address Kit. "It's a bit culty, a drug-addled stream-of-consciousness song written in the flower-power era. You know, 'There is a frog upon the lake…' I think it's on *Yellow Submarine*."

"Magical Mystery Tour," Kit corrects. "The Beatles had three albums that really were kind of rubbish, they had leftover scraps. But I like that song, too."

A black Corvette dangerously cuts ahead of us. "Jesus!" Gene says after he gives the bonehead an angry honk. "'Blue Jay Way,' yeah. Shari could write a second dissertation on them Beatles."

I cringe at the unwelcome *D* word. My dissertation. Oh fucking yeah. How can I face the shame when I tell my family my research has come to a sudden halt? Man oh man. I'll wait until I'm back from England. Not having a passport in my hands is stressful enough.

"Every obscure Beatles song," Gene continues. "Yet somehow she doesn't appreciate the genius of the Beach Boys."

"Well, as I said, I don't know much about them either," Kit says. "I know their hits of course—"

"Your lucky day! I have a CD I burned. Can I play it?"

"Brilliant. I look forward to the liner notes."

"Okay with you, sis?"

"Brilliant," I say, and Kit pokes me on my neck from the back seat. Gene's wrong. I've always enjoyed the Beach Boys. It takes a far bigger snoot than me to dislike the Beach Boys. But he's teacher now, and why undercut his authority?

"It's right on top of the glove compartment, Shar, can you get it for me?"

I hand it to him, and while the door is open I quietly shuffle through his books on tape collection, *Winning Every Time, The Da Vinci Code,* and the bottom one he quickly tugs out of my hand and puts back, *Mars and Venus in the Bedroom.*

It's not long before we fall under the spell of the Beach Boys' most singalong pop.

"'Can't remember what we fought about,'" Gene sings along to Brian Wilson's falsetto in "Kiss Me, Baby," and Kit even joins the party during "California Girls."

"'Wish they all could be California girls,'" he sings in his own Oxbridge take on falsetto.

After "Help Me Rhonda," Gene leans away from the steering wheel and dramatically pauses and says, "When I first heard this next one it made me cry."

"Let's hear it then," Kit says congenially.

It's a song that's always destroyed me a bit, too. "God Only Knows." As Carl sings that as long as there are stars above he will always love the nameless listener, a lump forms in the back of my throat; I know what's to be sung next, the bit about how if the person in the song ever leaves, life would still go on, but it would really suck.

"It's really breathtaking, isn't it?" Kit says to me at song's end.

"Yes," I say. He's surely noticed that the song has me in knots. I'll explain my mood shift later. Gene probably links this song to some woman he dated, but I relate breakup songs to the loss of my father's life. I wrote my entrance essay for Binghamton (and Yale), and summarized: *My father exists somewhere between the vivid minutes and the vaguer minutes, his true self in the unknowable spot between a dead man's invented greatness and reality.*

Gene manages to joke despite his wet eyes. "Brilliant?"

"Brilliant," Kit says after a little laugh. "But for the record, what do you like about it specifically?"

Gene holds back a sniffle and says, "It's very clever musically and it's also good pop."

"It's a smashing song on any level," Kit says.

"It's more complex mathematically than you think. If you learn music you can't help notice things like that."

"You noticed." I try very hard not to let anyone see my one telltale tear that has stubbornly managed to drip. "And you never learned music."

"I play piano now," Gene says quietly. As he did during the song, he once again stares straight ahead at the road.

I look at him, more than surprised. Dad, who was also great with math and engineering, played the baby grand piano that just fit in the nook at the far end of our apartment. Add that to his way with a joke—that he was a surprisingly okay pianist. An image pops back into my head: Gene's face when the neighbors Mom sold it to came by with two movers. As the "man with van" drove off, Gene stood silently under the door, his face chalky-white in this latest of many sad developments that year. Dad had no formal training, but he could work with a fake book, and he taught Gene the most basic songs like "This Land is Your Land" and "Yankee Doodle." I'd thought Gene never touched ivories again, even electrified ones.

"Doesn't surprise me," Kit says. "You've heard that math and music are connected halves of the brain?"

"Yeah?" Gene says. "I have heard that. You're backing up the theory?"

"Yes," Kit replies. "One of my mates in Cambridge was doing a lot of work in that area."

Once again I'm convinced that Gene will make a crack about privileged existence. Instead he really surprises me with what comes out next: "The lyrics always remind me of my father. He died when we were still kids."

"There's the exit," I say quietly.

So him, too? That's the reason for tears in my stoic brother's eyes?

"Did Shari tell you we lost our father when we were kids?"

"Yes," Kit says. "She did. I did, too, you know."

"Did what? Lose a father?"

"Yes."

"It really fucking sucks when it happens, doesn't it?" Gene says shakily.

"Yes."

"Your father was a good man?"

Kit says nothing, and smiles sadly and emphatically.

"There. Turn on this road," I say.

As Gene twists the wheel, I am still amazed. Tears. I have never seen my older brother cry, not once during the time he had acute tonsillitis nor even at Dad's funeral. Alan and I thought we heard him once, that same year. He was in the bathroom with the door locked, and there was an awful-sounding whimper emanating from under the cracks, but we mutually decided to leave him alone and do our homework. When we saw him again he acted cool as ever.

"Turn here," I say again.

"And again," I say a few seconds later.

My final direction: "There's the sign."

We can see tiny gravestones marking several acres of land shaded by low and gnarly trees.

There's nowhere to park but on a bit of side road. As we emerge, Kit lends us privacy by walking a few hundred yards away toward the cemetery to roll a cigarette.

I hold Gene. "Dad really loved you."

"He loved all of us," Gene says, and then manages: "I didn't mean to do that in front of your new boyfriend. Sorry about that."

"You had a Dad moment. Happens to me all the time, but I lose it more. I started welling up a few months ago when Cathy ordered Beef Lo Mein—"

"Dad's favorite dish," he cuts me off.

"Yes."

"Except it was chicken with cashews. Lo Mein was his second favorite dish."

"Hey, you're the big brother. Any memory you have goes."

"That's right. Pop quiz: The one day Dad went shopping, he bought seventeen boxes of what?"

"Jell-O. I helped Mom unpack them."

"Ten points," he laughs with red eyes.

I hesitate a second and Gene catches my expression. "What?"

"What side did he comb his hair on—I honestly can't remember anymore."

Gene considers the question as he moves hair out of my eyes with the back of his hand. "The left," he says. "Like you."

"Thanks," I mumble gratefully.

Gene coughs uncomfortably. He hates mushy sentiment, especially from himself. "By the way, do you want me to race ahead of the two of you to talk to the family?"

"Why?"

"I'll save you the embarrassment. Mom is certain your boyfriend is named Kevin—"

"No, she knows about Kit. I told her on the phone last night when I called to say I was coming to the funeral. I was seeing a Kevin, until about a week ago." I quickly ease out of the big story. "I'll tell you about it another time, when there's not a hole in your heart. What brought this on, Gene? Was it really that song?"

"Well, yeah, but—don't you know what today is?"

I nod slowly. God. It's the anniversary of Dad's death. How could I have blotted that out?

Gene straightens. "Come on, let's get Kit. We have a skunk to mourn."

I give him a kiss on his cheek. His breath is curiously free of tobacco. What's that familiar scent in its place? Oh, gum. "Big Red or Trident Cinnamon?"

"Big Red."

"Does that mean what I think that means?"

"It's true. I stopped smoking."

"Gene! That's great!"

"Yeah. Listen, I like your friend a lot even if has no clue who Gene Wilder is." He pauses for a second and then adds, "If you really like this guy, you should tell him not to smoke. I just hope I wasn't too late. Mom's working on Dot. How crazy is it that the two women Dad loved the most smoked after his death?"

After my lack of answer he says, "I wasn't thinking. I meant two out of the three women."

But I hadn't even thought about that slightly careless sentence. The rest of this conversation is what's getting at me. Sorrow is always at the surface, but those deepest horrid memories that threatened to come back during Kevin's mother's illness are pounding the inside of my head again even after I'd thought I'd finally sealed them up again during these last few glorious days with Kit.

Gene slings an arm over my shoulder. "Dot's already down a pack." An omniscient guide returns, the one who led me down the rope-and-plank corridor to my first grade class when Mom and Dad had to work or get docked.

As we walk to Kit, his back to us, a perfect cube of smoke, the kind old-fashioned magicians puff, rises above his head.

CHAPTER 11

Requiem for a Skunk

In my solemn mood from Gene's emotional outburst, I walk past animal headstones to the funeral office a hundred yards or so into the grounds. I stop to read a few of the memorials, and soon can't help my amusement at the names people come up with for their pets. Sure I feel a bit guilty, as they were not laid out for anyone's day of fun, but one reads: *Here sleeps our beloved little schnauzer,* and even the head of PETA would have trouble not smirking at a headstone that reads *Pussy 1921–1937.*

As I walk about ten more feet past the Pussy grave, I'm struck with an awful case of giggles. Despite its inconvenience, the laughing fit is a great release from the intensity of a few minutes ago. Kit hears me, and is at my side again with a helpful, intuitive understanding of the immediate task required of him as boyfriend.

"Nuclear holocaust," he says to get me solemn again. "AIDS in Africa. Rwanda."

As Kit holds open the door for the cemetery office, I spot Mom, coat off, so featherlight in her black-knit dress. Gene kisses Mom and then my aunt. Dot's big belly curves out like she's in her second trimester. Her eyebrows are particularly gruesome today, and I'm sure Kit blinked. Maybe I didn't prepare him sufficiently.

"Thank you for coming, kids," my aunt says in a gruff voice. We hug and kiss.

After my own kiss for Mom, I say, "Sorry we're late. We got a bit lost."

"But Shari navigated us here," Gene says for his passengers' amusement.

"Shari with a map?" my mother says.

I ignore the slight. "How are you holding up?" I say to Dot.

"They're about to let us view his body."

Kit is remarkably composed at that, but I'm fighting the sardonic smile threatening to take over.

"This is Kit," I say quickly, just to let some, any, words come out of my mouth. "Kit, this my aunt, Dorothy Diamond."

"Such formality," she says. "Dot. Just Dot."

"I'm sorry for your loss," Kit says, always the man of manners.

"Oh, you're British?" Dot says, and I pray she won't continue. She doesn't.

From somewhere, Eric puts out a hand that Kit shakes. "Eric Fine. Nice to meet ya." My aunt's nerdy boyfriend of ten years has no idea how many Kool Kats obsessed with killer fifties-wear would ironically dig the red Slim Jim tie that peeks through his olive green parka. He has had on a variant of this dated tie every time I've met him. There's probably an unironic vintage era tie rack back in the Catskills condo.

"Kit Brown," Kit says.

"Hi there, Eric," I say. Another hug.

"Shari. Nice to meet you, Kip." Eric pumps Kit's hand up and down like he's gone a-milking. "I tell ya, folks, Galoot was like a son. I know that sounds a bit strange, but it's damn well true."

"Kit," Dot practically screams into Eric's ear. "His name is Kit."

"I don't have good hearing," Eric screams to Kit.

"We're going in the viewing room," Dot yells toward Eric again. "Straighten your tie, honey."

"I buried a dog once," Kit says after a self-conscious group pause. "It killed me."

I guess Eric heard that well enough because he says, "Dogs are nice, but I tell ya, skunk ownership is an even longer commitment. Think at least twenty years if you buy a skunk."

Dot adds, "You learn to love them even though they chew up your bedspread." This memory brings on a big flow of tears. "Tell them, Eric, there's nothing nicer than feeding your skunk a vanilla wafer as you watch *Access Hollywood* together."

"And he was much better than a cat," Eric follows.

Dot nods her head vigorously. "All skunks are better than cats. They appreciate you more."

Gene is admirably straight-faced as he asks, "How did Galoot pass, Aunt Dot?"

"Listen to me, kids, never give any animal chocolate. I left out an open bag of bittersweet chocolate chips and—it killed him."

Kit winces. "Theobromine. A woman I lived with had a dog that ate it once. He had to have his stomach pumped."

"He lived?" Dot says earnestly.

"Just barely," Kit says.

Who's this woman Kit lived with? File that detail away. Now's not the time to grill him.

"What did Galoot normally eat?" Gene quickly asks Eric.

"He liked boiled chicken," Eric says. "And tuna fish."

"Vegetables, fruits, low-fat cottage cheese, yogurt," Dot manages to add. "We gave him goodies like the wafers occasionally. But usually we were hyper-careful. Our first one was a fat skunk because we didn't know how to feed him. At least Galoot was fit during his life." She clutches her boyfriend's hand. "He did, though, leave us an unfortunate gift after his death. Maybe it's his payback for the chocolate."

Eric shakes his head after his girlfriend speaks. "Oh, Dottie, please, Galoot would never want anything bad to happen to you."

"What do you mean?" Gene says.

"We're still suffering from bellyaches. Turns out they were brought on by skunk worms he picked up off the veterinarian's table. But we're on medicine now, so don't worry about shaking our hands. All this *tsoris* coming on the heels of Eric's pinkie accident a few months ago."

After digesting the bit about skunk worms, my carload of three look to Eric's hand. There is a pinkie gone. *Indeed,* I say in my head, in Kit's voice.

"What happened to your pinkie?" Gene says.

"He chopped it off while slicing a cucumber," Dot answers for him.

"Made it through the Korean war with just a bloody nose," Eric bellows. "I got a lot of use from that pinkie, it did me proud, but I don't really miss it. I'd rather have Galoot back than a pinkie."

When Alan arrives, Mom pounces on him, feathering her delicate son with kisses. There's an almost-gorgeous woman with long hair behind him, no doubt the commune girlfriend. This gal's looking mighty uncomfortable. With Alan's usual lack of social grace, he has forgotten to introduce her. But everyone in his family knows to let that be. He will introduce her on his own terms.

For a skunk funeral Alan has decided on blue jeans and a black sweater under a jean jacket. Alan looks—somewhat ironically considering our car-ride soundtrack—much like the noticeably cutest Beach Boy, Dennis Wilson—that is, before Dennis got old and overdosed as a way out of his headlong slide into self-destruction.

Gene sticks out a hand to his little brother and punches him in the tummy. "What are you up to, guy?"

"Nothing much," Alan says quietly.

These two brothers—talk about night and day. I assume that Gene's knack for self-perseverance has greatly helped him in the banking industry. He certainly didn't have any contacts going in. He spoke of colleagues kick-started with a nepotistic post, but Gene was not too proud to entry-level himself as a mail clerk. He has never once looked back or made a lateral move: A–Z is his life strategy. As a teen he applied that same stick-to-it-ness to Pac Man—he was the champ for our entire neighborhood, and shortly thereafter king of our neighborhood's Asteroid enthusiasts.

I carefully check Alan's face. He's definitely afraid to ask what his brother is up to, especially since Gene has landed a fat job that Mom has hinted scored him serious bucks.

As much as Gene strived through our childhood, Alan retreated. After Alan dropped out from the Queens College philosophy program, he swore blindly to my mother that he would try to earn an honest living. But he was just too shy, too nervous. After a few executive assistant interviews that didn't go well, even a humiliating termination from a summer gig of Popcorn Man at Coney Island, he retreated from day jobs with a fatalistic weariness. In his view, every conceivable profession in New York was a competitive sport, and he cited as evidence that even social workers raise an eyebrow when another one among them has that master's degree from Ivy League Columbia.

(I thought about it once, briefly entering his mindset. If you want to live in New York City and don't want to compete for jobs, your basic choices are squeegeeing and sandal communes—and I haven't even seen a squeegee man for at least ten years.)

The sight of Alan carting along a girlfriend is un-nerving; Alan has never brought a woman home to meet his family, not one. So who is this mysterious woman with long hair? Her brown eyes are startlingly intense. She would be gorgeous in a hippie-dippy *Love Story*-era Ali McGrawish way if not for her unfortunate nose that verges on a snout.

"By the way, this is Summer," Alan finally says to the collective family.

A group hi.

Summer opts for a sympathetic hug to both Eric and Dot instead of a handshake. "I know the pain when a pet dies. My cat died last year and a part of me shriveled."

Dot gives her an appreciative peck on the cheek.

Alan breaks us down into individuals. "This is my mother," he starts.

"Summer," Mom says in her quiet yet congenial man-ner, "do you live on the commune with Alan?"

"Down the street, actually, but I've considered joining."

"This is Shari, my little sister by a year."

"I heard you had a nice time at the commune," Sum-mer says politely.

"Yes, I did." Well, a time, anyway.

Dot audibly whispers to Mom, "Is Summer Jewish?"

How will I make it through this without Kit aban-doning me?

"Nice to meet you. This is my friend Kit."

"We're ready," says a smiling representative of the cemetery, a man in a dark funeral home vested suit with a tucked-in pocket watch. The director of the cemetery is by our side, ready to lead the eight in our mourning party to the viewing room.

Dot waves Kit and me ahead. "We'll go last."

We see what I was afraid we'd see: a skunk, belly-up in a two-foot-long open rosewood casket.

"My little man," Dot says, and she holds Eric. Gene beckons my family, Summer and Kit out of the room, leaving Dot and Eric in their tearful embrace.

"So, that was an experience," I say to Kit repentantly after we're back in the waiting parlor.

"A little oddity doesn't bother me."

Gene emerges before Mom, no longer able to keep his lips pursed as he fights off his own brewing laugh. "Now I've seen it all. So what do ya think of that little ceremony?"

Kit raises an eyebrow. "I found it very sweet, actually."

Gene says, "You're right. It was. Sometimes I'm just a bit of a jerk."

"You were just chatting. Think nothing of it."

I feel like a jerk, too. Gene is mildly appalled by this family circus, but certainly not mortified. And Kit looks fine with the most outlandish relations I have to offer. I'm the only one suffering here. I quickly remind myself about his gong uncle and feel better.

"Did you ever have a skunk buried here before?" Gene asks the respectful man from the cemetery.

My mother is out of the viewing room now. Exploiting her most uncanny talent, she reads my mind. "Be respectable, Shari."

"We're mostly dogs and cats," the director says to Kit

as he scratches at his arm (flea bite?). "We have one lion cub here, and there are squirrels, ducks, turtles, ferrets, birds and hamsters in the smaller leftover spaces on the plots—the plot owners can use every inch they bought if they want more than their dog buried."

"No skunk?" Gene says with considerable irony.

"First one," the man says just a bit conspiratorially.

"But how can you keep from laughing every day?"

"Don't be so rude, Gene," Mom says.

"Don't think I haven't heard that question before, sir. I've been director of Hartsdale since 1974, and anything you can ask I can answer."

Gene has his patented stupid grin on as he asks, "So come on, why do you bilk money out of suckers like my aunt then?"

"Idiot," Alan mutters toward Gene.

"He's not bilking her," Mom says firmly. "This burial is Dot's decision."

"Yes, I would agree with that assessment," the director says with fine diplomatic skill. "Celebrities choose us, but the majority of people who bring us their animals are everyday folk who for whatever reason, feel this is the right thing to do. The pets buried here were their friends."

Gene snorts. "And they can get a new friend at the pound. Or the skunkery or whatever you call it."

The director shakes his head. "What do you think you would say if you lost a friend, and were told why don't you go to a bar and get a new one? We let people grieve in whatever way they want to. Some choose to cremate, some choose to bury. They can use the viewing room for however they want to say goodbye. If they want a service, that's okay, too. We hold no judgment at Hartsdale because the death of an animal has a deep effect on many people, in different ways. That's exactly why a lot of pet owners hold in their grief—people don't understand what they're feeling. Yes, animals probably could fend for themselves in the wild, but we choose as a society to domesticate them, and many people who don't have families of their own view their pets as children."

The skunk funeral is becoming less tragic to me by the second. I'm even proud of Dot that she is not one of those that has chosen to "hold in her grief." She is a woman of action. Okay, a slightly senseless woman of action, but look at me, I could use a little of her gumption. And Kit's.

Chastened, Gene concedes, "Aunt Dot to a T. Galoot is her surrogate son."

"As I said, this doesn't surprise me in the least."

"So how many animals do you have buried a year?" Kit asks the director.

"This year we buried about eight hundred," he says. The conversation abruptly ends as Dot and Eric emerge. The director looks kindly upon them and says, "You can walk over, and we'll bring Galoot right to the grave in just a few minutes."

"Thank you for what you're doing," I say in parting to the admirable director.

He nods appreciatively.

The clear blue sky of people and dog heaven shelters us as we head down the sloped path to Galoot's open grave. With a backward glance I notice that Kit has stopped the owner to ask him another question. Now what?

Summer's winter clogs *clop, clop, clop,* as we walk. I'm too embarrassed to look Kit in the face, what the hell is he making of this insanity? The newly-aggressive sun is blinding. It's easier on my eyes to study feet. Eric's gangly legs splash through puddles of leftover morning rain, reminding me of those nature shows when giraffe legs amble through brackish savannah water. My mother's ankles and lower legs are admirably slim after three children; she always wears stockings and skirts and pumps, in a cemetery or the laundry room. Dad once called her the best-dressed gal in Queens, and she made us all rice pudding from scratch that night. The heels of her delicate pumps leave tiny footprints in the soil.

As I tramp by more graves with residents like Grumpy or Tinkerbell I'm reminded of the Wednesday afternoon nature trail walks I participated in the summer I went to sleepaway camp. The soil on that path led to curious finds, a caterpillar living in a deserted cobweb, an orange newt with two heads. This one leads to a sad-faced cemetery worker in a large mended sunhat next to Galoot's grave. Aside from the sunhat he wears nothing but an undershirt and torn, soiled pants. Despite his lack of clothes and the nippy day, he's sweating from his action-packed afternoon. A bird braving the cold snap watches him carefully.

When Kit is at my side I whisper, "What did you go back to ask the director?"

"I just wanted to know what celebrity dogs have their final resting place here."

"And?"

"Mariah Carey's pooch. George Raft had one here, Diana Ross, Joe DiMaggio."

He gives my hand a reassuring squeeze.

When everyone is ready, Dot announces that she is going to read the Hebrew Kiddush to begin the ceremony.

"In the viewing room," Eric explains, "we tossed in Galoot's favorite toys before they closed the casket."

Summer is close to tears. "What were they?"

"Three whiffle balls held together by purple yarn, and a stuffed cat missing one of its black eye buttons."

As Summer breaks into a full sob, Alan, looking a bit embarrassed, goes to her and rubs her back. It's slightly wonderful to see Alan worrying about someone other than himself.

After a prayer is read, everyone gives Dot and Eric space by walking back to our cars parked on the gravel outside the gates.

Gene is ahead of us, again with his arm around Mom. My mother lights up with Gene's extra attention. He's always been her favorite. I've never had much of a problem with this—he was literally her savior at the time of Dad's death. But I'm betting Alan doesn't forgive her for her not-so-subtle predilection.

"Do you remember Dad's funeral?" Alan asks in an almost inaudible voice.

"Of course," I say.

"How are you doing these days?" he asks. "I haven't seen you since you came to dinner."

"I've had a rough week, but my friend Kit and I are

probably going to England for a little bit. It will be good to finally see England."

"You're going abroad? Gene paying for that?" I'm surprised by the jealousy in his voice. But then again Alan and I have never been abroad, not even to Canada.

"Gene? Why would Gene pay for it?"

"Didn't Mom tell you? He's—a multimillionaire now."

"C'mon, he's well-off, but—"

"More than well off, I hear," Alan says.

We both know firsthand that Gene worships money. Even before Dad's death he bolstered our family coffers with a paper route, and after the funeral he was determined to fill his father's role. Yes, Mom had admitted that the last three years he has given her twenty thousand dollars, the legal limit for a tax-free annual gift. She wanted me to know she was okay with her bills. But a multimillionaire! A Diamond of the perpetually broke Diamonds?

"Has he been giving you any money?" I carefully ask. Am I the only one missing out?

"He hasn't offered. I was thinking about asking him." He looks earthward in embarrassment.

"Are you in trouble?" I'm genuinely concerned now. It takes a lot for Alan to ask Gene for a favor.

He looks up again and decides to continue. "Summer is pregnant. I haven't told Mom or Gene yet."

"Alan! That's wonderful, I hope."

"Wonderful if we keep the kid. That's what Summer wants but we really can't afford one. We have our rent paid through our work but that's all."

"Do you want to stay on the commune?"

"Truthfully? Not really. It's old hat for me. It gave me what I need when I needed it."

"Maybe you should talk to Mom. See what she thinks is the best way to approach Gene."

"Talk to Mom about what?" my mother presses me. Gene is back in the office, probably to pee. Mom slips a hand around both of her youngest children's waists.

I look at Alan.

"You tell her," Alan says. This plea for aid is probably harder on him than he thought it would be.

And I do. "You're going to be a grandmother."

"Shari, you're pregnant!"

"No. Alan and Summer are—"

"Expecting? You? Alan?"

"We don't have any money for a kid, but Summer doesn't want to give it up. I was thinking of talking to Gene—"

Mom breathes out heavily. Her eyes are tearing.

"Momma's going to take care of this, Alan, let me talk to him. You absolutely need that money, and I know best how to put the hard word on him."

For the next few minutes Alan fills Mom and me in on the details.

I glance around the grounds to see where Kit is. Smoking. Shooting the breeze with Eric.

"You're a funny fellow!" Eric is screaming. Maybe Eric was not as moved by the ceremony as Dot was.

Summer stops to pick up a dandelion growing out of a pocket of dirt near the road. She blows the white spores off. What's her wish?

I look over at Kit. I know what mine is.

CHAPTER 12

Like Old Chums

A funeral procession of three cars drive back to Eric and Dot's Catskills condo located over an hour away from the Northeast's finest animal final resting place.

When we're back in Gene's car Kit says, "I know the actor now, the one Eric resembles. Gene Wilder was Willy Wonka, right?"

"You got it," Gene says after an amused grunt.

"The resemblance *is* mind-boggling."

Gene nods appreciatively.

We enter Dot and Eric's modest foyer and then their living room anchored by an enormous maroon couch. There's also a tacky table lamp with a dolphin-motif lampshade, and a mantel of bad skunk and tugboat art that's been added to since the last time I was here.

"Where's your mother?" Dot says after she's brewed fresh coffee for her fellow mourners. "Or Gene?"

Good question. "Mom did want to ask Gene something," I say neutrally.

"Nothing we can hear?"

Alan shrugs. Summer blushes noticeably, and walks to a window.

Alan explains to Eric that Summer specializes in dewdrop photography, which Eric mishears as glue drop photography—the mistake starts him off on an animated discussion of epoxies and resins that Alan can't stop.

I try not to worry as my aunt engages Kit in conversation. I sit on the maroon boat and determinedly pick up a loose photo of Dot and my father playing together as kids. I've never seen this image. The photo looks newly framed, and is not at all dusty, so she must have been looking at it recently. I flick it over. There is no Kodak timestamp or handwritten explanation of where or when this was, but when I look at it again, I'm guessing Dad was twelve or so, and Dot around ten. At twelve Alan looked exactly like Dad does in the picture, that great skin and the blackest, thickest hair imaginable.

When Mom and Gene emerge from the den, Mom sneaks Alan a sly thumbs-up, and soon Gene walks over and gives Alan a big slap on the back.

Eric sits down next to us. "Your friend is charming the pants off of your aunt."

"What could they possibly be talking about?" I ask.

"Food."

I strain to hear what Kit is saying. Why has Dot just laughed so loudly? Moving to the kitchen I ask, a tad suspiciously, "How's it going?"

"We're making jelly omelets," Dot announces. "Kit

asked me if I had any bread to tide him over until dinner, and to tell you the truth my fridge is threadbare. I was supposed to have gone shopping at Stewart's but then as you know—" Dot sighs. "We didn't think any of you would come to this funeral. I was shocked you're all here for me. Such a generous display—"

"Of course we came, Dot," Gene says. He follows his sugary words with his ingratiating smile. I didn't see him there by the door frame, back from a long visit to the toilet. "We love you."

Dot blows Gene a kiss after she dollops a big spoonful of grape jelly into the middle of Kit's omelet.

Kit cackles loudly. "Oh, it's jam, Dottie! I thought it was gelatin you were talking about. I was a-*ghast*."

Dottie?

"Jelly omelets are yummy," my mother says to Kit as if she's been talking to one of my kindergarten classmates. "You have them in England?"

"No, not really. But if it's jam on the inside, that's better than gelatin."

"Hey! You're making jelly omelets over there?" Gene says. "Do I get one?"

"It's a little weird but good, Kit," Alan pipes up.

"Okay, I'll give it a go," Kit says. As he backs up to the wall with a plate and fork in hand, he almost breaks Dot's favorite plate in her water nymph plate collection. How could I never have noticed before that all of her nymphs are nude?

Dot, extraordinarily against character, says absolutely nothing about her beloved plate, and when it stops jiggling, asks, simply, "Do you like it?"

Kit speaks through bites. "Surprisingly, yes."

"What do you mean surprisingly?" Dot says, playfully defensive.

"A few seconds ago I was thinking that the problem with a jelly omelet from a British point of view is that it messes up the sensory order of the world. If you want sweet I think chutney with its sour-sweet taste makes more sense."

"I just love hearing you speak like that," Dot coos. "Did you know I loved all the British books when I was a kid?" She swoops her fork toward Kit's plate to steal a bite of omelet. I don't believe it. Aunt Dottie is flirting with my new boyfriend.

"You're like Shari then, eh?" Kit asks after his own bite. "An Anglophile?"

I bite my tongue. Where is this false history coming from, Auntie?

Dot brings her fork back to Kit's plate. "You mean Shari is like me."

Gene stifles a laugh. Alan is clearly amused, too, and he whispers something into Summer's ear. She smirks.

Is Dot, in fact, a secret Anglophile? Maybe that's why she's dropping her Deputy for the Jewish People act. Christophers from America bother her, but looking at that grin on her face I can just imagine her saying, "Christophers from England, well that's an exception, darling niece, because they're so damn delightful."

"Is chutney like hot dog corn relish?" Eric scream-shouts from behind us. He's looking strangely apprehensive at the way Dot is fawning over Kit.

Gene hoists his feet onto a leatherette ottoman.

"Hey," he says to me, "it appears Dot is dotty for your fellow."

"May I keep in touch with you?" Kit asks Dot. "To make sure you are okay?"

"What a lovely boy," Dot replies. "Do you use e-mail?"

"I certainly do."

Dot grabs a pen and scrawls her e-mail address on a piece of scrap paper. She smiles broadly. A stunning, artless smile.

Just before we get back to my apartment, Gene asks if we would mind stopping outside of the Citibank on First Avenue and Fifteenth Street. "Important transaction. A few minutes, that's all."

"You've been gracious enough to drive us," Kit says. "We can wait an hour if we have to."

"Of course we can wait," I say.

When Gene's walked through the bank door I ask Kit—who had switched with me for the second mate front seat—"So what did you make of my family? Loons, right?"

His nose wrinkles. "That's a bit harsh on them."

"So you like them then?" I say, in the same needy tone Dot used when asking after the taste-worthiness of her omelet.

"They're lively, not loons at all. I was enjoying them, with one reserve."

Oh no, what did he see? Who did he overhear?

"So what's your reserve?"

"You. Why are you so embarrassed by everything

anyone in your family says or does. They're very lovely people."

Despite the dressing-down, I smile. I'm considerably relieved. "I'm happy to hear you say that. You know, I was especially surprised at how much you clicked with my aunt."

"She's a pip, I'll have you know."

"And I think she has a bit of a crush on you."

"Well she did emerge from the loo with perfume on."

"When was *this?*"

"At the end, just when we were leaving."

"Okay, let me tell you why that is so hilarious and a bit fucked up. Eric has no sense of smell. She never wears perfume."

Kit smirks. "So even if the skunk was not destunk it wouldn't have mattered to him."

"Welcome to my existence." I lean over the car divide to give him a quick snog. He climbs his way over to the back and tackles me down.

"So very un-British of you," I crack.

"What is?"

"Motion. Aggressive sexual overtones."

"Take this, you bitch!" After he kisses me again, for a longer count, I give him a grateful hug.

"What's that for?"

"I was sure you were going to run a thousand yards in the other direction when you met them."

"I'm saying this for the last time, the only one with a problem here is you. What do I have to say to prove this to you?"

My eyes tear up, and this time it's not the wind.

"You're crying?" Kit says. He wipes one of my tears with his thumb.

"I'm really happy with you," I say. Have I jinxed myself by saying that out loud?

Our third kiss is so wet and passionate that I could use one of those slobber rags from a championship boxing match to dry off. I'm not sure how long we are at it, our legs braced against the back car door, but a flustered Gene is knocking on the door.

"That was fast," I say.

"What are you talking about? It was a long line."

Kit climbs up front again, and I can't help noticing Gene's mild scowl at the footprint. Kit may be nice to meet, but I know my brother well enough to know what's going on in his brain. Gene worked hard for that car. He stops in front of my building on Seventh Street, and I give him a kiss as Kit immediately hops out and rolls another cigarette.

Gene slips a Citibank envelope in my pocket.

"What's this?"

"For England."

"Money?"

"It is. I have it and you need it. Alan told Mom and Mom told me. You can come to me directly."

"I don't know how much is in there but—"

"Three thousand dollars."

"What? You're joking. No way—"

"I want you to have a wonderful trip. You deserve it. You've been working so hard on your dissertation, and Little Sister never asks anyone for anything. Don't make a man you hardly know pay your way."

"Gene, you're being so unbelievably generous—"

"If Dad were here it's what he'd tell me to do."

About that dissertation… I think. When will I actually inform them that as soon as the wonderful Christopher T. Brown entered the scene, my love life improved, but the rest of my life has officially gone to seed?

After we have all said our goodbyes and Gene has driven off, Kit snuffs out his home-rolled fix. "So what was in that envelope?"

"Gene is funding me for the trip. Three thousand dollars!"

"Really?"

"No shit. So I'm not a harlot now."

"With the money he's giving Alan and Summer—does he have that kind of money to throw about?"

"According to Alan he does. But what really shocked me was how sweet Gene could be."

"Well, I still won't let you pay for the plane ticket. I've already called in our seat numbers."

"Okay, be magnanimous if you like, but after that we go Dutch."

CHAPTER 13

A Different Take

I rest my eyes after devouring several chapters of my British guidebook. A little boy of around three is circling his tower of Legos on the Terminal Seven floor. "Come with me to the potty, Brian," a nearby mother says firmly. "Mommy knows the pee-pee dance when she sees it."

I wish Kit caught that hilarious coinage. *Pee-pee dance.* I laugh to myself as I crunch my pickle slice, about the only thing edible in my turkey sandwich bought at the terminal. I was doing that very dance until Kit and I finally got through the security line. Who would be desperate enough to go through that snaking nightmare again? A smoker like Kit, apparently.

It's the first day of my thyroid treatment. I pop open the childproof bottle and shake a pill into my hand. I examine the little *L* on it, remembering that Dr. Zuckerman told me I'd probably be taking a generic version of Synthroid, and drop it into my mouth.

"Shari?" I hear as the drug washes down into my stomach.

The voice is distinctly American. I crane my neck around. It must be high season for retirees—the only youthful man I see in my near vicinity is a probable bridegroom sleeping in his tux, withered red rose boutonniere still attached.

"Over here!"

I catch the eye of a man around my age. He has soft blues framed by dark brown hair, and a very appealing square jawline. There's something familiar about his good looks.

"Owen," this unknown man says, his handsome face now beet-red. "You probably don't remember me. Owen Zuckerman."

But I do. That crippling blush. For a split second I see his childhood features morph into his adult face. "Owen! I was just recently talking about you with—"

"My father. So I heard! How great that we run into each other like this. I was going to call you anyhow."

"Where are you headed?"

"Me? I have research work overseas. Hey, you like pickles? I have one saved from my sandwich."

"Hand it my way. I'm a pickle fiend."

He drops a green strip on the open wrap that holds my sandwich. Still bright red he says, "You're in good company. Cleopatra was also a big pickle fan."

I laugh. "Did you read that somewhere?"

"I sort of just know that." His color is inching back

to normal now. "I'm a historian so I sort of know a lot of things."

"Your Dad said you were doing that."

Owen nods. "So you know I'm not lying."

"Hey, I never said you were."

"And I hear you're a linguist. Esperanto, is it?"

"Volapük. It's a—"

"Predecessor to Esperanto."

I nod my own head in amazement. "You may be the only layperson to have ever filled in the blank."

"I told you, I sort of know a lot of things."

"So where are you off to via plane? To Alexandria to unearth some pickles?"

He smiles. I know he thinks I'm holding my own. Only since grad school have I been able to reference back and forth without feeling ashamed that I have a half-decent brain. My friend from back-in-the-day is as academic to the bone as I. And he's Jewish with white teeth. Since I know from his dad that he's single, I suppose if I'm really a good friend I should immediately send him over to Cathy. "No, I'm writing a book on the secrets of the British and American collaboration in World War II. I'm going to be at the British Museum for a few weeks."

"That's great! Congratulations on the book. Your father told me a little about it. I heard Oxford is publishing it?"

"Yes," he states proudly. "But Random House is talking to my agent for a book directed at a more general audience."

I smart a little, remembering my Big Publishing

House plan I forged in Starbucks. "That's incredible," I manage.

"And you?" Owen picks up. "What are you doing at the airport?"

"I'm a tourist, plain and simple. I'm trying to pick good places to see in England."

"I know a fair bit about the place—what's the budget?"

"Well, I do have a place to stay in London. The friend I'm staying with is outside the terminal with a cigarette."

"She better hurry up."

"He," I correct.

I'm flattered by the slight look of disappointment on Owen's face at my reveal. "It's good to have a place to stay, because hotels in London are so expensive. Where to then?"

"My friend and I are duking it out."

"I lived there for three years. I did a postgrad degree at Cambridge."

"So I heard. You know, so did my friend I'm traveling with. I know it's a big place, but you might know him, you never know—he did his undergrad years there, and I think some postgraduate work. What do you call the postgrad degree in England?"

He smiles knowingly at the question. "In Cambridge, you just say *read*."

"I actually know that, but how do you tell if they are talking about a master's or Ph.D.?"

"You tell by their age. It's tacky to ask. It's wearying at first, but once you get in the mindset, you cringe when you hear Americans ask such details."

"Did you cringe when I asked?"

"Shari. You don't mind me telling you these things do you?"

"No," I say half-truthfully. "So how about my friend. We never discussed—"

"You're right. I probably never crossed with him. You know how it is. There *are* a hell of a lot of students there." He goes on: "So what degree did you end up with after school? Oh and where did you go? Someone from the neighborhood thought you went to Yale—"

Who did I ever confess the Yale application to? Could he have talked to my guidance counselor? "Nothing so posh as Yale or Cambridge. I went to SUNY-Binghamton, and NYU for the master's, and that's where I'm doing my dissertation."

"Don't say the *D* word ever again. Glad I'm through—"

"Good evening, ladies and gentlemen traveling on British Airways flight 1702. We are now boarding our first-class passengers. First-class only, please."

Only a few people respond, including a woman in a mink leading a well-dressed toddler toward the gate. I spot Kit and motion for him to hurry up. Enough with the slow British perambulation the actors from Monty Python so hilariously mocked. We're in New York, and they've announced boarding.

Kit picks up his carry-on briefcase holding his terminal seat for him and sits down.

"You got through!" I say.

"I feel a thousand times better."

"We're about to board, so you're lucky. Hey, I want you to meet an old childhood friend of mine. This is—"

When I turn back to Owen his lips are twitching ever so slightly.

By the look on Kit's face, he is about equally disturbed.

"This is Kit," I say. What is this about?

Owen speaks first. "We do know each other. You should have said your friend went to Trinity College, Shari. I wouldn't have brushed off your question."

"Yes, we do know each other rather well," Kit says harshly.

"Passengers for British Airways flight 1702. We are now boarding business class."

There's more of a rustle this time.

"That's us," Kit says.

"It is?" I say. "We're business class?"

"It's a surprise. That's why I wouldn't let you see the tickets. I said it's my treat."

"Well, I'm lowly economy," Owen says finally. "I guess I'll talk to you after we land."

Kit is remote as we clamber on board and enter our plush business-class cabin.

"This is amazing!" I say. "Kit, this is far too nice a gift for someone—"

"Sleeper seats, too," he interrupts, patting the armrest.

His demeanor continues to confuse me even after he chirpily assures the female flight attendant that all is well. He stares at the laminated emergency directions, miles away in thought.

After a gang-up of planes, it is our turn to taxi down the runway.

"Was he a good friend of yours?" Kit says as we lift off, a clear view of Queens below us.

I haven't been on too many flights in my life—six including the trip back and forth from Chicago—the off-we-go moment is still very hard for me to talk normally through. "Sort of." Was anyone really Owen's friend? He was so, so shy.

Kit swallows air for a second as we continue upward at a forty-five degree angle. When we level off to horizontal he says, steadily, "He was a bit of a problem in Trinity, if you must know. A bit of a fragmented personality."

Owen Zuckerman, a troublemaker? Does a person change that much? I look at him blankly. "Did you have any problems with him?"

"Why, did he say anything to you?"

"No, it's just the weird glance you gave each other."

"We just didn't like each other."

"Is that really it?"

I wait.

"I can't abide him. Leave it at that."

"Why?"

No answer.

I tug at his shirt. "Seriously, Kit, why?"

He stares ahead as he answers. "Threatened by my background is my guess. He was pulling pints to supplement his income, and I never had to do that. First of all we don't have that kind of tuition you have, and then, well, as I guess you know, my family has money."

Kit is so close-lipped about most of his personal details that I don't know much about his history yet, except that he lost his virginity around eighteen and that his family has country property. Maybe he is a bored lord looking for more in life than beagling for partridge and grouse. I imagine when we visit his home I'll get the full picture. But meanwhile, Owen pulling pints? Jealous of money? Nothing he's saying squares with the facts. I think of Owen's gilded youth in that huge mansion in Queens. How many New York City families have an English Tudor to begin with?

I feel vaguely sick. What's unfolding has all the earmarks of deception, and I'm worried that it's Kit's. Owen's never had a reputation as either a rabblerouser or a fibber.

He raises his head again. "Come. Let's get on with the trip."

He tries to kiss me but I just look up at him. "You look troubled," Kit says.

"I am, a bit. Did you ever read *The Talented Mr. Ripley?*"

"I saw the movie. What, you think I'm going to drive you off someplace steep like the White Cliffs of Dover?"

I flinch, and he adds, "That was a joke. What is this about?"

"No, I'm just worried that I am traveling around a new country with someone I don't know well."

Kit curls his lip in disgust. "Considering that I have just met every member of your family, who seemed to get on with me rather well I might add, I'm going to choose to ignore your silly comment. Your friend and I just hated each other's guts, that's all."

"He was a very shy guy in school," I say, quietly and tautly. "That just doesn't sound like Owen." My head's in a considerable tailspin. Is what I perceived as British reserve in fact a well-oiled slipperiness?

Even though I haven't seen Owen in fifteen years, I trust him. He's from *back in the day*. I've met his family.

"Maybe he was shy as a kid. Let it lie. You've just been watching too many wonky psychodramas."

PART 2

Britannia

CHAPTER 14

A Magical Mystery

A majestic royal blue sky jeweled by a bright red sun greets our plane as we touch down for our early-morning landing.

Even the captain's weather forecast for the day is perfect, a crisp spring day with no rain.

Unaware of my brewing distrust, Kit leans over to peck me on the cheek. "Welcome to England. No lips until I brush my teeth."

One dream I had about him last night was so horrific that I feel guilty when I smile back: Kit was chasing me through Heathrow, brandishing a fork (sure, it sounds ridiculous now), only for me to find out at the ticket counter that my pocket was full of useless wet credit cards. I also keep to myself that after Kit dozed with my dog-eared copy of Martin Amis's *Money* in his lap, I fixed his sleeper seat for him, and then mine, and I lay prone, riddled with fear until I finally fell asleep. I wonder if Owen is peeved that I didn't go back to look for him. Surely he must have realized that I was in an awkward situation.

We're off the plane well before Owen's rear-end economy row. We need to collect our bags for customs. Kit lifts his expensive gray Samsonite suitcase, and my $29.95 bright blue duffel bag from Kmart, and places them on the British version of a Smartecarte.

My foreign citizenship slows us down. Kit fidgets a few feet ahead of me until I've cleared customs with my newly minted passport. Even though there's some Chicago hot sauce in his suitcase, Kit thinks the nothing-to-declare line should do the trick for both of us.

The guard looks at our paperwork, and waves us on.

Once through, Kit has a guilty look on his face. "If you roll the cart down to the entrance to the tube, and wait, I'll be there in a flash."

"No taxi?"

"The best way to get in to London is by tube. There's a stop right here."

"Of course I'll wait, but what's the rush?" Like I don't know.

"If I don't get a smoke I may kill. Wait just outside the door to the tube walk. I'll try and meet up with you as quickly as I can."

"Go ahead. I'll figure it out."

Kit breaks into a grateful trot.

As I'm getting my bearings in the tumult of a foreign crowd I hear someone call out, "Shari! Wait up!"

Owen.

"Hey, hi," I say when he's next to me. "I was hoping I'd see you again."

"Where's Kit?"

"Cigarette. He wants me to meet him by the tube sign."

"Walk with me, I'll show you where that is. That's how I'm getting in, too." Owen looks like he's going to ask something else, but he doesn't. "Good flight for you up in business class?"

I force a smile. It's a good thing Kit's not seeing Owen and me talk again. Could the two of these overeducated gentlemen possibly get into a fistfight in the airport? "Yeah. No turbulence. Food was great."

"Oh, we had plenty turbulence in economy."

"You did?" I say, and then laugh at my stupidity a second later.

"Did you have the chicken or fish?"

"Actually we had filet mignon," I say sheepishly.

"Oh, *man*. We certainly didn't get that choice."

"At the end of the day it's just a plane ride. You're here. And I'm here."

"I'm not too jealous. I got the rear bulkhead, so I had room to stretch even if there were some awful scents from time to time."

I force my lips up at the wisecrack. What would Owen say if I shook him and said, pleadingly, "Why should I suddenly be afraid of this lovely, well-mannered man? Why should my skin now go all goosey at his touch?"

Instead Owen and I catch up on innocuous Queens gossip; what stores have closed and which kids we went to school with have married. My old classmate has not kept up with *anyone,* which is even more pathetic than my sole contact with perpetually unemployed Danielle Spivak, a single woman who I run into every now and then because she lives across the street from my mother's building.

"I'm guessing we're the most successful people from that class," Owen says.

"Depends how you define successful. Who knows how happy anyone is?"

"Oh, come on, Shari, we were the ones with a future. Be as modest as you like, but it's true. Maybe they're happy, but what the hell could they be doing with their lives when half of them refused to go to college?"

Was Kit right? Was Owen much more competitive than I remember? I'm certainly not going to remind him of his running head start fuelled by family wealth. And has he forgotten the trio of science whizzes in our graduating class, two immigrants from Russia and one from China, all finalists in the national Westinghouse Search?

"What *is* Kit writing these days?" Owen not-so-subtly fishes.

Kit writes? "Papers, I'm assuming. He's a linguist, like me."

Something about my answer bothers him. "A linguist? Are you sure?"

"I'm very sure."

"Is he affiliated with a university? Is he a professor?"

I grin. "Now that we're in England, isn't that a little tacky to ask?"

"I'm doing independent research," Kit answers from behind me. "That's all you need to know, Owen."

"You're back," I say.

The tension is palpable but Owen is anything but shy now. "Where are you living these days, Kit?"

"Westbourne Terrace."

"North Side? South Side?"

"South. Near Hyde Park."

"Nice area."

Kit's facial expression screams, *Scram!* "Yes."

Owen coughs to save face. "Well, I'll be spending the week in the British Museum reading room. You can look me up, Shari—that is if you want an alternative tour guide."

Kit's eyes are peeled on the revolving belt as he says, "Take care, Owen."

"He's going on the tube, too," I say.

"I need to use the restroom. You two go ahead."

"See ya," I say appreciatively.

The walk from Paddington Station to Kit's place, a third-floor one-bedroom flat in a tall white stucco-fronted building, is short. The flat is somewhere in the middle of the street surrounded by many residences that look exactly alike.

After a cup of loose and strong green tea in what Kit calls the reception room, his demeanor brightens. Has he put the morning's encounter behind him? "Green tea is good for the brain. Gets you going."

"You're looking alert."

"I'm thinking we should sneak a morning activity in to reset our clocks."

"I'm up for that—I read that you're supposed to go

directly out in the morning light even if you're sleepy."
I really hope I'm sounding normal here.

"Good. Are you sleepy?"

"A bit—" A lot.

"You didn't sleep well on the sleeper seat?"

"I'm just excited to be finally here."

Kit smiles. "So, then, what do you want day one's activity to be?"

I don't know why I am still so unnerved by his peculiar reminiscences about Owen, but I am. Could I even back out of this arrangement now? Kit and I left this trip so open-ended—even my ticket home has an open return date. What could my excuse ever be? My stomach feels queasy. How could I have misjudged this person so much?

"Changing of the guard, and London Bridge," I manage.

"That can be day two," Kit says as he sits on an impressive Victorian couch with mahogany legs and plush red cushions that he earlier admitted was an authentic antique. "I'm going to hold you to your rule. There are certain sites you'll have to see on your own, like the Yeoman Warders—"

"Do I know what that is?"

"That's the Changing of the Guard tour—I thought you breathed this stuff."

"Missed that term."

"Well, anyhow, you can easily get there by tube when you want to go."

As he unpacks his black leather suitcase, Kit finishes the leftover half of a bacon and onion muffin he bought at Heathrow. I discreetly discarded mine in the airport women's room. My first overseas lesson: the savory muffin. Just like their film and book endings, the British like their pastries salty and not sweet. My American tongue was not happy.

"By the way, we'll have to go shopping if we stay in London for a few days. All I have to offer are month-old frozen chops. I eat out a lot these days."

"Do you shop in Sainsbury's?"

"I do," he says, a touch of confusion in his brow.

"It's the supermarket in a lot of British sitcoms."

He laughs like he did back in my apartment. "Please think about what you want to do while I shower."

I scout around Kit's flat as I sip my tea. Since he couldn't have expected to bring back a New Yorker from his conference jaunt, I have to assume the place is always this neat. He has a trio of inoffensive decorative objects set out on a coffee table—a deep blue glass bowl, a green-and-white complete glass chess set, a vintage tin clown toy on wee stilts—but other than the amazing couch and the strong scent of some manly brand of soap I noticed while peeing in his spotless bathroom, this home seems devoid of any real sense of hearth and familiarity. It's unnerving. Even in his decorating, he gives nothing away.

There is some very pricey video-editing equipment on a desk. I know from the many NYU film students I cross paths with that the G5 Mac that's part of the package is the most expensive option on the market. His silver mouse lays on a three-inch-long Persian carpet, the only nod to Kit's dry sense of humor.

I panic when I spot a room decor detail I definitely didn't see before: a display case of monarch butterflies stuck to the surface with thin pins. Thinking about it more, I shudder slightly. Weren't pinned butterflies in the serial killer's house in *Silence of the Lambs?*

Get yourself together! I chide myself as I catch myself tracing S.O.S. with my finger on my lap.

When Kit emerges from the shower he sports a white Turkish robe.

"Any more thoughts on where to go?" I say with skimpy enthusiasm. "I'm going to let you be lead attorney."

"Yes, I've been thinking of something that I could enjoy, but you would love, too."

"So what tourist activity will least offend you?"

He hesitates a second before he speaks. "I'm appreciative that you have accepted that a trip to the teapot museum is not top priority. If we're fixing our jet lag, I thought a drive out to Greenwich might be nice."

"As in Greenwich time?"

"Yes. It's nice there by the old observatory, and you can see the telescope Halley used to find the comet."

"That's sounds pretty good—"

"Or we can plan a lovely walk down Abbey Road for my favorite Beatles freak."

The thought of touching the gates of the most famous recording studio in the world thrills me and instantly quells my paranoia. "Abbey Road!" I breathe air out loudly.

"There we go. There's my girl. Welcome back."

"What do you mean welcome back?"

"You've been so—off."

I smile big. The Beatles' stomping grounds! "I'm really in bloody London, aren't I?"

"You really bloody are." His own big smile warms me up all over again, and I say, in a sudden swerve to receptive, "I want to do it all, make the most of things while I'm here."

"Don't exhaust yourself. We're not strangers who just met on a train. I'm assuming we can do more another time—"

"Well we did just meet three weeks ago on a tour…"

Kit raises an eyebrow. "That was then. Aren't we an item now?"

"Of course we are," I say as reassuringly as possible.

"Let's flip a coin then for today's agenda. Heads, Greenwich. Tails, John and Paul. So what will it be?"

"Let me see that coin first. Whose head?" All of my money is still American—Kit had plenty of pounds and was insistent that the foreign exchange stations rip you off at the airport.

"Are you kidding? You know that without even looking. Who do you think?"

I curtsy to the twenty-pence piece and flip it over. On the other side of the queen is a crown nesting on some sort of roselike plant.

"Heads or tails?"

"Tails."

He slams the silver coin on his knee. "The Beatles then. There's a man I've heard about that might interest you—"

"Yeah?"

"I think he's called the Beatle Brain of Britain, and he takes you around to the important London Beatles sites. Touristy, but he's supposed to be good."

I grab my red Danish bookbag and unroll the *Time Out London* Kit bought me in the terminal. I read the two Beatle Brain tours out loud, then call the number listed to find out more information.

After the last of Kit's socks and jocks are in his drawer, we're headed out for a quickie breakfast and the Tuesday option, the guided walk the magazine dubs *The Magical Mystery Tour.*

"You want a flannel?" Kit asks.

"I thought we weren't sleeping yet. Jet lag cure, remember?"

"Not pajamas, silly. For your shower—"

"Oh, you're talking about a washcloth?"

"Yes, a *wa-a-a-shcloth,*" he repeats in a long nasal tone that's really not fair to me at all. I couldn't be deceiving myself that much about my lack of Queens accent.

The buzzer rings and when Kit goes to answer it there is a quite elderly woman at the door.

"I saw you coming in, Kit."

How could she see anything? Her eyes are clouded with age, and I'm betting she's half-blind.

"Hullo, Mary, this is my friend Shari."

"Oh, this the girl you called about, the one you extended your stay for?"

Kit blushes a little. I'm not sure he wanted me to hear that. "Yes," he says, and turns to me. "Shari, Mary is my amazing neighbor, and friend."

"It's nice to meet you," I say.

After a bit more of this innocuous exchange Kit says, "I'll be traveling again. Can you water the plants for one more week? I feel so terrible about this."

"Oh please. How long do you think you'll be traveling again, luv?"

"We're working that out now. A week? Two weeks?"

"Take all the time you need, sweetheart."

As Kit sits on his couch, another horrible thought sneaks in my brain, even though I thought I'd banished the willies: Well if he's dangerous, *someone* saw my face. Didn't she?

According to the woman I talked to at the London Walks office, we're supposed to look for a guide carrying a company sign.

I nudge Kit.

In front of the theater opposite a Burger King is an earnest-looking white man of about my age; he's in a Yellow Submarine T-shirt talking to a slightly older white man holding a sign over his head. The second man has to be the guide. The presumed Brain has slightly fuzzy short brown hair, is of medium build and has a large black carrying case swung around his shoulder. He is dressed like many men I have already spotted on the tube and at the airport; apparently there's an unofficial London uniform going of white jeans and a short black leather jacket over a solid dark sweater.

As we approach the men their voices become clearer. The Brain's arms stay up with the sign, and his legs remain steadfast in position as he is apparently lectured silly about his own area of expertise. I'm sure that the guy in the T-shirt harassing the Brain is from New York, more specifically a native of the Bronx.

"John was shot and killed on my thirteenth birthday, and dat spooked me. I played hooky from eighth grade and ran to da Dakota, and I was part of da can-dal vigil. Can I stump you here, Mr. Brain? Do you know da address of da Dakota?"

"I've been there, yes," says the Brain coolly, and loudly—the discreet little concert-style microphone under his chin is inadvertently turned on. "One West Seventy-second Street."

"Ya good," says the rabid fan.

"He'll get to us sooner or later," Kit says to me. I nod and we stand off to the side, waiting patiently to fork over our tour money.

The Brain continues to nod as he is battered with even more pop-quiz questions from his annoying first customer.

"How did they spell Paul's name on the 'Love Me Do' promotional single?"

The Brain's look as he speaks is commendably neutral. Does he get this obsessive pestering every day? "They left out the big *C*. Mc-artney."

"No fooling you, eh? A good bit of manipulation dat was. So-called mistakes are da cash cows for a record company."

"I'm not so sure," says the Brain. "They were unknowns then. I'm sure that was a genuine—"

"Have y'all been to Liverpool?" says another American woman inching up to our guide. "To see John's home? I almost cried."

"Southern?" Kit asks me discreetly.

"Texan." Even without the giveaway *y'all,* I've met enough academics from that state to be fairly convinced I am right.

When the Brain addresses customer number two, his tone is detached polite. "Liverpool is good of course, but I'll be showing you Abbey Road today, which is in my opinion, also very good."

"Oh, don't *y'all* know it. My husband and I were up early today. Believe me, we couldn't sleep."

"Excuse me, ma'am, we'll pick this up later, eh? I reckon right this second I need to tend to more customers." At that he looks over at Kit and me with a beseeching glance.

"Yes, all right," says the Texan woman. "But afterwards I must tell you about our trip to the Beatles museum in Liverpool."

"Well, c'mon, lady, that's in England, you know he's been there," the creepy Bronx submarine T-shirt guy says to her.

Kit rescues the Brain with, "We have two for you here—"

Kit's greeted with an almost euphoric, "Oh, right, you're from *here.*"

"Yes," Kit says. "But watch out, my girlfriend is American."

The Brain smiles with a closed mouth as he collects our money. "Hullo? Beatles tour?" he says to each new arrival. Soon there's twenty-five of us for him to shepherd.

He tests out the little microphone and frowns when he realizes it's on already. "Can you good people hear me?"

"Yes," comes the group mumble.

"So, yes, everyone can hear me. Wonderful. My name is Richard, and I'll be your guide today. This is the Original Beatles Walking Tour and the only one sanctioned through the famous London Walks. We'll mostly be walking to sites today, but you will also need to pay your way on the tube as we will end up at Abbey Road near the St. John's Wood station, and I'll be happy to direct you back to wherever you have to go from there. I'll take your money from you now, if you haven't already paid. Five pounds for most of you, and there's a three-fifty concession for students and seniors."

A double-decker is caught in the heavy traffic on our street. "Beatles tour?" a young very English male voice calls out.

Richard looks up towards the upper level. Who yelled? Blinded by the sun, he calls out to the top level, "You need to hop out now if you're going to join us."

From my position in the shade, I can see better than anyone on the tour that there's an empty paper cup shying toward our group.

"Watch out!" I call, but the troublemaker has a direct hit on the crinkly white coif of an elderly British woman with a precise accent I can't place. Cockney? Something lower class.

The old woman twists her neck around and up. "Piss off," she screams at the culprit.

From the bus: "You old bat. Shut up."

"What wouldja mother say if she knew what'y're saying to nice people!"

The boy calls out something nasty again; but I doubt

if anyone on the street near me could make it out as the bus pulls quickly away with the green light.

The look on our kindly lady's face has graduated from cross to terrifying, like the look on the old woman in the shoe as she's about to hit her brattiest kid's behind with a hefty rolling pin. The tour group is helplessly mute as she mutters obscenities until Richard says, subtly, "Right, we'll ignore that awful man and begin. You are standing here where the Beatles performed on their first tour on December 9, 1961. This is the world-famous London Palladium, where one could say Beatlemania really first began. Their actual first London gig was played in the Blue Gardenia. Unfortunately I can't show you where that was as it was an illegal club and if the manager has forgotten, what hope do we have? One place we do know is Paul McCartney's London office, MPL. So we are headed to our first major stop, Soho Square."

As we cross the street, I'm easily amused by new icons in a new land: a little red man on the traffic light that changes to a little green man walking.

Richard pulls me to one side. "Watch the pram, my friend!"

A speeding mountain stroller with impossibly-blond twins in tow barely misses me.

Kit breathes a sigh of relief and motions for me to check out the tour's weirdo taking pictures of everything that moves. "I think Richard's first customer is even more excited than you."

Richard overhears us and chimes in with: "Enthusiasm hits all ages. I had a six-year-old on the tour last week who asked very specific questions about the Beatles recordings, and I thought, hold on, how do you know this?"

Kit and I both laugh appreciatively at his anecdote; Richard looks pleased that he has found his comrades on this tour.

Has Kit completely forgotten the run-in with Owen? Seems that way, by the relaxed look on his face. Truthfully, I'm feeling infinitely more comfortable than I did upon my arrival on British soil. We've spent so much time alone over the past three weeks, and in charged family circumstances, that I'm quite relieved to see that in a neutral group setting, Kit is still a very pleasant person. I feel silly that I got myself so worked up over Owen's cryptic comments. But okay, my mood is better, so then why am I so clammy on a brisk London morning?

In a few minutes' time Richard stops us and says, "Right, this is Soho Square, a great place in London to chill out."

Kit prods my elbow and points to the initials on the building: MPL.

"The office of MPL is not named for McCartney Paul and Linda. Rather these are the initials of McCartney Production Limited. They are a large holder of music rights, including most of Buddy Holly's estate, and the lyric rights to such celebrated musicals as *Annie* and *Grease*. Unfortunately as the world now knows, Michael Jackson bought many of Paul and John's songs, this by the way was after McCartney affably suggested to Jackson that as far as investments, lyrics were the way to go. He didn't think Michael would buy *his* own lyrics."

"Richard, have you ever seen him?" someone from the back of the group asks in a gruff American voice.

"I take it by *him*, you mean Paul. It's not going to happen. To promise otherwise would be false advertising. It only happened once or twice, but we've seen *him*, yes."

"Do you have a picture of *him* on this tour?" a German (or possibly Swiss) tourist asks.

"I most certainly do." He holds up a black folder. "Here we are in 1983—aren't we a lovely couple? I've seen Paul only five times in fourteen years, and if I could guarantee you that we would see Paul every time I'd charge more than five pounds, believe me."

"We can hope," says customer number one. Despite the kook who voices the sentiment, all of us, even Kit, sneak a peek upward to the second story of MPL, where there's a large glass mezzanine window.

"Is that Paul!" the Texan husband calls out excitedly. Even with three short words the big fellow manages to drawl.

Richard shakes his head, "No, sorry, that's not him I'm afraid."

Disappointed, we still doggedly take our tourist pictures outside MPL. After a few minutes, Richard rounds the troops.

"Our next stop was at one time considered the most fashionable street in the world. It was *the* place to buy Italian suits and fashionable leisurewear. The likes of the Who, the Beatles, the Small Faces and the Stones shopped here. The Street became legendary when an article came out revealing that these folk were hanging around. Well, let's carry on down Carnaby, shall we? Let's see what it looks like today."

There's no way I'm going to concede to Kit how excited I am to walk down this street or that somewhere in my mother's place, there are sixteen bundled vintage issues of *Petticoat*—a swinging sixties magazine devoted to the Carnaby set. I'm let down when we're on the actual famous stretch. Although there are a few funky shops like Diesel, they are not authentic to the era, and can be found in any happening city. The rest of the stores hawk items more suitable for a low-class hooker than a mod or a rocker. Half-priced imitation shoes are for sale in almost every window, as are psychedelic-era bongs. I take a picture of a sign:

Carnaby Street
City of Westminster W1

"Don't waste your film," Kit says. "I'm betting that's one of those photos that seem like a good idea at the time but never make it into an album and eventually get thrown away. I warned Helen on our safari, but she came back with a dozen photos of a hippopotamus arse."

"Who's Helen?"

He pauses. "My ex."

An African safari is a pretty extreme memory to hold and not have mentioned. But who am I jealous of here, Kit or, wait a second—"Is that the one with the dog that died?"

He looks up and over to me with a strange expression. "When did I tell you about that?"

"At the pet cemetery."

"Right. I did, didn't I?"

I look at him hard. Any more bits coming? Not a word. "We haven't really talked about her."

"No, we haven't," he says without emotion.

"Did you break up with her?"

"She broke up with me."

"Why?'

"Like you, she met someone else."

Kit bringing up Kevin, even in a roundabout way, knocks me for a loop.

"You're the cuckolder," I throw back. The second I say that I wish I didn't. He was just stating a fact.

Kit looks at me with genuine surprise. "Not really. I didn't know you had a boyfriend. I don't think you're cuckolding if you don't know the girl you're with is cheating."

My mouth drops. "You know what? That was a really vicious thing to say."

"Ease up. You pressed. I'm just letting you know that we'll have plenty of photos to take this trip. If you start taking pictures of signs and every British power station, you're going to fall asleep when you get everything back from the chemist."

"What about all those shots of graffiti you took in New York?"

"Graffiti's a sad symbol of a broken America."

"You spent less than a month in my country. Do you have the right to make that statement? New York is booming right now, by the way."

"I have the right to think whatever I bloody well think."

"It's a digital camera. I can delete whatever I *deem* junk." This is my London I've waited a lifetime for, and no one is bursting my bubble, so even though he rolls his eyes theatrically as I open my lens, I stubbornly take the shot of the big mural Richard stops us in front of, even though he hasn't even said a word yet about the mural.

"Was she pretty?" I say as I close the automatic lens.

Kit grins and, maybe to punch back a little, he says, "Extremely."

Of course I want more details now that Kit has leaked out a teensy bit more about his love life—but he is saved by Richard's new information: "This mural is called the *Spirit of Soho.* You might not know this but Soho was a hunting call. You'd shout out 'Soho,' and that became Tallyho. So, anyhow, now, right, we're all here, I've counted the lot of you, so let's walk down to where John met Yoko." We walk through an enclosure, and stop in front of a building that once housed a gallery called Indica, where the famous couple first met.

"John was quite taken with one of Yoko Ono's pieces. He had to climb a ladder and look through a spyglass to see it—it was a little tiny word the artist Yoko had printed. *Yes* was all it said. John said later what piqued his interest is that Yoko had written something positive. He thought it would say something negative. What happens next is history."

"Buggered if I care what anyone says about Yoko," the salty older British woman says, the one who was hit by the paper cup. "She was his great love."

Richard nods with vigor. "John was once asked what

attracted him. Now you may think John and Yoko went together like chalk and cheese. But John said, 'She's me in drag.'"

As we walk toward Three Saville Row I try to nail exactly what attracts me to Kit. Besides the obvious British stuff. Do I know his internal side at all? A safari? That choice nugget of life history would have come out of me right away.

And what exactly is it about me that he likes? Has he dated a string of bubbly Jews? Does he think I'm funny? I'm sorry to report to myself that I honestly don't know what he thinks.

Another American tour member who hasn't spoken before sums up what he's feeling as we leave the site. "I find this story enfeebling and ennobling to hear." He speaks so elegantly, like a youthful Walter Cronkite letting the private man out of the corporate anchorman as mankind landed on the moon. "We're dots in history, aren't we?"

The highlight of our next few stops is in front of Apple Records' old headquarters. Its rooftop is the sacred spot the Beatles played a surprise free concert for the people of London, their last-ever public appearance. After we're done soaking up the site's glory, we head for the tube and together take the short ride to St. John's Wood.

We emerge at St. John's Wood station and still a unit, turn a corner and walk in a steady pace. In the near distance, a slew of tourists is crossing backward and forward on a street I already know from countless photos.

I gasp a little. "Have you been here before?" I whisper to Kit.

"Can you believe it? I never have."

"This little scene plays itself out every day," Richard says after we stop right in front of Abbey Road Studios, on, as one would expect, Abbey Road.

By the look of the many grins on my tour, I'm not the only one vastly pleased.

Richard continues: "All day people cross and their friends photograph, to prove they were here. And then the tourists about-face and do it again, motorists be damned. Be careful when you cross, it gets a bit dicey now and then."

Our group's attention falters when a middle-aged man drops his pants, his backside toward us. He's doing something naughty against the metal gates that holds back the tourists. Yellow liquid soon drips down onto the curb.

The hit-by-a-cup woman on our tour rages again. "Ya taking a whiz?" Kit and I exchange slightly worried and amused looks.

"I'm doing it for the Stones," the public pisser says in a London accent as he finishes his pee.

"You're a disgrace to England."

"Go fuck yourself, lady."

"What am I today? A hooligan magnet?"

(Apparently.)

"Let it be known, you're a fuckin' wanker," says a familiar northern English voice.

"No fucking way!" another American man who is not from our tour says. "Oh, Jesus, Lisa, it's actually Ringo!"

The urinater zips up and turns his head, his eyes wide as twenty-five pence pieces.

"How are you today, Guv'ner?" Ringo Starr says to the guilty party.

"Fine," the urinater manages, before running in shame.

The Beatle Brain struggles hard for his own composure. "Oh, hello."

Ringo offers his hand to Richard. "I read about you in the papers. I hear you do good work."

Where did he come from? It's as if Ringo dropped in by jetpack. When my heart recovers, I note a limo a few feet down the road, and a BBC crew filming our awe.

"Dis is da craziest—" our group nut in the T-shirt is too freaked to finish his tearstained sentence, but the cup-on-head woman pops right out with: "Sign me Bristols, Ringo!"

She opens her coat, lifts off her brown blouse, and hands Ringo a ballpoint pen. He bravely leans toward a large exposed shriveled bosom stuffed into a bra. He honors her request as nonchalantly as a man who has spent a lifetime around fawning womenfolk, even fawning womenfolk missing three front teeth.

"What's your name, pretty woman?" Ringo asks.

"Pe-nelllllll-o-pe," our gal lets out in a long drawn-out rapturous mewl. "I want you to spell every letter, please. I won't clean me Bristols for a year."

Ringo gives her a kiss on her wrinkled cheek, too.

She sobs, and kisses the floor.

"What brings you back here?" the Brain says on our astounded group's behalf.

"A project for the BBC. A tribute song for George."

Ringo is a real trooper and offers to take a photo with everyone on the street who has paid a fee to Richard.

The other tourists gathered at the Abbey Road shrine moan, but Ringo repeats his rules, "I'm helping out a working man."

"You're as nice as they say you are then," Richard says with grace.

Ringo grins, and asks Richard to nod if we're with the tour.

When it's my turn, I say weakly, "It's nice to meet you."

"Where are you from in America?" Ringo Fucking Starr says to me.

"Queens, USA," I manage.

"Played a concert there once."

I'm still too starstruck to laugh at the Shea Stadium joke. "Un-huh," I manage. But I regain enough composure that Kit and I take turns taking a picture with Ringo.

Ringo glances at the gates daubed with international sentiments, smiles at a particularly obscene bit of graffiti and waves goodbye. The last time I saw and heard spontaneous public clapping was in October of 2001, when several firemen with sooty faces took a lift uptown on my New York bus after a hard day's night toiling at Ground Zero.

Ringo walks up the stairs, and past two large topiary spheres in terracotta pots outside of the fabled Abbey Road doors. The door opens and closes. There is a brief silence as we process the awesome surprise of the afternoon, and then there is a collective giggle from our group and more groans from the unfortunate without a London Walks ticket.

"Amazing," I say to Kit. "We just lucked out, matey."

"That was superb," he says.

"Brilliant."

"Yes, brilliant." Kit nods his head toward white enamel lettering on the section of black gate. "Did you see this?"

"The Japanese graffiti?" I ask.

This time Kit points precisely where he wants me to look, and I read a rather famous English language sentence out loud: "The Love You Take is Equal to the Love You Make."

"I didn't even see that when I took it," Kit beams. "I'm sure I got it in frame with Ringo."

"A keeper," I say. "I'm going to make everyone I know a coffee mug with that photo on it."

Kit nudges me and directs my eyes toward Richard smiling contently as he leans against a rail; his euphoric customers have left him alone.

We walk over to get the world's biggest Beatles expert's opinion on this almost, but not quite, impossible day.

My eyes are moist with emotion as I think of my spot in a centerless universe. Is it the drugs? I feel like I'm PMSing times ten. Talk about an emotional seesaw. First there was the horror of last night's dream, and now the memory of a lifetime.

I sit on the curb and cry as Kit rolls a cigarette, and addresses Richard. "That must have been a life highlight for you, no?"

The Brain and Kit grin as my quiet tears become less quiet.

Could someone please tell me what distinguishes me from the insane guy on our tour? Why I am such a bloody wreck when I should be in a constant state of bliss?

"Quite odd, that. But quite nice, yes. Never met Ringo before. I'm rapt."

You'd think the Brain would call it a day, but he *is* a hardworking man: after a few more minutes he blows into his mic and announces, "Well, folks, I still have some words to tell you. Originally *Abbey Road* was going to be called *Everest* after the cigarettes smoked by the Beatles' favorite recording engineer. It was suggested that they take their photo at Mount Everest, but here was nearer. And that's that. This was an extraordinary day for me really, and I'm very glad to have shared it with you. As John said at the end of the *Let It Be* album, 'I hope I passed the audition.'"

The Bronx fan is not taking in any of Richard's final words. He walks back and forth across Abbey Road, having somehow cajoled the shorter of the two Japanese women into snapping his picture as a trio of impatient cars wait it out.

Kit rolls and lights a cigarette, and seeks out my eyes. "So now that you're standing, I guess you want to take a photo crossing, too?"

I'm severely embarrassed at my previous emotional display. "Isn't that too embarrassing for you?"

"How's that?"

"A bum photo of a road? And what's the point after the gold we got a minute ago?"

Richard overhears us. "Do it. I get e-mails from people who wish they listened to me, and were too cool about it."

"Okay," I say. "Can you help us match the photo up to the album cover as much as we can? Might as well get it right."

Kit snuffs out the cigarette, gets my camera ready, and says, "Take as long as you want. I want the woman I love to be sated."

I swallow air. This is the first time that Kit has used the word love. Three hours ago I would have bristled even more than I did after Kevin abused that emotive, but after an incredible day, I kiss his neck, and hear myself utter, "I love you, too, mister."

I am delighted with myself how that fell out of my mouth so easily, but I am concurrently so, so ashamed of my previous thoughts about my sweetie. Thank heavens I did not think out loud. A serial killer? That was the lowest low of many stupid thoughts.

Richard maneuvers our bodies into the correct angle to shoot and be shot. "If you look at this photo you will see the top of the road here, and there's the wall of Abbey Road through the lens of Iain Macmillan when he took the famous photo in 1969. So you see you are now exactly in the right place."

CHAPTER 15

This is the Church, This is the Steeple

With my internal pendulum swung back to happy romantic, I'm eager to get on with my grand tour of the British Isles. Even despite the dream I had last night, which for a few minutes left me more than a little shaken when I awoke this morning. Kit brought me to an old gem he knew about in London, a glassblower's shop chockful of hourglasses and gorgeous goblets. There was no shopkeeper present, and when I stepped inside he locked the door and tried to strangle me.

Unaware that he's stalking me at night, Kit's still firmly discouraging a swing through Stonehenge. "Give me a half hour. Read. Watch some telly. Let me call some friends and cook up an alternative. They might have some recommendations for day trips I haven't thought of."

"Go for it." I've been secretly dying to watch British TV and commercials.

While Kit makes a few phone calls from his bedroom, I happily watch *Breakfast Time* on the BBC.

"What's a zebra crossing?" I say when his door opens.

"A pedestrian crossing. Abbey Road is one."

"A kid in Surrey got killed on another one. That's the headline. And a new mutation of strep that warrants a flu shot if you haven't gotten one already."

"I did, back in December. Awful about the kid."

He joins me on the antique cushions, and presents a handwritten itinerary for me to approve.

"Hackney," I read. "What's there?"

"Not much," Kit admits. "Outermost East London, none too pretty, but there's a Burberry's outlet to spend some of your brother's money. You can buy him a scarf or mackintosh if you like."

"Great idea," I say. Continuing down the list, I read: "Lunch in Canterbury. Simple Simon's—"

"A fourteenth-century pub. Not too touristy, I hear from a friend."

"No McDonald's?" I say good-humoredly, watching Kit grin. "Would we visit the cathedral in Canterbury?"

"That's what I was thinking. I've never actually been, but it must be good, Julius Caesar was a tourist there."

"Whitstable," I read. "Never heard of that either."

"Probably not a place you Yanks have heard of yet. An oyster town once, still is, but it's in danger of getting trendy. I've always bypassed Canterbury and gone right there to the best battered cod I've ever eaten."

I say in my awful British accent (surprisingly not much better than Gary's): "I do believe I've never eaten battered cod."

"Then Whitstable is a must. The skate at the Oyster Bar is great, too."

"Skate? Is that a fish?"

"You've never had it?"

"No."

"Very tasty. And oh, it's not on the itinerary, but I've tentatively booked us lodging at the town we're getting the chips, on your approval of course. There's terrible traffic near Canterbury Castle."

"Approved."

"Scarfs and castles, fish and chips. How does that bloody sound?"

"Perfect."

You don't expect too many fashion Meccas after driving past kilometers of sprawling housing projects. But there, like a mirage, is a bona fide Burberry's.

And there on a silver rack of last year's items is the bona fide white leather trench coat I spotted only a month ago in New York while pretend-shopping with Cathy in the intimidating Burberry's SoHo branch. Here is the beautiful coat at only seventy-five pounds! By my trusty pastel pink Hello Kitty calculator's calculation, that's only one hundred and thirty dollars, seventy-five percent off what I saw on the New York rack at five hundred and twenty dollars! I hesitate for a moment too long and a young black fashionplate type wearing a silver sweatshirt with the word "Cutie" picked out in silver glitter scoops the prize up. *Shit*. She's wavering between purchases, and drapes the prize over a rack of clothes. Is she done?

Should I yank it from the rack? She picks it up again. *But that's my size, lady, not yours!*

I stalk her, hoping she won't notice. She tries the coat on once more, preens in a mirrored panel, and then goes instead with a dress cut from beige barkcloth fabric blocked with a pussy willow print. When she's about to rehang *my* trench coat on the wrong rack, I lunge—only to have a fingertip pressed hard against my shoulder by a rival shopper, a woman tall, pinch-nosed, sharp-toothed, and angry. "Now, now, hand it over. We know who got to it first, don't we?" I'm guessing by the Princess Di accent and the smart black ensemble, Lady Bitch is slumming it here in East London, a bit of diversion here from her life all silver and gold.

"First of all, ma'am, get your hand off me. And this is not yours. I was three feet away."

"Don't ma'am me." She won't let go, and I've no backup troops: Kit's in the men's section, unaware of my combat.

A worried manager finally comes over, his heavily pockmarked face lightened by warm brown eyes. Using Burberry Judicial Power, he has a security minion rewind the security camera.

Before the winner is determined, Kit is back by my side with a stuffed shopping bag. "Did you find anything?"

I show him the coat.

"How much dosh?"

"Seventy-five pounds."

"Quite a good steal, I'd say."

"If she gets it, it certainly is," my still-livid competition says.

We stare each other down until the manager emerges from a back room with his verdict: "We're giving it to the American."

Triumph.

"I'm from the British wool marketing board," the Defeated One says with considerable wobbliness. "I'm certainly going to report a horrible shopping experience to the people that matter." She opens her cell phone.

The manager nervously pantomimes for her to close the phone as he holds up a similar coat that he has at the ready slung on his arm. "We haven't even tagged it yet," he confides loudly when she closes the phone. I continue "shopping" nearby just to get the full scoop on the developing story. She picks it up with her well-manicured fingertips to take a look. In a peripheral glance I assess that this second choice might even be a bit nicer than mine—is that actual horsehair trim on the white collar? She is smiling as she models it to a mirror, but I'm not going to acknowledge anything short of triumph, and as I leave the shopping area to pay for my item, I am the recipient of the iciest stare of the twenty-first century.

Our cars are parked several spots from each other. I offer a simpering smile through my left-side front passenger seat window. The woman is so angry she almost backs into a parked minicab directly behind her.

As Kit revs the engine, he laughs about the discount department store as the new battleground. But he soon loses the grin. The traffic jam by Canterbury Castle is alarming, and we sit and sit and sit.

I take my shoes off and try a little Chaucer toe theater, one big toe the knight in the *Canterbury Tales,* the other the maiden.

Kit says nothing.

"Where did the London broil get its name? Was there a celebrated butcher in your country's history?"

No response, not even a grunt.

And even less of one when I demand to know the difference between a hill and a dale. Gene's influence? Kit has too much road rage to play.

Kit offers an apologetic kiss when we finally get to the town my guidebook calls "the Pearl of Kent," an apparent play on the many oyster towns around the county. Canterbury, as any literature major knows, is the home of the cathedral where one fateful night in December 1170, four knights burst through the doors and killed the archbishop, Thomas à Becket on St. Augustine's chair. Without that event, Chaucer would never have had even one tale to write about, for there would be no travelers paying homage to write about. I've also checked off the medieval Eastbridge Hospital, a twelfth-century hostel for those fatigued tourists, apparently now a private retirement home, but I read out to Kit, "You can still see the undercroft, refectory and two chapels."

We're both famished, so instead of going directly to undercroft and refectory touristing, we detour to that fourteenth-century pub.

When Kit proudly declares that his friend who recommended the establishment promised that tourists have not found out about the place because it's off the beaten path, I keep to myself that the pub has a prominent paragraph about it in my guidebook.

I can see why it's so beloved by Fodor's on our arrival. The architects from Disney would probably love to photograph Simple Simon's medieval workmanship. According to my book, those windows, brickwork and timbers on the outside are authentic. Equally perfect on the inside is a sloping beamed ceiling, and a working fireplace that warmed drinkers of centuries past.

Kit heads to the bar to order us two pork pies in Kentish cider, and two "real ales." When he returns to our table he says, "So how much do you know about ale?"

"Just a little."

"If you need a refresher course, ale is darker in appearance and heavier than lager. What we're about to drink is what locals call an English bitter."

"Okay—"

"This one is called Hopdaemon's, it's brewed right in town. Ale should be brewed as close to where you're drinking it as possible."

What's that expression? *It's not what you drink, but where you drink it.* The Shakespearean word *thereupon* pops into my head. *Thereupon, I drink the ale.* After my first-ever bitter sip of the stuff I hide my displeasure with a palm—and briefly recall Kevin's much more amusing beer lesson that he gave one of those few days I thought we could actually even make it over the long run. "There's dark ales. Strong-flavored European beers. Can't stand them. Beer is like ketchup, Shari—it should have one flavor. If you add anything to beer it is only going to fuck it up. The only exception is Corona which is okay to throw a lime into."

"The pies come with a side of runner beans," Kit says after a long sip of his own.

"What are those?'

He looks confused. "Long? Green?"

I'm guessing string beans. I notice the words Simple Simon printed on my cocktail napkin. "This pub's name must come from the nursery rhyme."

The young hipster bartender hovering over us has skulls tattooed on his skinny arms. He sets down our place settings and jumps right in with, *"Simple Simon met a pieman going to the fair. Said Simple Simon to the pieman, let me taste your ware!"*

"I haven't heard that in years," Kit says.

"I hear it six times a day," the bartender admits. "The owners were right in changing the name. Tourists like it better than the old name."

"I thought there were no tourists here," I say with a wink in my voice.

"Where did you hear that?" the bartender scoffs.

"I heard there was a regular clientele, too," Kit says hopefully.

"Well, that there is. For a few centuries it was called St. Radigund's Hall. Our resident customers don't care what we call the joint, as long as we serve good brew."

I have to agree with him. Maybe they get many tourists, but other than myself, I don't see anyone here that fits that bill. For a pub over five hundred years old, this clientele does looks lively and hip. Leaning against the bar, two groovy musicians are loudly discussing the history of

Moog synthesizers over their own pints of Hopdaemon's. I kind of hear another conversation nearby, but not quite.

"Stop listening," Kit says softly.

"I can't help myself, I'm a linguist."

"Seriously, it's a bad habit. I understand the appeal, but others might find it very rude, especially in England."

"Oh really? How did you know I wasn't with Gary in Chicago?"

"I eavesdropped."

At my self-satisfied grin he says, with a serious quality to his voice, "But I was alone. We're here together. Let's listen to each other."

The smell of heavy smoking and recently chopped onions permeates the air, and I'm tearing slightly from both. I would probably tear anyway at the poignant conversation going on at the next table between two drinkers, a college-age kid and the man I quickly determine to be his father.

Kit is listening to the ever-loudening conversation too—so much for his just-touted manners.

"You had a poor show in school, and you need to apply yourself. But my son couldn't stick the job."

From my angle and lightning-quick glance to their table, it looks like the son is cleaning a bit of dirt out from under his left thumbnail with his right one. "You don't know what you're talking—"

"When you pop yer clogs, you want to be known as a lazy fuck? You're too fond of the dole. Fun when you're twenty but when you wake up from the stupid years no longer a kid the dole doesn't pay too many bills."

"You wanted to relax with a pint. Was this the plan?"

"I'm your concerned father."

The son picks up the bill and slams down some pounds. "A concerned father who beats the shite out of his mother—"

"*Sup* ya drink and stop your *scryking,*" the father says. "You're not going anywhere."

Kit looks ashen, as if witnessing this father-son altercation has released a "something else" sullying his memory.

"What you gawking at?" the father says, as he catches Kit's stare.

"I'm sorry you have to hear this pig talk," Kit says loudly to me, the harshest comment I've ever heard this exceedingly well-mannered man make. Even when he was trying to get rid of Owen at the airport, he was technically polite to him.

The son laughs appreciatively at Kit's acerbic commentary and rises for the door. His dissed father sneers at us, and pounds the table with a hairy fist. He refocuses on his son. "How are you going to get anywhere?" the father bellows to the entranceway.

"Shank's pony, mate!" the son half screams from the door. The hipster bartender arches an eyebrow at me.

"Shank's what?" I ask Kit discreetly, like a woman who needs more details after witnessing a horrific car accident.

"He's walking, as he well should. There is something about this country that makes hitting acceptable."

The father drinks silently with a shatterproof face.

To calm Kit, I shift subjects. "So tell me about the

place we're staying at tonight. Is there a bed-and-break-fast there?"

"We're staying in a hut," he says sharply.

"I don't think we should keep in this man's business," I say adamantly.

"Sorry," he softens, trying hard to get out of his snit. "Yeah, um, they are renovated fishermen's huts. Part of the Hotel Continental, but their huts are much more highly desired by guests—"

The barman, doubling as waiter, plops the two pork pies down for us. I eye mine suspiciously.

"Would you like me to take a bite first?" Kit asks with forced cheer, perhaps guilty for his public anger.

"Would you? Pork is always a bit iffy for me. I was sick for two days over a nasty little eggroll."

"It's very good," Kit says, after the bit goes down the hatch.

I lift my own cutlery. "More about the huts please."

The father leaves the pub with red eyes and a hateful look for Kit.

"Yorkshire man," Kit says once the door is closed. "In case you were trying to pick the accent. His son is probably going to school in Canterbury, escaping him."

"Keep your pecker up," a father says to a bored ten-year-old on this long line to get in the Cathedral. At my shocked look, Kit wryly says, "That's a mouth in that expression, not a cock."

"Oh, thank God."

According to the handout, we can see where Saint Thomas was buried (before Henry VIII plundered his tomb), and the tombs of Henry IV, his wife Joan of Navarre, and the Black Prince's effigy.

The cathedral is beautiful, as is the music from the enormous pipe organ, the soaring architecture, and especially the stained glass the locals so shrewdly hid during World War II. We've opted for a self-guided tour, and when we hang up our headphones after a well-articulated blitz of architectural details, we hear some good news from the headphone rental clerk.

"If you stay fifteen more minutes, you'll be here for a service."

"Would you like to stay?" Kit asks me.

"Sure. It'll be probably be very interesting."

"It will," says the clerk.

Am I the only one at mass who doesn't know exactly what to do? If this isn't Catholicism, is this service called mass? Why is everyone going up for the bit of wafer?

Kit rises, too, and heads for the center.

"I thought that was a Catholic thing?" I quietly ask.

He shakes his head no.

"Am I supposed to take a sacrament? Isn't that a big sin, to eat the Body of Christ? What's the policy here?"

"Sit," Kit whispers harshly, when he sees I'm about to follow him. "You don't have the training."

"The *training?*"

Kit puts a finger to his lips.

"Are you confirmed?" a helpful woman says.

"No."

"Sit," her husband imparts to me.

I feel my face flush as I walk back to my pew. There's a few curious looks, but I happily spot a handful of others staying, including an Asian family and the man who told his son to keep his pecker up.

Inside the gift shop, Kit explains that the Church of England is closer to Roman Catholicism than to Protestant churches.

"I thought Protestant is Church of England."

"No, you're thinking of Episcopalian, I think that's what it's called in America. Canterbury is the seat of the whole system. Technically the queen is on top, she's the supreme governor, but the archbishop of Canterbury is the chief cleric."

"And that would be?"

"Rowan Douglas Williams."

I look at a picture of a clean-shaven man on the Church's tourist handout. "Is this him?"

Kit looks. "Yes."

"'He is an accomplished pianist and lover of opera as well as a keen tennis player and traveler; he has also written some hymns.' What is this, a personal ad?"

"Hey, that's my spiritual leader you're disrespecting." Kit gets his Zippo ready to light up the second we are out of sacred ground. My mother used to ready her lighter, too, whenever we were ready to leave my father's hospital for the night.

"Okay, I'm really confused. You've got to tell me again about when this whole Anglican thing happened."

"Old Henry wanted to marry someone he shouldn't have, and—you know, it's rather complicated to boil down to a minute." As I look through a rack of religious postcards I definitely won't be sending to Aunt Dot, Kit buys me a souvenir guidebook that he says has what I need to know, and a little teddy bear with an archbishop's hat.

The ride to coastal Whitstable is a short, tired, but pleasant one.

Along the route (from A299 to M2) Kit tells me a few things he knows about County Kent, including the rumor that Ian Fleming's selection of "007" for his Bond character was from the bus number from London to nearby Deal. I gobble up the always-appreciated Bond trivia but soon, with considerable magic out of the window, I'm a less receptive trivia recipient. Kit senses I'm tiring out from a long day, and he switches into silent-driver mode, occasionally smiling as I soak up the view of the marvelous countryside of Kent.

A whistling man alongside us for a few yards, carting a wheelbarrowful of potting soil, turns toward a roadside bed-and-breakfast decorated with colorful buckets of spring flowers. A few kilometers later I spot another B&B with a wishing well, the old stone kind, not the gray plastic kind you buy at a Long Island mall.

As we exit the car at our parking spot in Whitstable, the strong scent of the sea wafts up my nostrils. We take a brief walk down stubby streets to the Hotel Continental on Beach Road.

"It looks art deco-ish," I say.

"It is. A break from medieval."

"But it's a hotel, not a hut."

"The Fishermen's Huts are in the back."

The perky Hotel Continental receptionist greets us with a smile. "If you're eating at the Oyster Bar you'll miss the sunset if you don't hurry. We can put your things in the Anderson Shed for you."

"Do you need our credit cards now?" I ask. "We're splitting the bill."

"You look like trustworthy folks. And remember, I'll have your luggage! Do you know which one is the Anderson Shed?"

"Yes," Kit says. "I've been here before."

She studies him. "Yes, I thought I'd seen you before."

She hands us each a passkey. "I'll leave a note for my replacement who'll be doing the overnight. You can fix it up with him in the morning."

"That's champion," Kit says. "Very helpful."

"The sunset is what it is all about. Oh, you can move your car later. There's private parking."

"I forgot," Kit says.

I am staring at him when he looks at my face.

"What?"

"I know you recommended this place, but who exactly have you been here with before?" How did it not occur to me to ask earlier? "With Helen?"

"Yes. Does that upset you?"

"Why should it?" My voice betrays my annoyance.

"Good. Because the hut overhangs the seascape. In the morning everything is, well—I want to share this with you."

He looks so hurt that I squeeze his hand. "You sound charmingly earnest."

He squeezes back. We hurry over to the Oyster Bar, and are seated near the water.

"Are you ready for that battered cod?"

"I'm ready, Freddy."

Before we place our orders, Kit excuses himself for the men's room.

Out of Kit's minding, I'm free to eavesdrop again.

"Personally, I think she's got a very commonplace face, don't you?" says a nearby woman with a rather commonplace face; her features include droopy eyelids, and a boring slit for a mouth. Even though it is a warm but not hot day, the woman speaking is wearing a sleeve-less shirt, and when she scratches her nose I can see that one of her underarms is shaven and the other is not.

"Oh, no, I think she is gorgeous. You're mad! And frankly, his life has certainly been on the uptick since he met her, don't you *think?*"

When Kit is seated again, I lose the conversation, and join him in looking over the menu. As always, he's forth-coming with advice. "Your basic choices are cod, had-dock, huss, plaice."

"I thought the plan was cod."

"Yes, you should absolutely order it. There is a dire lack of codfish left in England—overfished, I guess. Cod might not be a culinary option the next time you're on my soil."

After our order we are silent. A good silent. Holding hands. A sunset. Again I chastise myself. My recent para-noia must have stemmed from jet lag. I've never been far enough away to actually have hardcore jet lag, so how would I see that coming? Maybe I let a little ugliness slip, but I stopped short of revealing my ugliest suspicions. Thank God for that. I wouldn't miss this moment. The colored skies out the window are perfectly hued: the pale blue of heaven melting into the early red of the evening sky is alone worth the three-thousand-mile journey to the British Isles.

According to my watch, still on New York time, it's time for my thyroid medicine again if I'm keeping a consistent hour. I pop another pill into my mouth and wash it down with a glass of room temperature water. Why ruin the moment and ask for ice?

Our waitress puts our meals on the table, and when she is out of view Kit leans over to hand me salt and malt vinegar. "Turner came here to paint the sunset," he says softly.

I nod.

After I have finished my first forkful of fish, he asks nervously (which I find touching), "What do you think?"

"It's so, hey, this is *really* good," I say like a television hostess visiting a famous restaurant. It is good, but as that sort of talent knows, a little theater never hurts.

"If we were in the north," Kit says, after a bite, "this would come with mushy peas."

"Mashed?"

"Yes."

For once I am the one with the silencing finger. I kiss him on the lips and the women from the neighboring table sigh at the sight of new love.

"Ain't getting any of that from the old man," one says.

★ ★ ★

We walk back to our hut through the narrow streets, our kissing ever intensifying every few feet.

We stop to watch the buskers in the square. I usually hate mimes, but with stomach full and love brewing, I love the mime. An hour passes of doing nothing. Doing nothing with your fantasy man is a wonderful thing.

The night is dark, and Kit lets a butterfly land on his finger. "This is a Woodman's Follower," he says. "Very rare, especially so early in the spring."

I jolt, remembering that butterfly collection in London again. The right side of my brain begs my left side to block the reemerging gnawing thoughts about Kit. But there they are again. How could I possibly harbor any suspicion about how lovely this man is? I didn't realize it would be so isolated at night. Does anyone know I'm here?

I count six weatherboard huts clustered near us, maybe seven.

A man hard to make out in the poor light addresses me. "Hi, there, Shari."

CHAPTER 16

We Meet Again

"I thought you were researching in a dusty room at the museum," I say to Owen after removing my hand clapped over my mouth. I quickly glance at Kit. Even in the darkening light, I can see the supreme displeasure in his face.

"Great out by the water, isn't it?"

"Did you tell him we were coming here?" Kit demands.

I sway my head no. "We haven't even—"

Kit drops my hand.

We're close enough to see Owen's lips move as he says, "Nothing like Whitstable for an easy getaway from London." After a tension-filled pause, he says, "How's the trip been?"

"Well for starters, we met Ringo Starr on our Beatles walking tour." Anything but silence.

"No way!"

"Seriously! We took a picture with him. Everyone on our tour did. He was doing some kind of tribute to George Harrison at Abbey Road."

"That's incredible." Owen glances to my companion. "Kit? That you? It's hard to make out your face."

"Yes," is the curt reply.

"You like Ringo?"

"He was a nice man."

"Did Helen introduce you to these huts?"

This time Kit doesn't answer.

So that's what this is about. A love rivalry. As uncomfortable as the situation is, I'm relieved. It appears no one's strangling anyone anytime soon.

We stiffly stand until Owen asks, "Where to next on your itinerary?"

Kit glares at me, and storms into the hut.

Should I follow Kit? We're all exhausted after that plane flight. Should I give him room to breathe? Is it betrayal to reveal any details? "We were going to maybe go to Kit's family's house," I divulge against good judgment.

"In Yorkshire?"

"His family lives in the Cotswolds."

"That's curious, because I thought our friend Helen told me his dad was a northerner."

"His research was somewhere near Yorkshire, that's what she probably told you."

"And what research is that? Linguistics, right?"

How can I back out of this conversation? The motormouth in me keeps going: "Yes. We both study Volapük. You know—the predecessor to Esperanto?"

Owen touches my elbow in the dark. "You mean like his father speaks? That's his field of research? I kept quiet when I met you, but our friend Helen—"

"His ex?"

"Yes, you could say that. Last time I spoke to her she said he was hard at work on a novel."

A novel? This is like a game of telephone. I'm sure Owen's got this all mixed up. "You're mistaken. Kit's father is dead. There is a man who speaks Volapük near Yorkshire, but that's not his dad. He's an elderly man, there's no way—"

"I'm sure it was. But it's been a while now since I've seen—his dad could have died in that period of time."

"Trust me on this, Owen. Kit's father isn't alive, and he does not speak Volapük."

"You're arguing with a historian?"

It's dark enough that bugs are buzzing now. I press harder: "Do you think Kit could be lying to me?"

"I think I've opened my mouth plenty," comes the reply in the dark.

"Go on, for god sakes. You're telling me Kit is a compulsive liar?"

The poison is practically dripping off Owen, but there is something curiously believable about what he is saying. Owen's obviously thought a *lot* about Kit, and once again I admit to myself that I've known Owen a hell of a lot longer than I've known Kit.

"Depends. What else has he told you?"

I struggle for a memory. "When I met him, he was talking about a Cambridge reunion, with Andy and some other guy."

"Reece."

"Yeah."

"Those were his roommates. They were very dubious of him. Thought he was a loner."

"They did?"

He shrugs his shoulders. "What can I tell you? Sounds like Kit's been feeding you an artful tale. Wish I had something nicer to say."

A memory flash. That moment that Professor Dave picked "something else" in his Cambridge accent—could it be a telltale vowel that gave him away as a Yorkshire lad? Has my wooer been faking a life? What else has he faked? I excuse myself and head the few feet toward my hut. I still feel frightened, but once and for all I'm going to sort this out.

When I key into our room, Kit is staring out the window into the dark.

"We need to talk," I say like a TV detective about to expose the charlatan.

"Tomorrow. I'm in a foul mood right now. I really don't like your friend, I'm sorry to say."

"I'd be talking if I was you."

"And why's that?"

"He let me know a few things about you that have really disturbed me."

"Oh, really? What did that tosser say to you?"

"Maybe exactly what you didn't want me to hear."

He pulls a chain on a standing lamp and light floods the room. "And what would that be? I'm a bit put off by your entrance, you know." At the *p* in "put" I feel his angry breath on my neck. "Why were you so chatty with him when I've told you how much I despise him?"

"I went to school with the guy. I know him from childhood."

"And I'm the one you're with right now, or at least I thought I was." He pours himself a glass of water in the sink. After a gulp, he says fiercely, "I'm so mad right now I could—" His words peter off mysteriously.

"You could *what?*" Am I baiting a madman?

No response.

"Kit, who are you really?"

"Pardon me?"

"You heard me. What is your plan for me? Are you going to threaten me so I can't let the world know the truth about your big research lies?"

"My *plan* for you? To see England together—"

"Oh is that it?"

"Are you *insane?*"

"You tell me. I just heard that the man you presented to my colleagues as your great academic find is your father who supposedly died when you were little. Remember that compassion you hurled at me? What a fucking crock!"

I spring back, scared. I'm even terrified at the psychosis in my own voice.

But Kit looks at me right in the eye as he answers: "You've got a very febrile imagination. And when you calm down, I think you will rue the day you said all of this to me."

I can't stop what's been welling up inside me since we

first ran into Owen. I rock my head derisively. "That's your explanation? I note there is no denial—"

He slams a door hard as he leaves our highly desired hut.

What have I just done? My forehead is covered in perspiration. I shudder. Maybe I *am* insane. I'm definitely confused.

I run to Owen's hut and knock on the front door.

Owen answers with sleepy eyes, "Sorry I was just dozing off—" One look at my face and he forces himself to attentiveness. "What happened?"

"Kit and I had a nasty fight."

"Over what?"

"Over you."

He seems just a bit pleased. "Me? Can you throw out a bit more info here?"

"Over his lying. He made up friends, he made up an existence. I'm scared he might hurt me—"

"I don't think he's going to hurt you—"

"With all the lying he's doing, why not? Who knows what he's capable of?"

Owen gulps. "Well, it's not like they all hated him in Cambridge. That was a bit of an exaggeration, I guess."

I look up nervously. "Exactly how much of an exaggeration?"

"Like I said, a bit."

I lock eyes with him. "Tell me more."

"Some days, I guess. We all have our months we fall out of favor."

"What about the father connection? Is that real?"

"Now hey, I didn't say I was certain about that. It's just what I think I remember from Helen."

"You said you have a photographic memory—"

"I said I was a historian. I never said anything about a photographic memory."

I gasp loudly.

"I was getting caught up in the—Kit and I have a historical rivalry going, if you haven't noticed."

I rhythmically blow out air, lost for what to do or think. "How long did Kit go out with Helen?"

"Well he went out with her through school, but he was married to her for—"

"*Married* to her?"

"Yes."

"What happened?"

"We always had a spark going."

"A spark?" I say shakily. "You and Helen? Does that mean she cheated on him with you?"

"Frankly she found Kit boring, it was never going to work. She wants guys with New York energy. She was always going on about moving to a loft in the—"

I have a flash of clarity ending my paranoid rage. I've completely blown everything out of the water. Kit, what the fuck have I done? "Owen. I've destroyed—" I can't even finish the sentence.

"Calm down. This will sort itself out."

"I have to find him!"

"He'll come back. He'll calm down. How nasty did it get?"

Instead of answering, I rush back to the Anderson hut in the dark. The windless night is chill and grim, matching my mood. I key in and open a door to find a black room.

I'm spooked. "Kit?" I call, timidly at first, and then with no answer coming, I yell his name. Still no answer.

My pulse feels like I'm hooked up to a rowing machine, practicing for the Olympics.

I knock again on Owen's door.

"Still no sight of him?" Owen says. He's plenty awake this time, and beckons me in when I shake my head no. "I feel awful about this mess. Why don't you just stay here until the morning? You can take the bed, and I'll take the sofa. We've been traveling, we're all jet-lagged, and everything will straighten itself out."

Eventually I agree to the plan.

In the bathroom I wring a bit of Colgate out of Owen's half-empty tube. In lieu of a proper brush, I swish it with a slug of bottled water. I look in the mirror. With all the sweating and crying going on, everything applied on my face has smudged. I'm a wretched raccoon.

I lay on Owen's bed in a fetal curl. I feel every inch the fool. I think I see a face in the window. Wasn't Heathcliff freaked by Cathy's visage in *Wuthering Heights?* I need to get my shit together.

"This is lunacy," I sleepily tell myself. "Why the hell am I staying in Owen's room?" A better plan: when I go back to see if Kit is back, this time I stay. Wait for him. Alas, that plan never transpires—footsore and heartsick, I am utterly exhausted, and I fall into a dead sleep.

After a loud knock on the door, I leap up from the bed. I can tell it's early morning by the light glowing into

Owen's bedroom. I've left my watch on: it's 6:00 a.m. It has to be Kit calmed down. I hesitate a second to smooth the quilt, sure the sight of me in his adversary's rumpled bed would roil.

It's a shorter line from the couch to the front door, a geometry lesson I learn when I spot Owen opening the door.

"Hello? Kit?" Owen says.

There's not even a ghost for Owen to do any explaining to. Kit's not there, but someone's plunked down my suitcase. Taped to it is an envelope that contains no note, but the remainder of the three thousand in cash from Gene. (After I admitted I always lose things during trips, Kit nicely offered to hold the pounds we transferred after the Beatle Brain tour in his wallet.)

"Kit?" I scream into the morning air, my naked feet wet in dewy grass. "Where are you?"

One of the other hut guests opens his door in white boxers. He implores me to keep down the volume.

Again I return to the Anderson hut. There's no one there. Outside. Inside. Outside. I silently scan the vista and hear the swish of the surf hitting the pebbled beach. I see now how beautiful the huts are and why Kit risked coming here despite fragile memories of his past.

The car! How could I have not checked? Opportunity gone, probably hours ago: on the unpaved parking spot assigned to our hut I see nothing but dust.

CHAPTER 17

Dogs of the Chase

Dr. Zuckerman calls on Owen's cell phone only minutes after my third round of sobbing subsides.

"Dad? Can I call you later? I ran into Shari Diamond from New York and—"

I sniffle as he listens for a minute.

"Yes, really— What?— No, she's here now— Yes, well we met at the airport— What?— You're joking— Sitting on my couch—sure, hold on, Dad—"

He holds a hand over the receiver. "My father wants to talk to you urgently. You better pick up, it's *very* important."

Of course with wording like that, I oblige. What could this be about?

"Dr. Zuckerman?" I say tentatively.

"Ms. Diamond, the next time you leave on an international trip, you should give your roommate and your family a number to be reached."

"What's going on?" I ask apprehensively.

"You are on the wrong medication. Your drug store called—they have another Shari Diamond who lives on Avenue A. You have your poor neighborhood pharmacist terrified you are going to take down his family business with a lawsuit."

"What have I been taking?" Can my day be any worse?

"Larium. It's primarily used to prevent malaria. The other Shari Diamond is probably going on an African safari or to Southeast Asia, somewhere like that. It's not going to kill you, but it causes delusional thinking. Bad dreams.

"Hello?"

"I'm here," I peep up.

"You can also have vivid nightmares."

"That's exactly what's been happening. I've been a trainwreck ever since I left New York."

"Just what I—of course it's not your fault. But you didn't read the label?"

"I saw an *L* word. You said there might be an *L* on the pill, some generic substitute for Synthroid."

"Oy, I did, too. That was Levothroid. Listen, stop taking your pills immediately. You still might have a bit of a roller-coaster ride for a day or two. The Larium is in your bloodstream."

The bottle of pills is within reach, and there on the label is the word Larium. My lord. As I recap everything for Owen, I flush the cause of my misery down the loo.

★ ★ ★

"Don't give up ship. Whitstable is small. We'll have lunch, he'll probably be having a smoke on a dock." Owen has been to the town enough times that he knows of a prize café table that offers excellent people-watching as well as a grand vista of the waves.

"What would you like?" Owen asks when a diminutive waitress appears before us with her pad.

"I'm not hungry."

"You're eating something," Owen orders. "How are you going to do detective work on an empty stomach?"

"Side salad of greens," I say.

Owen shakes his head and orders a swordfish shish kabob on a lemongrass stalk and chips. "You'll eat some of my chips," he says to me after the waitress has left our table.

Just as our orders arrive, a toddler girl manages to climb the reasonably high cement divide separating us from the sand, and sprints toward the beach as fast as she can caper. Owen jumps to his feet, hurdles the divide and winches the kid to safety.

A woman from two tables over greets the unlikely couple returning.

"You're a saint, a hero."

Owen smiles at the mother, and commendably doesn't gloat about the incident when he's reseated.

Like *Animal Planet* cameramen waiting for the ocelot, we continue to stalk from our determined spot.

Owen attacks the bulging weekend *London Times*. He

offers me the Book Review section. "A new Martin Amis book is out," he says. "This should get petty."

I sway my head no, preferring to listen to England as I plead with the sea to return my man.

He's thinking of a run for Parliament, he's potty.

Can you do the cheque, Alistair? I was never very good at maths.

No, Larry, I think those birds are sandpipers. In fact, I'm quite sure of it.

I think I'll give that one a miss—I'm not big on fig, really.

Saved tot and grateful mama long gone, my American dining companion touches my hand. "We should go."

CHAPTER 18

The Face That Launched a Thousand Ships

"You seriously don't remember the number on Westbourne?"

"Tell you the truth, I was so jet-lagged I wasn't paying very much attention."

"You're not good with addresses are you?"

"It was somewhere in the middle of this block." *This block?* I second-guess inside my head. This block of white stucco flats looks the same as the one we just passed.

"I'll start at the light, and we'll drive down again. Something will spark your memory."

But nothing does. We head back to the large serviced apartment that Owen's leased for the month, not far away in Paddington.

I'm nearing defeat. "Maybe you can call the Cambridge alumni office. They'll have his number, and they'll send a message from you, you're an alum."

If only to calm me again, Owen answers, "Excellent idea. I'll do that after a quick shower."

We enter his flat, and I collapse in a chair. I'm not just physically exhausted from my last two sleepless nights, I'm famished and mentally spent as well.

When Owen returns from the bedroom with both a towel wrapped around his waist and a downcast face, I ask anyway, "No information?"

"Zilch. The only thing they have on the computer is the year he left."

"Don't you know *anyone* who might be in touch with him?"

Owen racks his brain. He only has two Cambridge classmates in his Palm Pilot, and apparently he's already tried them. Alas, there was no answer from either of their phones.

"I can call Helen," he says finally.

I perk up some. I hadn't known that was an option.

"I'll need privacy," he says as he reaches once more for his Palm Pilot.

This time when the door opens, he has very big news: "Helen wants to meet you for a cappuccino. Suss you out."

"Of course. Where?"

"The Boogaloo Bar, near the Highgate tube. She likes the jukebox there."

"Are you going?"

"She doesn't want to see me," he admits, looking a little forlorn. "But I'll drop you off and you can call when you're ready to leave."

★ ★ ★

"You must be Shari?" the woman standing above me says.

The first thing I notice about Kit's ex (and Owen's ex for that matter) is her mouthful of impossibly white teeth—so much for the British stereotype. And illuminated by our sunlit window, Helen's eyes are bluer than a cloud-free sky. She's ineffably gorgeous as she walks gracefully to an open booth. No matter how she turns her head, she's posing for the one toothsome headshot that will land her the starlet gig.

I order myself a Hopdaemon's.

"That's Kit's brew," Helen says knowingly in her upper-class accent.

I'm wearing jeans and a gray Gap T-shirt and feeling very plain Jane—Helen's dress, stretched tight against her almost perfect curves, has a fabulous vintage seventies polyester chevron pattern of black, red, white and brown. She's perfected the look with knee-length brown-leather boots. I flatter myself that she's dressed to the max to impress me.

I nod.

After she orders a white wine and seafood tapas she says, "He's a very private person."

"What happened?" I start.

"What happened?" she echoes softly. "I betrayed a man who does not like to be betrayed. I feel badly about it, but we were a mismatch from the beginning. I'm far more adventurous than that man. I find him rather dull."

Kit? Who flew me to his country on a whim?

I tell her a barebones story of how I met her ex-husband, and the pitiful tale of my paranoia drugs.

Her facial expression is polite, but not especially kind.

"Do you know where he lives on Westbourne?"

"He lives on Westbourne now?" she says with a worried glance.

"Yes."

"He didn't before. He lived in Maybury. He must have moved."

I gasp. Is my last hope gone?

She empties her glass. "If he's not in Maybury, I'm not sure where he can be—" At my crestfallen face she adds, "I could possibly take you to someone who might know where he is."

My heart races. "Who would that be?"

Instead of answering, Helen eyes the jukebox, scrounges in her bag for a pound coin, and selects Bob Dylan's "Simple Twist of Fate."

"Owen could come with us," she says on her return. "I'd pack your bags for an overnight trip. If I can arrange it, I'd like to do this tomorrow."

"You can't tell me any more?" I say just as she is about to leave. She looks at me so indignantly that I nervously ask her a replacement question. "That's a really nice bracelet. Is it Indian?"

With a not-kind face she says, "It's from Kenya. Kit bought it for me on our honeymoon." She pronounces Kenya *Keen-ya,* like someone who's actually heard the proper pronunciation on location.

"Oh," is my meek reply.

She hands me a card with her name and number engraved on heavy cream stock.

Helen Chattleworth-Brown.

Did I make a face at her hyphenated name as I quickly imagined my own card with Kit's name hyphenated with mine in union?

I must have as Helen's last words for the "ex date" are: "Our divorce came through, you needn't worry."

After two days, I'm back to full meals, but nearly as miserable. Once Owen has extended his rental car for us we drive directly to Helen's place straight from the carhire shop.

"She's a drama queen," is Owen's reasoning for Helen's mysterious nonanswer of where we are going.

He may have long-ago ended his affair, but he is clearly affected when he sees her approaching in, what from pretty much any angle, is a skintight black Catwoman suit minus the ears and tails.

She allows our eyes to take in her fine figure, and then with a big smile, she zones in on my new Burberry coat. "Did you get that in the outlet?" she says with the false kindness of the competitive dresser.

"In SoHo," I say. "New York's SoHo."

The itinerary is finally revealed. It turns out I will meet the man whose existence has practically ruined my life, the man Owen is convinced is Kit's father.

Helen immediately dismisses such nonsense. "Owen, you never listen, do you? He's Kit's *grandfather.*"

"You must have met him then," I say slowly as I discard my earlier thoughts on where we were headed. I'd thought a hideaway hut they may have gone to in their married days.

"No, I never did. But we drove by here once, and Kit was too nervous to go through with his plan. He must have come back after our separation."

Owen and I try to engage her more, but she grunts her answers. She seems singly focused on getting us there. Owen rolls his eyes and leans over to ask how I'm doing in a concerned whisper.

I give him a grateful peck on the cheek.

This seems to have engaged Helen's attention more— a spectacular blaze of hostility follows—not a word for twenty kilometers.

Somewhere in the moors of England, three disconnected souls get out of the car. An old man is plowing a field with an expensive farm vehicle. Is he licensed at his age? And then boom! That face! I recognize it now from Kit's Chicago presentation.

"Yes?"

"Robert Royden?" Helen says calmly.

He smiles at her. How often does a woman in a catsuit approach a farmer?

"May I have a word with you?"

His eyes look delighted as he walks closer. "Of course."

"We're looking for your grandson."

He stops in his tracks. "Has something happened to—"

"Kit," Helen says. "We were hoping that you've heard from him."

"I was hoping you had. He appeared here, but never gave me a number."

"Then you are Kit's grandfather?" I ask in Volapük, and the man looks at me in surprise.

"You speak Volapük?" he says in Volapük.

I explain my studies, and my friendship with Kit.

I struggle for the romantic sense of things as Volapük was conceived as a language for businessmen.

Owen looks at us like we're speaking an alien tongue. Helen must have heard Kit speak this language before because now she's back to looking as disinterested as ever.

I ask the Last of the Volapük Speakers if there is somewhere I can send the two others.

"The house," he says, and calls his wife on his cell phone. After a brief conversation he points the old lovers her way.

Owen and Helen seem relieved to have a period of time away from me. I imagine they have their own issues to tackle.

I'm relieved, too. I am free to tell Kit's grandfather everything I know.

Maybe he, as Helen suspects, can help.

Robert Royden and S. Roberta Diamond rest on an almost rusted-over farm bench.

"Would you like to talk in Volapük or English?" he starts.

"English," I say. "I might not know all of the words I need."

"I didn't know he was married to that woman."

"It didn't last long."

"You are friends though?"

"I wouldn't call us friends. It's just that she thinks you're the only one who can help me find him."

"What more can I tell you? I don't know where he is."

"He talked about growing up in medieval watercress. That his father died."

"Yes he did. I never met my daughter's husband, but I understand he provided well. I only met my grandson three years ago, and he kept things formal."

"Why wouldn't you have met him before that?"

He shrugs.

"I need to contact him," I press.

"I told you, didn't I? I don't know where his mother lives."

"You don't know where your daughter lives?"

"I did some terrible things to her once, I'll leave it at that. Even my wife knows I can't take back the past." He picks up the bottom of his shirt to wipe his wet brow.

This is more truth than I sought out.

"He did give me something."

"Yes?"

"It's in the house."

His wife, Kit's grandmother, is in the kitchen with Owen and Helen.

"Are you here for a cuppa?" she calls from her seat.

"Yes, dear," says Kit's grandfather.

He leaves my side to track down whatever the item is that he is looking for. I sit at the table with Owen and nod my head. His wife is back at the stove making a fresh pot of tea.

Robert Royden pokes his head into the kitchen. "Have you seen the poem?" he asks after an unsuccessful hunt.

She looks at him curiously, and reaches for a sewing basket on top of the refrigerator. She removes a darning egg, knitting needles marked on the end from years of use, a package of eyes and hooks, thimbles, a sock darner and finally, a cream-colored envelope, which she hands to her husband.

He passes it on to me. "He gave this to us when he left. Maybe you can make sense of it."

He unfolds a poem I instantly recognize as a James Merrill jewel. I've always loved this poem about how naming animals brought about their destruction. The poignancy of a poem given to a man who cares more about language than flesh is not lost on me.

But as Owen points out in the car ride back to London, we still don't know where Kit is.

CHAPTER 19

You Can't Always Get What You Want

"So here we are, ten Jews, in a German restaurant at Christmas time," Dr. Zuckerman says in Rolf's of Third Avenue after a gulp of wine. "And we've almost got us a *minyan* around here." In one half hour he's cracked as many corny jokes as a gagwriter on the rubber chicken circuit.

The line for seats is long. In the same week, both *Time Out New York* and the *New York Times* gushed about the impossible number of decorations at Rolf's at holiday time. It was my mother's idea to check the place out for a fun family meet-up. (Although she's implored me to use my noodle and not drop the setting in any report to Dot.)

On my direct left is Owen's sister, Wendy. She takes it upon herself to offer Summer an explanation of her father's weak witticism. "You might not know the word *minyan*. Ten Jewish men are needed for a proper prayer session."

Summer smiles at her: "I know the word. My last name is Moskowitz."

Dr. Zuckerman is entertained. "*Summer* Moskowitz?"

"Leave it alone," Owen says to his father. "Don't mock her name."

"Who's mocking? Did I just offend you, Summer?"

Gene spins the Lazy Susan toward his sister-in-law. "Your first name was originally Barbara, right?

Summer smiles. "It's okay, Dr. Zuckerman. I hear it all. People find my name change very political. I was reborn the day I chose my own name."

Gene kicks me under the table. I know the code: he's unnerved by flakes, even if he's related to them.

I'm glad Summer is finally joining in on the conversation. She had her hands full before when Noah, my tiny niece with a boy's name, screamed louder than anyone could imagine a little baby could. At least screaming herself silly silenced her to sleep.

And now, with her granddaughter calmed, Mom can finally talk to Becky, Gene's newest interior designer girlfriend. Gene cracks his neck nervously as they speak. With the new baby, and my engagement, I'm guessing he feels left out of the mix. I wouldn't be surprised if another engagement comes soon. His year with Becky is a miracle unit of commitment.

"So I hear you're giving my son's place a fresh look again."

Becky's smile is proud. "Donna, I have awesome plans for the place in Queens."

"Yes?" Mom nods.

"I'm a movie buff and I was thinking of recreating the lunar look of the old *Star Treks.*"

Gene coughs uncomfortably. I like Becky, even if she borders on loopy. I know that if Kit could hear the newest Forest Hills bachelor pad game plan, he'd have something funny to say. I shush my thoughts.

Kit's absence has been a bitter pill to swallow, but I've swallowed it. Haven't I? Can't I once, in this setting, finally stop thinking of him? A marriage is no place for dwelling on lost opportunities.

After all, who wouldn't trade places with me? My brilliant author-historian fiancé can broach the weather and the Great Mongol Cavalry with equal aplomb. His family wealth insures a life of ease, and his religion of birth means no long lecturing from Aunt Dot.

Yes, late at night, I sometimes still search Kit's name on the Internet. But there are an infinite number of hits in all the variations: Christopher Brown, Christopher T. Brown, Chris Brown and Kit Brown. I open each page, just to be sure, searching the cyber universe as determinedly as a treasure diver hoping to catch sight of a Spanish-era relic glinting in a seabed impossibly tangled over with watery weeds.

I sigh inwardly. Yesterday, Google's images option had a new face for me to investigate. An English Christopher T. Brown no less. But this one had a salt-and-pepper beard, and sunken eyes and dark rings around his eyes. Not a chance that it was *my* Kit.

When I heard Owen opening the front door of the

new apartment we share, I closed out of my telltale screen with lightning speed.

"Working on your dissertation?"

My stomach burned with my lie. "Yeah."

"Did you get any interviews?"

"I have one with a temp agency near Wall Street. For a legal proofreading job. Pays pretty well."

Owen tried to be nice. "It should. Proofreading is skill intensive."

When he was peeing, I raced to check my name, too, my other daily masochistic ritual. Perhaps there was an orbiting fuck-you in cyberspace. I'd take anything from Kit.

I've only ever found one—from Kevin on his Manga blog. Since I'd checked his Web site last, he'd posted a chapter of a Manga novel with a villainess named Shari Dee.

Dr. Zuckerman taps my hand. "Did my son tell you about his uncle Mort and where he has to sit?"

"Dad—" Wendy cries preemptively.

Dr. Zuckerman looks at her firmly. "This is your family. Let's bring it up now."

"Mort is a handful," Owen explains.

"He's been half-deaf since he was a little kid and poured ten peppercorns in his ear and had to be operated on."

Owen laughs with a bit of goose in his mouth. "Have you been taking a continuing ed memoir class again?"

My mother turns to me. "So should we sit Mort near Eric?"

"I don't think you sit two half-deaf people next to each other," says Gene. "It's not like they both like model building."

Owen's father cuts in again. "Shari, you look a little tired, have you been taking the Levothroid every day?"

"Yes," I lie.

"It's great to have a doctor in the family," Mom says flirtatiously.

Dr. Zuckerman beams. "Well, with Owen's successful dissertation last year, you have two."

There is notable silence from my blood relatives. When and if I will ever finish that Volapük dissertation is one big question mark.

Professor David Mitchell's glowing report on Kit's presentation was published two weeks after the Chicago conference in the online newsletter that *Journal for Constructed Language* subscribers all receive.

Dr. Cox called me in for a much-needed powwow the week after I returned from the U.K.

I brought in a vanity pressing of Scot Gaelic proverbs I bought for a buck off a bargain bin bookrack outside the Strand.

"Maybe I can switch my expertise to Scot Gaelic," I said lamely.

"Nonsense. Stay with Volapük. You think no one can write about Shakespeare anymore? Every topic has a new angle if you think hard enough. Have you considered a dissertation addressing religious persecution as a reason the universal language was started? A Jew started Esperanto because he was sick of nationalism. You could explore the persecution of the Jew as it relates to Volapük…"

I have an appointment to see Dr. Cox on Monday, I

realize. I need to write that on a wall calendar some-where, before I forget.

"Bread?" Gene says, and I'm back with the table.

The table next to us is done with their meal. The waiters sweep in for a fast turnover during the high sea-son of this restaurant. The host in a Santa suit an-nounces on the loudspeaker: "Lowenstein Party of Six, please. Benjamin Lowenstein party of six."

The Christmas jingles resume with the first bells of "Santa Claus is Coming to Town."

"So how long have you been a widower?" my mother says to Dr. Zuckerman. She has rarely been so forward.

"Fifteen years."

She catches his eye with the empathy of a single par-ent who has suffered intense loss. "That's almost as long as my stretch."

"Did you ever remarry?" Dr. Zuckerman says kindly.

She breathes. "The right man never came along."

"Well, I remarried."

"The wrong woman came along," Wendy says after a sip of ice water.

"She sure did," Owen says.

Dr. Zuckerman eyes them intently and refocuses on my mother. "It was a record-short marriage. Vicki was too young to understand how precious marriage was."

"Twenty years his junior," Wendy says with obvious distaste.

"Okay, Wendy, that's enough," Dr. Zuckerman says piercingly. At the knowing looks from his two kids, he breaks down laughing. "Okay, she was a mistake."

"Thank you," Wendy says. "Finally."

"Why was she so awful?" I ask.

"For one, she was an awful snob about Queens. It was beneath her to live in her husband's house. She kept pressing me to move into Manhattan."

"A snob about Jamaica Estates?" Mom says. "Your part of Queens is extraordinary—leafy and lovely."

Dr. Zuckerman glows. "Well, to tell you the truth, *you're lovely.* If I knew such an extraordinary and beautiful woman lived so close, I might never have gone out with her."

Gene kicks me under the table again and I kick him back. Of course. Why hadn't the thought even crossed my mind before? Dr. Zuckerman is her quintessential type. Jewish. Funny. Warm.

"Anyone ever have the Starbucks maple scone?" Wendy asks out of the blue.

"What about it?" Owen asks his sister. "I eat that about once a week."

It's true, he does, thinks me, his fiancée.

"Perfection."

"At Starbucks?" Alan doubts.

Wendy shrugs. "I know. I feel so guilty buying it." She and Alan start a private conversation about capitalism I can only hear the odd word of. Now and then Alan stops to cherrypick the things he will actually eat in any given side salad, cucumbers and lettuce. Tomatoes, onions and peppers are strictly verboten to his precious palate.

"So what do you do for fun?" Gene says to Owen. "You fish?"

"Me? God no. Who has time to do that? I prefer my fish already dead and buttered."

"I'm hyper-busy," Gene says congenially, "but I find it relaxing. Maybe you can go with me some weekend."

"Thanks, but I don't really have time for play, I have a book coming out."

Gene can hardly hide his disdain as he sneaks a look at his expensive banker-on-the-rise watch. I wince. When I got back from my disastrous trip to England, Gene was eager to see if I could bring Kit over for a weeklong brown trout and fly-casting extravaganza. He'd gotten so giddy at the thought he'd already gone online and bought the three of us Buzz Off wide-brimmed hats from Orvis.com at fifty dollars a pop.

"So we need to decide, kids. Whose rabbi? What synagogue to go to? You like Rabbi Grossman, Owen?"

"Dad, can we do this later? This is just a family meet-and-greet."

"You don't like Grossman?"

"He is a comedian, not a clergyman. Who brings up Bob and Ray sketches in a service?"

"A rabbi who knows his comedy, that's who. Bob and Ray are geniuses."

My mother looks at Gene, who winks at her. My father lived for the old Bob and Ray sketches. He had every Bob and Ray record, and knew their routines backward. "Do you know *Matt Nuffer, Boy Spotwelder?*" she says to Dr. Zuckerman warmly.

Dr. Zuckerman scans her thin face. "You know *Matt Nuffer, Boy Spotwelder?*" He picks up my mother's hand. "By the way, Donna, I know a woman's family sometimes pays for the wedding, but I have to let you know, we will pick up the full cost."

Owen gapes at his dad. The current plan now is for the wedding to be paid for by him via a loan taken out against his trust fund, which will kick in when he's forty. We were never going to ask my mother for anything except her organizing skills that she's perfected as a secretary.

I'm sure Owen's surprise at his father's offer is genuine, and I am just as shocked. But I'm not feeling especially guilty about the bighearted proposal. Mom is ridiculously insisting that a bride's family should pay for a wedding and wants to cash in her retirement savings for her only daughter.

Yesterday I almost brought up eloping to Vegas on a supersaver fare to Owen as a way to remedy the conflict.

Owen insisted his sister would never talk to him again if we eloped. He said he'd talk to my mother and ensure her that in the long run he wouldn't even feel the wedding bills.

I shook my head in shame and said, "I can't imagine what it would be like to grow up with that kind of safety net underneath you, finance-wise—when Gene lost thirty-nine dollars out of his pocket once my mom reacted like he'd dropped thirty-nine hundred dollars." Maybe Owen had repeated my reaction to his father.

Another astonishment: "I'll pay for my sister's wedding," Gene says pointedly, proudly.

Now it's my turn to gape.

I suspect that even with Gene's portfolio in shipshape,

his net worth must be chickenfeed compared to Dr. Zuckerman's holdings. Owen briefly mentioned a summer spread in the Hamptons, and when my fiancé says the word spread, that worries me.

"Gene," Dr. Zuckerman says adamantly, "we have a lot of cousins, and they would be very insulted if they were not invited."

"How many is a lot?" Gene responds coolly.

"I have nine brothers and sisters. And my deceased wife had five, four of whom are still living."

"And they have kids," Wendy says.

His father takes a sip of red wine. "Defeats the law of averages. They all had girls. Owen is the only boy among thirteen girl cousins and a sister."

Gene keeps a poker face, but he can't be too happy.

"Our Owen is the prince in our family," Wendy says. "If any of them are left out, there'll be hell to pay."

Prince Zuckerman smiles as he admonishes his father. "You're being amazingly generous, but we just got engaged this week. Give us a minute to plan things out. You're not the bride."

"Eat your wienerschnitzel," Dr. Zuckerman says to Gene congenially. "We'll duke it out later."

"My dad's going to win out," Wendy says. "When he says he'll pay, he'll pay."

I smile as I eat another mouthful of trout. I really like Owen's father. He's a warm man, born into poverty but who advanced by sheer intellect (and continued luck with the stock market). I got the sense that big display of financial wealth was more about an assurance to my mom than a self-worth boosting brag.

"What's a good date?" Dr. Zuckerman asks.

Owen looks at my face—he knows I was thrilled to be asked, but even so I hemmed and hawed for a day before coming back with a definitive yes to his proposal. "We'll get back to you on that, Dad."

"Where are you taking your honeymoon?" Summer asks quietly.

I feel bad saying Paris because I know Alan and Summer took their honeymoon in Cape May. That may be New Jersey's prettiest seaside town, full of charming Victorian houses, but it sure as hell isn't Paris. That's why I feel bad about discussing my honeymoon, isn't it? Pity for a sister-in-law who married my poor brother? It can't be because I'll be taking a celebratory jaunt abroad without Kit. Would I have survived this awful year without Owen and his incredible patience and humor? The year AK, After Kit, as I think of it, started out sour but when Owen and I finally acknowledged our growing connection, I enjoyed my days. It took three months for us to sleep together, but then, we were rarely apart. I was thrilled the day he asked me to move in to his quite roomy place in the Gramercy Park area. Owen and I have tons in common, if not the status of our bank accounts. He loves that I can proofread for him, and I love that he is always ready with a book recommendation.

My future father-in-law pats his belly. "How did we all forget the toast! A Chanukah toast to marital bliss!"

"You're getting married in a synagogue?" Dot says. Knitting needles click from somewhere very close to her phone. "I never thought I'd see the day."

Eric is next with his congratulations. As he speaks, the clicking noise is farther way, and then it's back to the first level of volume. "Hold, on, darling," Eric says. "Dot wants you again."

I brace for the worst as I wait for her to speak. What could she say to bruise me now? Gene once said it best. Dot can't help herself. If given enough time on the phone, she hits you with the very thing that will hurt the most, even if she never has a clue that she is so automatically insensitive.

"So your mother is a locked box on the matter, but honey, you tell me. What happened to Kit?"

I grit my teeth before I answer. "Fell by the wayside."

"I have to say, he was a lovely man."

"For a Christian?"

There is a shocked pause at my insouciance. "I never spoke out against that relationship, did I?"

"No, but tell me Dot, if things had worked out, would you have approved?"

"Cookie, do you really care what your silly old aunt thinks? And there are loopholes as far as the rabbinate is concerned—"

"Loopholes?"

"For children. The child of a Jewish woman is always Jewish."

I let a few seconds go by, and try to mask my curiously intense reaction as humorous. "Now you remind me of this?"

"I had no idea you had any interest in a Jewish home."

"I'm not sure what I want, Aunt Dot."

She pauses. Breathes loud. "Enough nonsense, Shari. You're getting married to a scholar. *Mazel Tov.*"

I stand in my childhood bedroom, really a storage closet with a bed that was given to me. There was and is, as the expression goes, not even enough room to swing a cat. But I never minded, I loved my itsy-bitsy closet room and the privacy it offered me. If I closed the door I could hardly hear my brothers fighting.

I look up at the time on the swinging cattail hallway clock that has always been there. Mom is on a date. With my father-in-law to be. Except they're not calling it a date. They are shopping, as neighbors. Rolling individual carts down the gourmet oil aisle in the supermarket.

She wants me to take my best shot at the guest list so we can go over it together when she gets back.

Since I've visited Mom last, she's converted my room back to its original use of storage space. My bed is gone, but on the new shelving is my pillow sham with its fairy hovering over a girl asleep in a bed of flowers. I really would like to take that back with me to Manhattan. I put it on the floor so I won't forget it.

I remove a box off the highest shelf, and immediately spot some of her three children's camp Peanuts postalettes preserved in a see-through sandwich bag. The rubber band snaps with age as I try to wiggle one out.

Before Dad died we got to go for two sessions a year, but afterward only one session of three weeks. My mother forewarned us not to complain, as she and Dad never went to camp at all.

"Awesome time!" were Gene's two sole words on his Snoopy postalette.

"Camp sucks," Alan wrote after three paragraphs summarizing his dislikes and resentment at being forced to go. *"Please come get me now!"*

"I learned how to float in the creek," Mommy's good girl scrawled, sealing her news with a Lucy sticker.

Mom has piled up more remnants of our childhood on the lower shelf. There are our favorite board games including Basket, a lever-action game with "working" mini nets, baskets and backboards that popped up to shoot the basketball that we always felt looked more like a Ping Pong ball. The corners of the Basket box are taped together for strength. The old price sticker of eight dollars is still on Billionaire: The Game of Global Enterprise—I can almost remember the rules: you could try your luck at investments like diamonds or electronics, something like that. Whatever industry Gene chose he always creamed us in profits. There is Alan's favorite, Stay Alive! He loves moving those slides. A new configuration of recesses would appear every time a slide moved, and if you were unlucky, one of your five marbles would disappear into them. Alan always had the last ball left, and even back then I suspected Gene let him win at his game because Alan loved it so.

And yes, she's saved my favorite, every little girl's favorite, Candyland. The game box is dirtied with water stains. I smile as I unfold the board. I select a red gingerbread man to move around the rainbow path. I race my man through Peppermint Stick Forest to the candy castle. I laugh out loud. Whenever Alan tried to trounce me at my favorite game, Gene slipped me the "big advance" ladder cards from the pick deck.

A tongue depressor from my toy nurse's kit is on the floor. I pick it up and marvel; it must have been stuck in the side of the Candyland box for thirty-odd years. I was ridiculously sad the day I wrote off that piece of wood, and secretly never felt it was the same with a long adult-sized tongue depressor replacement from the drug store.

Countless other small family sorrows will never be fixed. As hard as Jack pitched his mother those magic beans, Gene begged Mom to buy circus tickets so he could see the Ringling elephant doing the headstand like in the TV commercial, and when Uncle Sam finally took us Gene bellowed at Alan for eating most of the big box of Sno-Caps and we missed the headstand. Oh, and what about the time I lost the seven-layer chocolate cake Dad handed to me from the bakery to hold— five Diamonds couldn't figure out where I could have left it if not on a car rooftop.

I fight the lump in my throat that you get from digging around in your past.

There's change in the kitchen. I forgot that Gene gave Mom money to spruce up her kitchen with a cheery yellow paint job, new white cabinets and a dishwasher. But there's familiarity, too, a comforting box of Wheatina on top of the fridge. I quickly run water in the kettle and put it on a burner. With no one to set my limits, I slather the serving with heaping tablespoons of butter and sugar.

I finish it quickly as if someone might catch me out. I wash my dish—God help us kids if we didn't wash our dish after a snack. A box is under the table, marked Shari in thick black letters. There's a fusty scent of old paper as I excavate my issues of *Petticoat* and a pile of my favorite childhood books that further helped set my identity.

The Secret Garden. I stare at my wobbly name I scripted on a *Cat in the Hat* bookplate inside the cover. *Shari R. Diamond*.

I put it down and stare at the ceiling. Yes, who on earth would not be happy to land a man like Owen? I'll finally override my wiring if I just let myself. The onward rush of time always works.

My mother opens the door with that quaint look that accompanies any woman's new crush.

"You like him," I say immediately.

"Does it show?"

"It does."

She flinches. "I haven't felt anything like that since, well, I met your father. I honestly don't know how to proceed. I don't want to step on your—"

"Mom, you have the spark. Proceed."

Without my blessing, Cathy proceeded with Kevin, but she had her comeuppance—as it turned out she couldn't stomach him either. But at least she knows now that she has crossed all of her *t*'s in her search for a Great Jewish Man. The short-lived relationship was uncomfortable for us roommates, even if all of it unfurled away from our apartment. Kevin still refuses to see me as a friend, or even to finally talk things out without the intensity of the day he caught me out. Am I vain if I suspect he dated Cathy as a way of hurting me without seeing me?

"How did you do on your wedding invite list?" Mom says from the couch just before she pulls off her high-heeled supermarket date shoes. She rests her feet on a twenty-year-old ottoman, arms in a stretch, toes stretched, too, the longest line my mother can be.

CHAPTER 20

Sayonara to Volapük

Velma motions for me to go into Dr. Cox's office.

"I had a brainstorm," I say preemptively as I enter the room.

"Let's hear it."

"I'm officially quitting the dissertation."

Anger flushes his face: "That's your brainstorm?"

"I want to write a memoir," I say meekly. I continue talking even though my dissertation supervisor is glaring at me. "So I didn't find a Volapükist in New York State. But I have had adventures. For better or for worse."

I await his answer. Finally, Dr. Cox is ready to speak.

"I needed time to find my true calling. I had two tries at my own dissertation, did I ever tell you that? We're going to see this Ph.D. through."

I don't argue with him.

Dr. Cox stands and offers me a pity hug I don't really

want. Maybe I should bring up my engagement so he doesn't feel so badly for me. My financial worries are over, that's for sure. I guess that's what you call marrying well.

"I'm actually excited about this," I bravely pipe up.

"I have tenure, sweetheart. I can get you any extension. I can put in a word for more funding. Don't give up."

"I'm done, Dr. Cox. No more dissertation."

I hug him.

There's no going back.

CHAPTER 21

The Garden Secret

"Owen, where are we going?" I say the day after we've landed in London. My fiancé's been driving for almost an hour now since we refueled our gas tank and stomachs at a petrol station that also sold stale ham and butter sandwiches.

"What do you mean?"

"If you want to get to Dover in time for your research appointment, you might want to turn back around. You took a wrong turn."

"No, I haven't," Owen says automatically.

"Owen, seriously, turn around." Since the trip to the pet cemetery, I've become a master of the road map. "We're *going* the *wrong* way."

"Not when I have a surprise for you."

"So then where exactly are we going?" I say, confused. There's been little tenderness between us lately.

Without even a glance at me, Owen answers. "Rolvenden, three miles southwest of Tenterden on the A28 on the Kent and Sussex border."

"Why there?"

"For my research."

"And this will thrill me how?"

"The old home we're going to is supposed to be magnificent."

"Then we'll continue on to Dover?"

I expect a firm yes. The last chapter of Owen's almost-finished book will focus on Dover, the site of so many important joint American and British war stories. He went there a month ago and he needs a follow-up visit. It was his idea to combine leisure travel and research, to shift the focus away from the very embarrassing lack of progress with our wedding plans. Instead, my driving companion mumbles incoherently.

A glance at his face tells me all I need to know. Jesus. I'm not fighting back. I'm mentally exhausted from the plane trip yesterday afternoon—although at least I'm not paranoid this time. I'm also exhausted from my engagement. Owen's sister Wendy is practically my enemy now since she spent hours finding the perfect band (after Owen said our specifications were retro hip, jazzy and under two thousand for the night) and on our end we've gotten nowhere. Yes, *mea culpa*—I've made a muddle of the big event, avoiding setting a date just like a woman fed up with housework who refuses to face any more pesky stains on washday.

What sort of defense do I have? Maybe we should just

go ahead and pull the plug. I know that's what Owen has secretly been thinking, too.

Since I've delayed setting the date again for the third time after the Christmas greet-and-meet, Owen has stopped making any form of sexual advance toward me, and prickles when I touch him in any place that might lead to more physical contact.

Last night after we checked into a bargain hotel he found on Orbitz, I stood over his armchair and optimistically touched his shoulders. We were thousands of miles away from his dad with the daily wedding instructions, and my dead thesis. He looked up from his crossword puzzle, forced a smile. When I went to kiss him he said, cruelly, "Did you know how long Jonah was in the whale?"

Okay, this isn't a honeymoon, but it is our first big trip overseas since we tried to hunt down Kit almost a year prior. With a lovely blue sky above us, I'm feeling proactive again; I suggestively put my hand on his thigh. Owen quickly removes it with an "I need to concentrate."

"What's the name of the house?" I say sharply a few minutes later.

"I told you," he says, just as coldly. "A surprise."

We've been through six couples' therapy sessions already, but why the hell *should* I get married if this kind of passive-aggressiveness is what I'm up against? If he really loves me, he should be willing to wait until all of my regret over Kit is gone.

Finally, there is a grand estate up ahead of us on the road.

"Do you know someone here?" I say when we park.

My voice has softened to neutral but Owen is still particularly unresponsive.

Eventually I spot a sign that will have to do the explaining for me. Great Maytham Hall.

A groundskeeper pokes his head in Owen's right-side driver window. "You're too early. It's only open Wednesday and Thursday afternoons May to September."

It's an April Monday.

Owen gets out of the car, motions the guard aside and whispers something. The guard nods his head. Even though I am despising Owen right now, I'm itching to know what this is all about. We step inside a gate, and walk on acres of land with flowering trees. A surprisingly large number of seniors are roaming the large grounds.

Owen's first words since we parked: "I forgot. He said they've converted Great Maytham into a senior's residence."

I stand firm on a mossy corner of grass. "Who said? Okay, O—why am I here?"

For the first time in hours, he makes direct eye contact. "Let's go inside the house and find out."

"Why are you being so crazy? Why can't you answer me?"

"You know what? I've changed my mind. Let's look inside later. Let's have a walk around the place."

Owen starts walking toward the formal green lawns.

I'm exceedingly pissed off now. I follow a few feet away and raise my voice. "These grounds are pretty, but tell me what's happening here."

"It is time for your surprise," my fiancé says significantly. He leads me by the hand to a brick wall. His long look is as devastating as the one Kit gave me before he stormed off, at turns pitying and hateful.

I'm inwardly shrinking, but outwardly calm.

"What is it?"

Owen hands me a brochure and then—Boom! "I'm leaving you now."

"What was that?"

"Shari, you don't really want to be married to me. Deep feelings of affection are not enough. I think that goes both ways."

I'm speechless. Between Kit's disappearance and my father's untimely departure, I've had quite enough with the dramatic abandonment.

"Read the brochure," he continues in a toneless voice. "We'll talk later. You'll have to figure out when and where."

"Where? *What?*"

He is gone. I'm too shocked to run after him. I stand silently, his strange words echoing in my head.

And then I read:

Great Maytham Hall, which inspired Frances Hodgson Burnett's The Secret Garden *is open Wednesday and Thursday afternoons in May. According to Ann Thwaite, biographer of Frances Hodgson Burnett,* The Secret Garden *is a book of the new century.*

Burnett lived at Maytham Hall from 1898–1907, and wrote many loved books here, including The Secret Garden. *This beloved classic, inspired by the old walled garden at Maytham, suggested children should be self-re-*

liant and have faith in themselves, in that they should listen not to their elders and betters, but to their own hearts and consciences.

What else can I do except listen to him? I angrily walk through a wooden door. Inside is a garden so close to the description of Mary and Colin's garden that I have to think, *Whose memory is this? A reader's or a filmgoer's?* There, under an abundance of greenery, is a man in a gazebo reading a copy of, of course, *The Secret Garden.*

I brave the chopping block. I touch a shoulder.

Christopher T. Brown sizes up my wet eyes as he holds a hand out.

"I didn't know you were here until a second ago," I push out.

"He didn't tell you?"

"No."

"Bloody hell! That wasn't the plan! You were supposed to be here of your own volition."

But I'm here. And you're here. I immediately start to weep.

I try to talk. "I wish we could wipe away that day we fought—"

Kit holds my hand to comfort me. "You know you're not completely to blame. I was going to get around to the whole story on my own schedule. Bloody English. We're such fools sometimes."

"I met your grandfather," I finally manage.

He stares. There's a long break before he answers again. The birds wait it out, too. "I was going to tell you about my family advantage over you just before we got there."

I let him continue at his own pace.

"Shari—my grandfather beat my mother when she was young. That's why I was so secretive about everything. I hate him, but his father is my great-grandfather, and he was by all accounts a remarkable man, a true enthusiast for the power of language."

"He told me he was awful to her. I have to know—did he rape her?"

"Boy you New Yorkers, you don't mince words."

"It's my very unpleasant theory."

He breathes out. "Now I know he didn't. My mother wouldn't say a word more other than he hurt her. I had to know, too. I became a Volapük academic just to find that out, and eventually I told Robert who I was. By then we were 'pals' you see, and he bared his soul."

"Did Helen know about the real reason for your academic research?"

"Unfortunately, yes. That's why her betrayal of me cut so deep. I have another story for you. Helen was my wife, you know."

"I met her, Kit. I know that, too."

He's so taken aback that he actually chortles. "What is it that Woody Allen's mom says in *Annie Hall* when she's horrified?"

I laugh, too. "'Drive a stake through my heart.'"

"That's it," he nods.

"You don't have to tell me anything else."

"I want to. You can tell me about the meeting later. First I want to say—my reserve—" He struggles for the right words. "My reserve is not by choice—my mother escaped Robert when she was seventeen. My grandmother sided with her husband. Mum met my father in London. She was beautiful, you know? There was that crazy obsession for language in my family, and she spoke well for a farmer's girl. She simply rewrote her past and married money. My father died when I was fifteen. We weren't as close as you and your dad, but I did miss him."

"I'm so sorry about what I said." I burst out crying again. "The way I accused you—"

This time he lets me cry. "Yes. You practically had foam on your mouth. Drugged, apparently. Or so Owen told me."

"Owen," I say distraughtly, remembering the rest of this mess.

"I tried to warn you. Owen is a complicated fellow. He is an angel or a son of a bitch, according to who he interacts with. He's been with—" Kit stops. "I shouldn't say this—"

"After what we've been through, you might as well say it all."

"He's been with Helen for a month."

"*What?* No way. He had a business trip here last month, to Dover, for his book."

"To London, I'm afraid."

It's my turn for stunned silence.

"As soon as he realized what he wanted, he carried on your search to find me. He wormed into favor with me. I guess he's not all terrible, mind you. He didn't want you to have another crack-up."

"Is that what he called it?" I say contemptuously.

"He said he knew you would be okay if he found me. He said you were still in love with me."

"Well, I guess he was right." I have to keep talking or I'll fall to pieces again. "Who came up with the plan to meet me here?"

"Dot."

My jaw drops for the second time in three minutes.

"We've been in touch by e-mail for a bit. She e-mailed me after you announced your engagement plans. Apparently you didn't sound so convincing.

"She's led the charge to get us back together. She wanted to be careful about your mother and Owen's father though. Your mother is very much in love, you know—"

"That I do know."

"So I think you'll be seeing Owen whether or not you want to. After Dot e-mailed, Nigel was the one who really talked sense into me. Funny how brothers can do that. I was moping and—" Kit pauses, slips the Zippo out of his pocket, and readies his rolling papers.

"I'd like to meet your family," I say, repeating Kit's words to me from so many months ago.

"And my mother wants to meet you, if you are coming home with me."

"What did she think of Helen?"

He weighs the question. "She thought she was pretty. And that was good enough for me."

"Helen is not pretty. You were right. She's gorgeous."

"She's got nothing on you. No one has those big brown laser eyes you have—"

I kiss him. I kiss his head. I kiss his cheek. I kiss his wrist. "Are you real? I missed you so much."

"So who's the loon now? You've got a loving family, and it appears I'm the one who should be ashamed of my bloodline—"

"We're both crazy then. I'm loving my family now, and I know I'll love yours."

He squeezes my hand. "Mum is going to drag every bloody photo of me out. I'm forewarning you, when I was eleven in my addicted-to-custard stage I got really, really fat."

Maybe Kit's previous confession about his grandfather and mother was too taxing. He starts to bawl. An Englishman is crying. An Englishman is crying for *me*.

I let him cry as I hold his hand. Five minutes of silence does my soul well. I may well get the knack of the stiff upper lip.

"I had a look about the place earlier," Kit finally says in a recovered voice. He points: "There's the old door Burnett found, but it's bricked up. And this is the gazebo she used to write her books."

I pat the wood.

"In this seat?"

My cell phone rings, my rich-person's phone Dr. Zuckerman has prepaid for the year, a really great engagement present. Owen has the same kick-ass plan with all the bells and whistles, unlimited international and national plan, photo capacity and texting.

"I'll get it later," I say to Kit.

"You should answer it. It's probably Owen checking to see if you're staying."

He's probably right. I flip open the phone.

"Hey, Miss S," Gary Marino's voice says.

"Gary! You're calling me in England—"

"What are you doing there? Finally living out your fantasies?"

"Sort of. Long story."

"I wanted you to be the very first to know, my parents haven't even heard this. I'm getting married in three months in New Jersey."

"I'm flattered. You haven't told your parents?"

"I first want to rub some serious shit in your face."

"What are you talking about?"

"I just got engaged to Sally from the tour. Let me put her on—"

"Gary! This isn't the—"

"Shari?" says a pert Midwestern voice. "Isn't this the most amazing thing ever?"

I'm forced into a reply. "Congratulations. Hey, I can say I was there when you met."

"You sure can. We're thinking of renting out one of the Frank Lloyd Wright houses in Oak Park. We're going with an arts-and-crafts-movement theme."

"Sally, I'm in England now."

"You are?"

"Yeah. I'm really worried about my battery running out. So congratulations again, but can you put Gary on for one second again? I'll definitely come to Chicago."

"Can't wait. Hold on!"

"Hey," Gary says for the second time.

"Incredible, my friend. I really thought she despised you."

"You can't beat chemistry."

Kit looks mighty confused that I'm continuing to talk on a mobile when he has just spilled out his heart-rending life abstract. "Yeah, you can't."

"So what about you? You still dating that nice Jewish boy?"

"Can I call you back later?"

"Just give me the quick update."

"Let me give you a call later to fully congratulate you. You caught me at a very awkward moment. Same number?"

"Same number."

"What was that about?" Kit is readying another home-rolled cigarette.

"Nonik!" I cry out. "No!" in Volapük.

"What's wrong?"

I grab the lighter and slip it into my purse. "We need to talk about your smoking."

"Is this going to be a lecture? I just had one from my mother."

"This is going to be an order because I'm not fucking losing you this time."

He smirks. "Maybe we need to break out the ice cubes again."

With stinging wet eyes, I kiss him. Tomorrow I will scream my head off at Owen, after I thank him profusely.

★ ★ ★ ★ ★

For this dyed-in-the-wool city mom,
life in the country is no walk in the park…

Wonderboy
Fiona Gibson

On sale September 2005

Urbanite parents Ro and Marcus are trading in life in
London's fast lane for a quiet country life in Chetsley.
As Ro struggles to adjust to the "simple life" though,
she learns that her husband's reasons for moving may
not have been so simple, and Ro must make a decision
that may change her and her son's life for good.

Don't miss

The Matzo Ball Heiress

by Laurie Gwen Shapiro

Q. How does Heather Greenblotz, the thirty-one-year-old millionaire heiress to the world's leading matzo company, celebrate Passover?

A. Alone. In her Manhattan apartment. With an extremely unkosher ham and cheese on whole wheat.

But this year is going to be different. The Food Network has asked to film the famous Greenblotz Matzo family's seder, and the publicity op is too good to, ahem, pass over. But the Greenblotz's aren't your average family, and an unexpected walk-on from Heather's bisexual father, his lover and her estranged mother proves just that. This is sure to be a family affair you will never forget.